stare noted 3-18-13 at

WEST TEXAS KILL

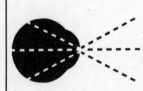

This Large Print Book carries the
Seal of Approval of N.A.V.H.

WEST TEXAS KILL

JOHNNY D. BOGGS

THORNDIKE PRESS
A part of Gale, Cengage Learning

GALE
CENGAGE Learning™

Detroit • New York • San Francisco • New Haven, Conn • Waterville, Maine • London

GALE
CENGAGE Learning™

LIBRARY OF CONGRESS CATALOGING-IN-PUBLICATION DATA

Boggs, Johnny D.
    West Texas kill / by Johnny D. Boggs.
        p. cm. — (Thorndike Press large print western)
    ISBN-13: 978-1-4104-3788-4 (hardcover)
    ISBN-10: 1-4104-3788-4 (hardcover)
    1. Texas—Fiction. 2. Large type books. I. Title.
PS3552.O4375W45 2011
813'.54—dc22   2011009947

Published in 2011 by arrangement with Pinnacle Books, an imprint of
Kensington Publishing Corp.

Printed in the United States of America
1 2 3 4 5 6 7 15 14 13 12 11

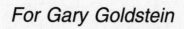

For Gary Goldstein

CHAPTER ONE

Hell, the man on the gray horse decided, does get cold.

He had tied a blue woolen scarf over his hat and under his chin, bringing down the brim of his battered Stetson to keep his ears warm. Ice crystals had formed on his stiff mustache, his nose was red, lips chapped, and his lungs burned with every breath he took. Behind him, over the monotonous clopping of hooves came the sniffling of his men, the creaking of leather, the chimes of spurs. But no complaints. The sixteen men riding with him would not whine, would never turn back. He had heard the saying dozens of times before: *The Rangers of Company E would ride through Hell for Captain Hector Savage.*

Indeed, they had.

Hell. Mexico. He sniffed. Same damned thing.

Dead stems rising from century plants

7

bent to the brutal wind as he led his men through rough, mountainous terrain, the ground frozen solid, the country so bleak that even the yucca plants looked worn out. No clouds. No threat of snow. As Doc Shaw had commented a few hours earlier, "Too cold to snow." Nothing but a harsh November wind, making the twenty-degree afternoon feel a lot colder. Behind him, to the north, rose the ominous peaks of the Chisos Mountains. Also behind him lay the Río Grande.

The wool-lined collar of his heavy canvas coat had also been pulled up, although he had not bothered to button the coat. Despite the gloves, his fingers felt numb as he gripped the reins with his left hand, keeping his right near the ivory grip of one of the silver-plated Merwin Hulbert .44s holstered high on his waist.

His pale blue eyes scanned the country. For the past couple hours, he had not seen any other living animal, not even a javelina or a coyote, as the horses picked their way around clumps of bear grass, catclaw, and pesky prickly pear. That would change soon. The Guardia Rural would intercept them shortly. He was counting on it.

Twenty minutes later, as he led the Rangers into a widening valley, he spotted a flash in the distance — likely sunlight reflecting off a saber. He spit out a mouthful of tobacco juice as he tugged slightly on the reins, stopping the gray. Five more minutes passed before he saw the dust, and the band of Rurales came into view a few minutes later.

Behind him, he heard an ominous click.

"Nobody cocks or pulls a weapon," Hector Savage said without turning around. A muttered sigh answered his order, followed by metallic sounds of a hammer being lowered on a Sharps, and the sliding of the rifle back into a saddle scabbard.

"Demitrio," Savage said.

"*Sí, Capitán.*"

"Best tie that bandana of yours to the barrel of your rifle. Let these Rurales know we come in peace."

"It is already done, *mi capitán.*"

Savage grinned. Half Irish, half greaser, Demitrio Ahern had been riding for the Rangers since Savage had formed his company more than a decade earlier, after the government in Austin had finally wised up, gotten rid of that insipid state police, and sent men onto the frontier to bring justice — often summary, by hemp or lead — to outlaws terrorizing much of Texas. Austin had formed companies of Rangers, called battalions, and sent them to various regions. Leander McNelly got the Nueces Strip, and much glory, before succumbing to consumption. Hector Savage left his ranch southeast of San Antonio for the sprawling expanse of nothingness west of the Pecos River. He hadn't been east of that river since.

Without being ordered, Demitrio Ahern eased his horse out of line, and trotted to Savage's right, a frayed cotton square, once solid brilliant white now faded and yellowed, popped in the wind from beneath the front sight of his .45-70 carbine. The stock was butted on his thigh against the worn leather chaps. He kept his gloved finger out of the trigger guard, but his thumb on the Sharps's big hammer.

Savage could see the Rurales loping across the desert floor in columns of twos, led by a thin Mexican wearing a French-style kepi. He counted eleven men, but just to be certain, he asked Ahern how many men he saw.

"Once," came the reply.

Satisfied, Savage straightened in the saddle, and pushed his heavy coat back behind the butt of the Merwin Hulbert on his right hip. "Reckon they left any up near that pass? To keep them covered?"

Ahern studied the terrain, then said, "No, *mi capitán.* They are too foolish. They believe this flag of truce will protect them."

"Hell." Savage spit again. "It will." He raised his right hand, bit the dirty, oily leather above his fingers, and pulled off one glove, which he stuck in the pocket of his coat before returning his hand near the .44 revolver.

The Rurales reached them, and slowed their horses. The one in the kepi and two others rode forward, the rest remaining back, their horses nervously stomping, snorting, waiting.

The leader looked young, probably still in his early twenties, with a handsome, unblemished face. He wore a gray jacket trimmed in silver, blue-gray britches with deerskin on the insides of the thighs and buttocks for extra protection, a billowy, white shirt, and a red cravat. A gold crucifix hanging from a rawhide string bounced across his chest as he trotted forward on a black stallion, and he raised a gauntleted right hand. He carried no long gun, just a saber that clattered against his saddle, and a pistol holstered on his right hip, butt forward, covered with a leather flap. The flap, Savage noticed, was snapped closed.

The other Rurales looked more like the

11

Mexican peace officers Savage was used to seeing — well-worn pants and jackets; bandoliers of ammunition draped over their chests, around their waists, and hanging from the saddle horns; revolvers stuck inside waistbands, or holstered on hips; knives sheathed in concho-studded belts; large sombreros pulled low on their heads. A few cradled old muskets — one carried an old fowling piece. Every one of them, except the young officer, appeared nervous, and looked like the damned bandits they'd likely been before forced into the police force, though not a one seemed cold.

"Buenas tardes," the officer said after he reined in his stallion a couple rods in front of Savage. *"Me llamo Jaime Bautista Moreno, teniente de los Rurales de San Pedro. Tu siervo, señores."*

"El gusto es mío," Savage said, and the lieutenant smiled and bowed. Savage spit, then asked, *"¿Habla usted Inglés?"*

The immediate one to Lieutenant Moreno's right answered. "I speak English, señores. You are *norte-americanos, sí?*" He was an old man, white hair underneath a battered sombrero, eyes suspicious, a few days growth of beard on his face and a mustache that, unlike the rest of his hair, had not turned completely white. His revolver was within easy reach, and his right hand never strayed far from the walnut butt.

With his left hand still gloved, Savage let the reins fall across the gelding's neck. He gripped just beneath the lapel of his coat and pulled it back slightly, revealing the star cut into a circle made from a Mexican peso pinned to his vest. "We're Texas Rangers." He said it loud enough for the soldiers behind the lieutenant and his two *segundos* to hear, and took a little pride in the reaction he got.

"Los rinches," came the nervous whisper. *"Los rinches . . ."*

The white-haired man began speaking to the lieutenant in Spanish. Savage couldn't savvy most of it, figuring if the old man said something he needed to know Demitrio Ahern would tell him, but Savage could read the lieutenant's young face. The Rurale straightened in his saddle, his black eyes never leaving Savage, and spoke in an urgent whisper.

The old Rurale turned back to Savage. "Teniente Moreno asks, 'Why have you traveled into our poor country?' "

Poor is an understatement, Savage thought. He tugged the coat back over his vest, gathered the reins, and answered, "We were pursuing the bandit, Juan Lo Grande."

13

"Lo Grande?" the old one asked, his face betraying him with a wry grin. *"No se corta un pelo."*

"He ain't a bit of a devil," Savage snapped. "He's *el diablo* himself."

The white haired one translated. Lieutenant Moreno's face hardened, his head bobbed slightly, and he sighed as he told the old man something.

Again, the white-haired one translated. "Teniente Moreno regrets to inform you that our *presidente,* Porfirio Díaz, would consider your presence on Mexican soil as an armed invasion. He must ask that you turn around and return to your own country. Leave Lo Grande to us."

"We've been leaving him to you bean-eaters," Savage said with bitterness. He took time to switch the chaw of tobacco to his other cheek, letting his temper cool. "Lo Grande's men raided the quicksilver mines in Terlingua. Killed a couple miners, made off with a whore and the payroll. That's an armed invasion, if you ask me. I'm Hec Savage."

Even as the old one translated for the lieutenant, Savage heard the whispers among the other Rurales. He smiled, and kept talking, "We've been on Lo Grande's trail for a couple days. I would be willing to

14

put my men and myself under Lieutenant Moreno's command. I think they call it a 'joint punitive action.' Between us, we could make Lo Grande pay for all the crimes he has committed on both sides of the border."

He listened to the old one's translation, saw an eagerness in Lieutenant Moreno's eyes, but the young Rurale's shoulders sagged, and he answered by shaking his head. Without waiting for the old one to speak, Savage said, "My understanding is that the Mex government and the muckety-mucks in Washington City have been allowing our damnyankee cavalry to pursue marauding Apaches across the Arizona border into Sonora. Makes sense to me, and maybe the government of Chihuahua, that we should be able to do the same thing. Lo Grande is worse than Geronimo and old Nana. At least in West Texas. And San Pedro."

Again, the old one translated, and the young officer considered it. He wants to do it, Savage thought with amazement, but finally, Lieutenant Moreno's head bowed, and shook. He spoke, and Savage listened to the translation.

"¡Ay de mí! Teniente Moreno apologizes, but there is a difference between the government of the United States and the govern-

15

ment of Texas. *Los rinches.*"

Savage smiled an understanding smile.

"Teniente Moreno says that although he would accept your generosity and end Lo Grande's reign of terror were it up to him, he is a soldier, and must follow orders. *Con permiso,* Capitán Savage, we will escort you and your *soldados* to the river and see that you reach Texas safely."

Savage's head bobbed, and he let out a weary sigh. "I figured as much. Worth taking a shot, though." He turned around. "All right, men. These hombres will take us back to the Río Grande. They'll protect us."

Dusk was approaching when they reached the border. The lieutenant used his saber to cut through the brush, and spurred his stallion into the gurgling river. Hec Savage followed on his gray gelding. The river was shallow and muddy, but wide, maybe fifty yards across, and bitterly cold. Halfway across, Savage reined in the gray, reached into his vest pocket, and withdrew a handful of cigars. Most of the Rangers eased their horses to the Texas banks. Most of the Rurales had stayed on the Mexican shore.

The white-haired one and the lieutenant took the cigars, muttering their thanks. The old one put his away. Young Moreno sheathed the saber, bit off an end of the smoke, and waited for Savage to light it.

Like hell, Savage thought, *I ain't your manservant, boy.*

But Demitrio Ahern eased his bay gelding near the lieutenant, struck a lucifer against his chaps, and fired up the cigar, before backing up his gelding a few rods. The bandana on the end of his rifle flapped in the wind.

Savage, who had spit out his quid of tobacco miles earlier, stuck a cigar in his mouth, and lit it with a match he had struck against the butt of one of his revolvers. The wind moaned through the trees and brush lining the riverbanks on both sides of the border. The bandana kept right on flapping in the biting wind.

"Demitrio," Savage said when his cigar was finally smoking to his satisfaction. "I don't reckon we need that flag of truce anymore."

"But, of course, mi capitán," Demitrio Ahern said. He removed the dirty piece of cotton, and while lowering the Sharps, thumbed back the hammer, and squeezed the trigger, blowing the white-haired Rurale out of his saddle.

Spitting out the cigar, screaming something, Lieutenant Moreno reached first for

17

his revolver, then, realizing the flap was shut, tried to draw his saber. By that time, Hec Savage had slipped from his saddle into ankle-deep water. Holding the reins in his left hand, using the gray as a shield, he drew one of the long-barrel .44s with his right and shot the stupid officer, seeing the white shirt explode crimson.

The big black horse wheeled, spilling Moreno into the water. As it bolted for the Mexican side of the river a bullet slammed into its head, killing it instantly.

"Pity," Savage said aloud. A fine stallion like that would have brought a nice price over in Presidio. He snapped a shot that spilled another Rurale on the far bank from his saddle.

Behind him roared the weapons of his Rangers. In front of him, Lieutenant Moreno tried to push himself to his feet, but slipped back into the reddish-brown waters of the Río Grande. Savage aimed again, squeezed the trigger. The Merwin Hulbert warmed his cold hand.

Horses and men screamed. The Rangers cursed, and shot. The air smelled of sulfur, of brimstone. Most of the Rurales lay dead in the river, or on the banks, but three spurred their mounts through the brush, and up a hill, only to be met by a dozen charging, bellowing Mexican bandits, firing revolvers and slashing down with machetes.

In less than a minute, it was over, the only sound coming from the river and the wind, and the occasional pop of a coup de grâce as a Mexican bandit shot a wounded Rurale in the back of his head. Then Savage heard a small groan. Pulling the gelding behind him, he slogged through mud and water toward the lieutenant, who had drifted a few yards downstream.

"Capt'n," Doc Shaw called out, and Savage paused briefly to consider the Mexicans riding through the brush. Some of them stopped to loot the dead. One, grinning so wide his gold teeth reflected the disappearing sun, kneed his horse into the river while he shoved a Colt revolver into the holster.

"Amigos," Juan Lo Grande boasted, "we work well together, do we not? 'O heaven! were man but constant, he were perfect.' "

Ignoring the bandit, Savage reached the lieutenant, whose fancy jacket had snagged on an uprooted sandbar willow in the middle of the river, partially buried in the mud. Blood seeped from both corners of the young man's mouth, and his eyes looked up, begging for mercy, while his right fingers fumbled for something on his chest.

Savage considered Lo Grande and the bandits for a moment, but holstered the .44. He knelt into the river, the cold water pricking his nerves, and gripped the gold crucifix in the fingers of his right hand. Spitting out the cigar he asked, "This what you want, Moreno?"

The lieutenant tried to speak, but couldn't.

Savage rose, jerking the gold cross from its rawhide string, then shoving it into his coat pocket. Juan Lo Grande said something, probably quoting Shakespeare again, but Savage focused on the dying lieutenant. He turned back to his horse and started for the saddle, thinking he might use the double-barrel Parker 12-gauge to finish the job before deciding he didn't want to waste any lead. With Juan Lo Grande, he might need every shot he had.

He turned back, looked down once more at Moreno.

"Remember the Alamo," Savage said hoarsely. He put his right boot on the Rurale officer's nose, and pressed down until Moreno's head sank beneath the muddy water.

CHAPTER TWO

Fort Davis was his favorite town.

Oh, there wasn't anything spectacular about the little burg itself, a few scattered adobe and stone buildings, some wood frame businesses with silly facades, a couple log cabins, and plenty of jacales, hovels, and picket houses. Yet it didn't resemble most of the parasite communities that sprang up around military posts, and the town's namesake fort was one sprawling compound with plenty of troopers assigned to guard the San Antonio-El Paso road. Hell, the little town boasted a Methodist church and Sunday school meeting house, an ice house, and a two-story saloon. Sergeant Dave Chance rode toward the latter.

Chance admired more than the town. The community braced against the Davis Mountains. Thick woods of piñon, juniper, oak, and ponderosa pine housed mule deer, rock squirrels, and white-winged doves. Rich grasslands fed thousands of Don Melitón Benton's longhorn cattle that watered in lovely Limpia Creek. Surrounded by the northern Chihuahuan Desert, Fort Davis had always been an oasis in the middle of Hades.

Much of West Texas would swallow a man, chew him up, spit him out. Water, when you could find it, often tasted like alkali or iron, and left lesser stomachs suffering from bowel complaint. The wind blew brutally harsh, and every animal and plant would bite, stick, or poison you. The same might be said of most of the men and women who hung their hats in the region.

A peace, however, settled over Chance whenever he rode into Fort Davis. He figured he'd like to be buried there when his time came.

That time, he lamented, *might be this morning.*

He came up from the southeast on the old Overland Mail Company road, commonly called the Butterfield Trail. The town was divided into three sections: Chihuahua, where the cribs were located on Chihuahua Creek; Fort Davis proper, the largest region, due south of the military post; and Newtown, just east of the fort. When Chance rode past the courthouse in Fort Davis, a

22

peon rode up beside him on a blind mule, giving him a curious look.

"*Señor,*" the rail-thin, gray-haired man said, tilting his head at the drab-looking building. "*¿Te gustaría pedir ayuda?*"

Chance answered with a calming smile, shaking his head. "I don't need any help. It's only one hombre I'm after, right?"

Grinning, the old man nodded, but Chance thought the smile was forced. The peon looked mighty worried.

Actually, Dave Chance would have given two months' salary for help, but he couldn't put any citizen of Presidio County at risk, not even some well-meaning lawman. Not against the likes of Moses Albavera. Nobody in Fort Davis cared how many men Albavera had killed in Galveston.

The aroma of baked apples, fresh coffee, and frying bacon wafted out of the Lempert Hotel as he rode on, tormenting his stomach. He hadn't eaten since the day before and that meal had consisted of the last of his jerky and a stale biscuit that had nigh broken a couple teeth. He'd have to stop by the Sender Brothers store for supplies on his way out of town . . . if he lived.

They rode on to Newtown, reining up in front of the saloon. The two-story structure had been built only a couple years ago, but looked older than dirt. It had gone through a number of owners in its short life, and from the bullet holes pockmarking the crumbling adobe bricks, Chance didn't think the saloon would live much longer. The hitching rails out front were full, but the gray Andalusian stallion stood out among the cow ponies and old cavalry mounts. A proud-looking horse, standing a good sixteen hands, it had a deep body, powerful hindquarters, beautiful mane and tail. The Andalusian looked like it could carry its rider a far piece.

Chance took in a deep breath, slowly exhaled, and turned to the peon. "*Gracias, Miguel.* You best get on home now."

He didn't need to tell the old man anything else.

When the Mexican and blind mule had rounded the corner, Chance swung from the saddle, and removed his red mackinaw and gauntlets. The fringed gloves went into the pockets of the wool jacket. The mackinaw was draped over the saddle as his horse stood patiently. There was no room at the hitching rails, and Chance didn't bother to hobble the gelding. After tugging at the Schofield revolver holstered on his right hip, he felt behind his back for the handle of the double-action Smith & Wesson .32 as he walked to the Andalusian. He ran his fingers under the cinch.

Most men visiting a saloon would have loosened the girth, but that one was tighter than Dave Chance's old man. He pulled on the latigo, loosened the cinch, then pushed up his hat, and stepped to the saloon doors, taking another deep breath before heading inside.

Sunday morning, not yet eleven, and Chance figured more people had congregated at the nameless saloon than at the churches in town. The place reeked of stale beer and sawdust, the cacophony of voices assaulting his ears as he walked to the potbelly stove in the center of the room, and held his hands out to the cast iron stove to warm himself.

A redheaded woman, rouge caked on her face with a spade, came up to him, and asked, "What'll you — ?" Her rye-soaked question stopped before she finished, and her eyes, one green, one brown, locked on the peso star pinned above the pocket of his black vest. "Aw, hell."

"You got any coffee?" Chance asked.

"Coffee?" Incredulously, she stared at him.

"With cream."

"All we got's goat's milk."

"That'll do."

"You ain't lookin' —"

"Coffee with a splash of milk. Milk helps keep my teeth white." He flashed her his smile. His teeth looked more yellow than pearly, but at least he had all of them. Other than in his mouth, he doubted if there were a full set of teeth in the entire saloon.

He watched her head to another stove on the other side of the bar. She didn't talk to anyone, not even the big beer-jerker working the bar, except to curse the rawboned cowhand with the new Stetson who slapped her buttocks as she walked past him.

Keeping his hands near the stove, Chance looked past the stovepipe, letting his eyes grow accustomed to the darkness of the saloon. Cowhands lined the bar, a bunch of muleskinners stood by the roulette wheel, and some officers of the Third Cavalry sat at a table by the window, sipping Jameson. Well, the label on the bottle said Jameson, but in an establishment like that, Chance figured the Irish whiskey had been consumed years ago, and the bottle was filled with forty-rod rotgut.

Past the roulette wheel, he saw the card tables: three faro layouts and a poker table. The faro players were segregated: whites at one, Mexicans at another, blacks at the last one. He studied the blacks, but found only

26

some cheering retired buffalo soldiers. The 10th Cavalry had been stationed at Fort Davis until the past spring. He was about to examine the poker players when the redhead returned with his coffee.

"Here you go," she said.

He took the proffered pewter beer stein with his left hand, and tested the steaming brew. Chance grimaced. "This tastes like crap."

"So does our whiskey. That'll be a two bits."

"For coffee?" He fished into his vest pocket for a quarter. "How much is your whiskey?"

"Same. Everything in here costs two bits. Even a poke." She grinned at him. Her teeth were darker than his, and she was missing a bottom front one. "If you's interested."

"If a poke's as crummy as your coffee and whiskey, I'll pass," he said.

Beneath all that rouge, the redhead's face flushed. Chance thought she might slap him, but she turned in a huff, and strode back to the bar.

Chance tried another sip of coffee, grimaced, and put the stein on the stove. Walking across the creaking floor, around the roulette table, and past the faro layouts, he leaned against a wooden column beside the poker table.

The poker table was integrated.

A fat white man with a whiskey-sodden Roman nose tossed down his cards with a curse, and reached for a bottle of tequila in front of the few chips he had left. He wore an unbuttoned blouse, with the chevrons of an infantry corporal on the sleeves, and a well-worn Army kepi. Across from him, a merchant in a black broadcloth suit, smiled, and raked in the pot. He was a dark-haired man, with a gold Star of David pinned on the coat's lapel. To the merchant's right sat another soldier, a cavalry trooper with blond hair and peach fuzz for a mustache. Although Chance could see only the side of the trooper's face, the kid didn't look old enough to be in either the Army or a saloon. Next to the trooper sat a Mexican vaquero, smoking a sweet-smelling cheroot. Chance couldn't see the man's face, but he didn't have to. To the right of the infantry corporal sat a woman, who gathered the cards and began shuffling. She wore tinted glasses — though sunlight was rarer than good whiskey in a bucket of blood like that place — and a fashionable ladies riding outfit of garnet and green. The jacket was double-breasted, a brooch pinned above her heart. A riding crop leaned against her chair. She also had a stack of chips larger than anyone else at the table. She looked a hell of a lot better than the redhead who had served him coffee, and Chance decided she probably had all of her teeth. Whiter than his, to be sure.

A handful of men — black, white, and Mexican — and one of the saloon girls had gathered around the table, watching the lady gambler. Yet it was the final man, sitting between the woman and the merchant, who interested Chance.

He wore a rakish double-breasted vest the color of Madeira, a black tie with a diamond stickpin under the collar of a fancy cream shirt with black stripes and a tapered bottom bib front. His hat was black, with a horsehair hatband of red, gray and blue. The brim curled at the sides, dipped in the front and back, and had a telescope crown. A linen duster and fringed buckskin coat were draped on the seat of his chair. Both hands rested beneath the table. His eyes locked on Chance.

He looked to be a large man, broad shouldered, probably would stand a good two inches taller than Chance, and Chance was six-foot-one in his boots. He was a black man, clean shaven except for a thick mustache flecked with gray. His hair was close-cropped. A Seth Thomas watch with a gold chain laid beside his pile of chips, a few gold coins, and some crumpled greenbacks. He hadn't won as much as the woman, but he had done pretty well. A beer stein was to the man's right. A slight Mexican saloon girl, probably in her teens, came over and topped the stein with black coffee. The man made no move for the cup. Just sat there, staring at Chance.

The woman shuffled the cards, passed them to the black man to cut. Without looking at the deck, he raised his right hand, saying, "Thin to win," and cut the cards. As the woman gathered the deck, Chance stepped away from the wooden column, and spoke in a voice just loud enough to be heard. "Moses Albavera."

The woman left the cards on the warped table. The vaquero slid his chair back, and studied Chance. The saloon turned quiet.

"Do you have business with me?" the black man said in a stentorian voice. He could have been somewhere between thirty and fifty years old.

"There's the little matter of a murder warrant," Chance said.

The merchant, trooper, and infantry corporal hurriedly left the table. The vaquero slid his chair a little farther out of the line of fire. That was good, Chance thought.

It gave him a chance to give the Mexican a quick glance. He was unarmed, merely curious. The woman removed her glasses, and laid them on the table. Her eyes kept darting between Albavera and Chance.

"Don Melitón send you?" Albavera reached for his coffee stein and took a sip.

The words surprised Chance, but his face remained granite as he shook his head. "Why would he send me?"

With a shrug, Albavera said, "He owns Presidio County, I'm told. Owns most of the Big Bend country." He took another sip of coffee. His left hand remained underneath the table. "And I killed his son two days ago. Down in Shafter."

Shafter was a silver-mining town on the eastern edge of the Chinati Mountains, maybe sixty miles south of Fort Davis. Spitting distance from Don Melitón Benton's *rancho*.

"You killed Prince Benton?" Chance couldn't hide his surprise, even though the old don's son had always been a heel and was bound to get killed sooner or later.

"It was a fair fight."

Chance admired Albavera's grit. He had killed Prince Benton, and instead of lighting a shuck for the Mexican border, maybe twenty miles from Shafter, he had ridden

31

north to Fort Davis. Not that it mattered. Don Melitón likely would have tracked Albavera all the way to Cape Horn to avenge his son's death, no matter how worthless Prince had been.

"I imagine it was," Chance said, "but I didn't know about Prince Benton. Don Melitón didn't send me." With his left hand, he tapped the circled five-point star on his vest. "I'm a Texas Ranger. Warrant I'm serving was issued in Galveston."

"The Marin brothers?" Now it was Albavera who looked surprised.

Chance's head bobbed.

"Hell, man, that was eight years ago."

"Reckon so. But there's no statute of limitations on a murder charge."

"That was a fair fight, too. Fairer even than that Benton punk. There were two Marin brothers, and one of them was about to shoot me in the back."

Chance shrugged, and straightened. "I don't care."

"Ranger." Albavera spoke in a tired voice. "I've no quarrel with you."

"Good. That'll make our trip to Galveston much more pleasant."

"I don't want to kill you."

The curiosity of the vaquero died. He rose slowly, and joined the crowd.

"You killing me wouldn't make our trip pleasant. But me killing you?" Chance dropped his hand by the butt of the Schofield. "You want to put your left arm on the table?"

The black man's head shook. "Can't. It's holding a sawed-off Springfield rifle that's pointed at your gut."

"That gives you only one shot."

Albavera smiled.

Probably has all his teeth, too, Chance thought.

The black man said, "That's all I need."

A momentary silence was broken by a shout from the bar. "Five dollars says the Ranger kills him."

"I'll take that bet!" came a reply from one of the old buffalo soldiers at the faro layout.

Albavera's eyes hardened. He gathered his money and the pocketwatch, which he dropped into his vest pocket, pushed the chips toward the woman, and spoke in a pleasant voice. "Miss Lottie, I'd like to cash in."

"One of you two's about to do just that," she said, but collected his chips and counted out a wad of greenbacks, which she shoved to Albavera. That money, too, he pocketed. Then rose.

The weapon in his massive left hand was,

indeed, a sawed-off Springfield, the barrel cut down to an inch past the forearm, the walnut stock carved into a pistol grip decorated by brass studs forming a star.

That impressed Dave Chance. If he tried to shoot a weapon like that, it would probably break his wrist.

Strapped to a shell belt filled with big brass .45-70 cartridges was a big holster, tied down on Albavera's left thigh. The man wore striped black britches tucked inside spotless stovepipe boots with white crescent moons inlaid in the tops. No spurs.

"Drop your gunbelt, Ranger." Nodding at the weapon he held, Albavera said, "Miss Vickie here will blow a hole in you big enough to drive a Studebaker through."

The Springfield, Chance noticed, was cocked.

"Shoot the damned darky!" another voice cried from the bar.

Seven tense seconds passed before Chance let out a weary sigh, and unbuckled the russet gunbelt, letting the Schofield drop heavily to the floor.

"Now, kick it under the table."

Chance did as he was instructed.

"Ladies, gents," Albavera said, taking a chance, laying the Springfield on the table as he donned his coat, then his duster. "I'll be taking my leave now. Please don't anyone stick his or her head out of the door or window. I'd hate to kill anybody on this fine morning. Grounds a little hard to be digging a grave."

He picked up the Springfield, tipped his hat at Lottie, smiled at Chance, and backed his way to the door.

"Why didn't you make a play for that bastard when he put that big gun of his on the table?" the infantry corporal demanded. "You could have at least tried."

"Why didn't you?" Chance watched Albavera nod once more, turn and run.

Chance was already sprinting, drawing the Smith & Wesson .32 from his back.

"Hooray!" called one of the white bettors at the bar.

"Watch out, mister!" warned one of the old buffalo soldiers at the faro layout.

"Ten dollars says the colored boy gets away!" someone bet.

"Five-to-one dollar says there'll be a double funeral mañana."

Chance ran past the door. Outside, he heard the nervous snorts of horses stamping their feet. He weaved around a couple tables, shoved a muleskinner out of his way, jumped onto another table, overturning a pitcher of beer, and dived through the window.

CHAPTER THREE

Slivers bit into his neck and arms as he fell in a cascade of broken glass. Horses snorted and stomped. Screams and cackles came from inside the saloon. Sergeant Dave Chance landed with a thud on the hard-packed earth in front of the building — the landlord had been too damned cheap to put up a boardwalk or porch — and immediately rolled to his right, the Smith & Wesson extended in front of him. Surprisingly, his hat remained on his head.

For a moment, all he saw were the hooves and saddles of the horses tied to the hitching rails. Finally, he made out the gray legs of the Andalusian stallion. Moses Albavera had led the horse away from the other animals and was swinging into the saddle. To Chance's astonishment, Albavera made no move to shoot him. *Saving his shot,* Chance figured. *He only has one.*

Scrambling to his knees, Chance dived

behind a water trough, caught his breath, and made his way to the right corner. He peered around the trough and hindquarters of a small blue roan.

Albavera threw his left leg in the stirrup, his right hand gripping the saddle horn and reins. His left hand held the sawed-off Springfield as he tried to boost himself into the saddle. He didn't make it.

With its girth loosened, the saddle slipped under the big man's weight, and he crashed to the ground with a thud.

Inside the saloon, someone groaned. A few of the patrons, the bettors, most likely, had chanced a few looks out the windows and doorway.

Chance fired a shot into the air, spooking the Andalusian into taking a few steps away from Albavera. Most of the horses at the hitching rails had already been frightened when Chance busted through the plate-glass window. The roan broke its reins, took off south toward Chihuahua. Another bay fell to its knees. On the far side, a claybank reared, jerking the rail from its post, which allowed the ten other mounts to slip free, and take off at a lope down the Overland trail.

"Hell's bells!" a cowboy cried out, and busted through the door.

"Stay inside, you damned fool!" Chance cried. He dived away from the trough, landed on his right shoulder, and drew a bead on Moses Albavera as the black man rose, swinging the Springfield in Chance's direction.

The .32 bucked in Chance's hand. Over the din of noise, he heard the whine of the bullet as it splintered the Springfield's forearm, and sent the sawed-off rifle spinning toward another water trough, knocking Albavera off balance. The man-killer landed on his buttocks.

He looked dazed, but only for a moment.

Chance came to his knees, brought the Smith & Wesson level, and pointed the gun's short barrel at Albavera's diamond stickpin. "Don't move."

Albavera didn't, except for shaking the cobwebs out of his head.

"Crap!" came a yell from inside the saloon.

Chance climbed to his feet, keeping the Smith & Wesson trained on the gunman, who grinned and sat with his legs outstretched, his hat still on, and the Andalusian a few rods behind him. Chance's own horse also had not run.

"Ranger?" a cowboy asked from the doorway. "Is it all right if we go fetch our horses?

The ramrod at the Backward-C-Lazy-Seven won't take kindly if we come home afoot."

"Go ahead." Chance's eyes never left Albavera. "Just walk behind my prisoner."

A half-dozen cowhands, soldiers, mule-skinners, saloon girls, and the woman gambler named Lottie stepped outside. All but the cowboys stayed close to the saloon.

"You're a good shot, Ranger," Albavera said. He pointed at the Springfield. "You do that on purpose?"

Chance shook his head. "I was aiming for your gut."

Albavera's smile widened. "I figured." He shook his head again. "Well, I guess I'm your prisoner."

Chance never lowered the .32. He watched as Albavera brushed the dirt off his hands on his outstretched pant legs, on the sleeves of his linen duster, then wiped them on the front of his vest. Chance started toward him, heard a cough, shot a glance at the saloon front, then looked back to Albavera. "Damn."

Moses Albavera had fished an over-under .41-caliber Remington derringer from his vest pocket. He fired once, the bullet tearing off Chance's hat as he ducked. Quickly, Chance cut loose, knowing he missed, as he dived to the ground. He rolled, came up, and saw Albavera rounding the corner of the saloon. Chance held his shot.

Someone in front of the saloon whistled with appreciation.

Chance's revolver was a five-shot, but he always kept the chamber under the hammer empty. He had fired three times, leaving him with one round. Fishing out a few extra shells from his vest pocket, he quickly reloaded the top-break .32, giving him five shots to Albavera's one round left in the double-shot Remington.

Unless, he realized, Albavera had reloaded the derringer.

He walked back to the water trough and picked up the Springfield in his left hand. The sawed-off rifle appeared to be in working condition. His slug had only splintered the forearm a bit. Stepping toward the saloon, he pulled back the hammer of the big gun. He tried to think.

The two-story saloon lay in pretty much open country, with some outhouses behind it, and a few adobe structures off to the north. More buildings lay south, before Chihuahua, but Albavera would be in open country if he made his run that way. Behind the saloon there was nothing but open prairie for a good three hundred yards, then a barbed-wire fence that would offer no cover. Beyond that rose a mountain, but the mountain was treeless. If Albavera went that way, he'd be a sitting duck.

Chance decided Albavera's only shot at escape lay right by the saloon. He'd want to get that Andalusian, if he could; if not, then one of the horses that hadn't spooked. He'd make his escape then. First, however, he'd have to kill Dave Chance.

"Reckon you got a choice, Ranger," a burly black man said, grinning a toothless smile. "Which corner of this building you wanna stick your head around. Which corner won't get your head blowed clean off."

Chance pointed the barrel of the sawed-off Springfield at the man's big belly. "Anybody here shouts a warning," he said calmly, "I'll kill him." He looked at Lottie. "Or her." He pushed his way past the crowd, and entered the saloon.

The beer-jerker behind the bar scowled at him as Chance made his way to the poker table. He couldn't blame him. Nobody in the saloon was ordering anything to drink, and the roulette wheel, faro layouts, and poker table were empty. Underneath the table, he found his gunbelt. He buckled it on, checked the Schofield, and headed for the stairs, feeling he had enough firepower to handle Moses Albavera.

All eyes were on the Ranger as he made his way up the steps to the second level.

He picked the center door facing the back, hoping the room had a window. Quietly he turned the knob, pushed open the door slightly, and entered — .32 first.

The room appeared to be an office. A lawyer's bookcase stood by the door, a roll-top desk was in the center opposite a couple of reception chairs covered in silk damask. Pretty fancy for a grog shop. Behind the desk was a window that drew Chance's attention. Leaving the door open, he eased his way across the creaking floorboards to the desk, then to the window.

The walls, of course, were thin. To his left, he heard the squeaking of bedsprings, and a woman's giggles — which was what he had expected to find in the room he was in. Apparently, the happenings downstairs and outside held no interest for the amorous couple next door. He started to gently push back the drapes, when a noise to his right stopped him.

Behind the walls came the groan of a window, followed by a woman's gasp. "What the hell?" He heard her clearly. Then, "Moses . . . what are you —"

He even heard Albavera's desperate

"Shhh. Quiet, Ramona. Quiet."

Smiling, Chance looked out the window and saw a ladder leaning against the saloon. Carefully, he set the Springfield and Smith & Wesson on the desktop, and quietly knelt, pulling off his boots, careful to keep the jinglebobs on his spurs from chiming. Finished, he rose, picked up both weapons, and quietly picked his way across the floor in his stocking feet, halting at the door. He put his left ear against the wall.

For a moment, all he heard were the clanks of glass and muffled conversations on the floor below. The squeaking and giggles from the room on the left had stopped, but the voices came clearly.

"How was that, Judy?"

"That'll be two bits, sugar."

The right-hand door opened. Boots creaked on the floor. The conversations and noise downstairs immediately ceased.

Chance held his breath, waiting, listening as the boots neared. Moses Albavera's broad back came into view. He held a Remington in his right hand, his left gripping the balustrade, watching below. The big man kept walking, not bothering to look at the doors on the east wall. Chance waited until the man's back was even with the Spring-field rifle in his left hand.

44

"Drop your derringer, Moses," Chance said. "Miss Vickie here will blow a hole in you big enough to drive a Studebaker through."

Surprisingly, Moses Albavera laughed, and dropped the Remington on the floor.

"Kick it under the railing."

"It might go off."

"It might. Kick it."

Albavera swept his foot, and the little hideaway pistol dropped to the first floor with a thud. It didn't discharge.

"Reckon we think alike, Ranger," Albavera said. "Guess that's my mistake."

"We're even then," Chance said. "My mistake was taking my eyes off you for a second outside. Gave you a chance to palm that derringer. Were you aiming at my hat?"

Albavera's head shook. "I was aiming for your head."

"Don't move." Chance stepped out of the doorway and prodded Albavera's back with the Springfield's barrel. The door behind him opened. Without looking at the prostitute, Chance said, "Ramona, would you be so kind as to go into that office and fetch my boots?"

No answer.

"Do it, Ramona," Albavera said. "Do it for old Moses here."

45

She did as she was told, and the other door opened. A young cowboy's head appeared in the crack. Behind him was the curious face of a whore.

Slowly, Albavera drew a quarter from his vest pocket and tossed it in front of the door. "Y'all go have yourself another quickie. Old Moses's treat."

The door slammed shut.

Halfway down the stairs Chance made Albavera stop while he hurriedly pulled on his boots. He gathered both guns, continued down the stairs, and headed outside, the crowd of men and women parting for them like the Red Sea.

The gamblers began paying off or collecting their debts.

Chance prodded Albavera past the horses and troughs, stopping to pick up his hat. He ran a finger through the hole in the center of the crown, and pulled the battered hat on his head.

"Walk to the sorrel," Chance ordered.

"Your horse?" Albavera asked.

"Yes."

"Nice looking mount."

"So's yours."

Albavera stopped by the sorrel gelding.

"Stand there, hands up," Chance ordered, and walked to the horse. He shoved the

Smith & Wesson behind his back, kept the Springfield trained on Albavera, and gathered his mackinaw from the saddle. "Open the saddlebag," Chance said, "pull out a pair of bracelets, put them on your wrists."

The black man did as he was told.

"Step away from the sorrel."

Again, Albavera obeyed.

Chance placed the Springfield at his feet, pulled on his jacket, and then drew a Winchester Centennial from its scabbard.

"Nice rifle," Albavera said.

"Uh-huh. Now, mount up."

"What about my stallion?"

"I'll ride him. I figure that gray can outrun that sorrel of mine. In case you get the notion."

"I don't know," Albavera said. "This little gelding's got a lot of heart, lot of stamina, I think. Might be a good horse race."

"Mount up."

Grunting, Albavera swung into the saddle.

"All right." Chance turned, saw the Andalusian, and remembered the saddle. Sighing, he barked an order at one of the loafers in front of the saloon to fix the saddle. While a cowhand did that, Chance grabbed the saddlebags from his sorrel and shoved the Springfield in the bag that had contained his handcuffs. When it was buckled tight he secured the bags behind the saddle on the gray stallion. Next, he withdrew a Winchester carbine from the scabbard, and tossed it to the cowboy who had saddled the horse. "Payment," he said.

"Thanks," the cowhand said. "But them stirrups might be a little long for your legs."

"They'll do." He slid his Centennial into the scabbard, gathered the reins, mounted the horse, and drew the Schofield. "All right, Moses Albavera, let's go to Galveston."

Albavera pointed toward the Butterfield trail. More than twenty riders were loping down the road, turning off, heading straight for the two-story saloon.

"I'm not sure either of us will live to see Galveston, Ranger," the black man said. "If I'm not mistaken, that's Don Melitón Benton."

CHAPTER FOUR

The bells of the mission Nuestra Señora de Limpia Concepción de Los Piros de San Pedro del Sur — Our Lady of the Immaculate Conception of the Piros of Saint Peter of the South — rang loudly that morning until the friar pulling the rope spotted the riders entering the village. As the ringing died the friar ran out in front of the whitewashed building, urging an elderly woman and her daughter inside, slamming the heavy wooden door shut behind them.

A dog barked once, before scurrying underneath an ox cart.

The streets were empty.

A shutter on a window facing the street quickly closed.

Captain Hec Savage and Juan Lo Grande led the column of riders down the quiet streets, stopping at the cantina. Lo Grande nodded at one of the riders, a thin man wearing the bullet-riddled, bloodstained uniform he had torn off a corpse on the Río Grande. The *bandido* pounded the butt of his battered musket on the door until a gaunt man still in his nightshirt opened the door. Shoving the man out of the way, he beckoned at the mounted horsemen and barged through the doorway.

"You must try the *mole de guajalote*," Lo Grande said casually as he swung down from his white horse.

"For breakfast?" Savage shook his head.

"Amigo." Lo Grande wrapped the reins around the hitching rail in front of the cantina. "We will be here much longer than for breakfast. *¿No es verdad?*"

"We'll see." Savage dismounted and found the makings for a smoke.

To the captain's surprise, more than half of Lo Grande's men headed for the mission instead of the cantina. Most of the Rangers led their horses to the livery across the street. That didn't surprise Savage. He should have done the same thing, but after he had lit a cigarette, he followed Lo Grande into the adobe building.

Lo Grande took a seat at a table facing the doorway, his back to the wall. The Mexican outlaw gestured to the opposite chair, but Savage grabbed another, and sat directly beside Lo Grande. Both men drew their revolvers and laid them on the rough tabletop. The man in the nightshirt immediately brought them a bottle of tequila, and filled two tumblers.

Lo Grande lifted his. *"A su salud, mi capitán."*

Their glasses clinked. Lo Grande downed his in an instant. Savage took a small sip, then set the glass beside his Merwin Hulbert. He told the man in the nightshirt, *"Café solo negro, por favor. Y agua."*

"Sí." The man in the nightshirt hurried to the kitchen.

"You speak our language *muy bien*," Lo Grande said as he refilled his glass.

"Had to." Savage exhaled, and took another long drag on the cigarette. "You damned greasers living in Texas won't learn our language."

Lo Grande's head shook. "I am no damned greaser, amigo. And I do not live in your humble state."

"Texas ain't humble, Lo Grande. And you spend enough time north of the river. Hell, you could probably vote in the next election."

Leaning his head against the wall, the Mexican let out a boisterous laugh, slammed his glass, empty again, on the table. *"Rinche*, you amuse me."

"You smile too damned much."

Lo Grande shrugged. " 'One may smile and smile, and still be a villain.' "

"That's the damned truth."

Two women, their hair a mess, clothes hurriedly thrown on, came out of the kitchen, and began serving Lo Grande's men who had not gone to Mass. Doc Shaw and two other Rangers hesitated at the doorway, but finally entered the cantina, taking a table near the window. They, too, put their pistols on the table. Savage looked through the window, scanning the low rooftops of the adobe buildings across the street, half-expecting to see a rifle barrel appear. He wouldn't put an ambush past a man like Juan Lo Grande.

The man in the nightshirt returned with Savage's cup of coffee and a glass of water. He set both on the table, then turned, but Lo Grande stopped him, ordering *huevos revueltos con jamón, té* and one *toronja.* With a worried nod, the man returned to the kitchen, glancing at the women as they took orders from Lo Grande's men.

"We should get down to business," Savage said, pitching his cigarette to the floor, sipping his coffee.

"Después de desayuno, mi capitán," Lo Grande said.

Two of Lo Grande's men began shouting at each other, rising from their seats. Savage shook his head. "Not after breakfast, Lo Grande. Now." He lowered his left hand below the table, and, taking advantage of the noise the two bandidos made, carefully drew his other ivory-handled .44, leaving it cocked on his lap.

Shaking his head, Lo Grande refilled his tumbler, but did not raise it to his lips. *"¡Cállate!"* he yelled at the two arguing bandits, and the men glanced at him, shut up, and sat down. He turned toward Savage, looked at down at the Ranger's lap, and grinned.

Man's got good ears, Savage thought. *Heard me cocking that .44 over all that ruction.*

"Very well," Lo Grande said. "The Rurales of San Pedro are now my men. I control northern Chihuahua."

Savage took another sip of coffee. "What about the Rurales in Ojinaga?"

He crossed himself. "They were killed last week, mi capitán. Without your help."

"That's interesting."

"*Es verdad.* So, again, northern Chihuahua is my kingdom, if you will."

"Till Porfirio Díaz finds out about it."

Lo Grande shook his head. "He won't.

Savage made no reply and switched from

53

coffee to water. He drained the glass.

"Can you control Presidio?" Lo Grande asked.

"Northern Chihuahua's your kingdom. West Texas is mine. Has been for better than ten years."

"Indeed. From the Pecos River to say . . . the Davis Mountains?"

"I'd put it farther west than that."

"But not El Paso, eh, amigo?"

"I don't get to El Paso much."

Lo Grande killed his tequila. "Murphyville and Marathon are the keys to our success."

Towns on the Southern Pacific Railroad. Savage understood that. For an answer, he nodded.

"And what of your *soldados?* The blue-coats, as you call them." Lo Grande grinned again. "Your *presidios.* Fort Davis, Fort Stockton, Fort Bliss."

"I'll take care of them."

"With sixteen men?"

Suddenly, Savage's shoulders sagged. He took another sip of coffee, and sadly shook his head. "When I first come out here, I had seventy-five men. Two lieutenants. Lost a lot of good men" — his cold eyes locked on Lo Grande — "to a lot of murdering vermin like you."

Lo Grande smiled again, lifted his glass in

a mocking salute.

"Austin got tight. Cut back. Hell, they even disbanded some Ranger companies. They think Texas is tame. It's not. Won't ever be."

"Your story is very interesting, amigo, but you digress. You have sixteen men, no?"

"I got twenty. Left four of them behind. Got to keep the peace."

"Indeed. Then sixteen men you can trust?"

"We'll see. Haven't told these boys everything. There's a couple I'm not sure of. Yet." He looked at Doc Shaw and the two Rangers sipping coffee.

"Perhaps you should."

"I'll do it. But there's another thing we got to work out before I agree to anything with the likes of you. You want this little deal to work, I can't have you or your men raiding north of the river, killing miners in Terlingua, making off with a woman."

Lo Grande laughed. "Amigo, she was a *puta.*"

"She's still a woman."

The outlaw leader shook his head. "You want her back?"

"That's why we crossed the border."

Lo Grande pushed his sombrero back, and scratched his head, then shrugged. "You are a man of principle, mi capitán. I thought

55

you came to Mexico to help us eliminate some Rurales." He slammed the bottle of tequila on the table, and called out, "Leoncio!"

A black-bearded man wearing the dead lieutenant's uniform rose from a table, crossed the cantina's floor, and stood in front of Lo Grande as the bandido barked out something in Spanish too rapid for Savage to catch. The man's eyebrows arched, and Lo Grande yelled something else.

"*Sí,*" Leoncio mumbled, and hurried outside.

"It is done." Lo Grande smiled again.

The man in the nightshirt returned with a platter, and served Lo Grande a plate of scrambled eggs, ham, and an old grapefruit, as well as a cup of tea. He also had a fresh cup of coffee for Savage. After depositing the breakfast on the table, he hurried back to the kitchen.

"Before I partake of this *magnifico* breakfast, amigo, I must insist that we reach our truce, and proceed." Lo Grande gathered knife and fork. "*¿Estamos de acuerdo, no?*"

Savage rose, the Merwin Hulbert in his left hand, which he switched to his right. He left the other revolver beside the coffee cups. "Let me ask my men over yonder."

We'll see if we're in agreement or not."

He crossed the room and stood at the table where Doc Shaw sat with Rangers Hamp Magruder and Wes Smith. "Lo Grande's man is fetching that whore," Savage said.

"That's good," Shaw said nervously.

"We've formed a little alliance."

Magruder pushed back his porkpie hat. "Figured that, Capt'n. After what happened on the Río Grande."

"You didn't tell us nothing about that, Captain Savage," Wes Smith said.

"I know it. Maybe I should have. But it's spilt milk."

Magruder leaned forward. "You can't trust a *bandido* like Lo Grande, Capt'n," he whispered.

"Reckon I know that, too." Savage stepped back and looked through the window.

Leoncio was dragging a woman, screaming, fighting, and crying, from the hotel, pulling her by her hair. The Terlingua whore. She fell, but Leoncio never broke stride, dragging her in the dirt. Savage glanced at the livery, saw Demitrio and the others watching, wondering, but staying put. Doc Shaw turned, rose, and cursed, his hand dropping for the long-barreled Colt on the table beside his beer.

"Easy, Doc," Savage warned. "Let him bring her in."

Hamp Magruder also muttered a curse — aimed at Savage — but the Ranger captain ignored it. By that time, Leoncio had entered the saloon, and let go of the woman's brown hair. She fell to the floor sobbing. Slowly lifting her head, her right hand pressed tight against her head, she bit back the pain. Her eyes drilled through the Ranger badge on Savage's chest. Lips trembling, she started to rise.

"Stay put, ma'am," Savage said. To his surprise, she obeyed.

Savage glanced at the .44 in his hand. "Boys, we've been risking our necks for years now. Nothing to show for it. I kinda figure Texas owes us."

"Capt'n," Magruder said, and pointed at the woman. "If this is part of your alliance with Lo Grande, I don't want anything to do with it."

"You helped kill those Rurales on the river," Savage said.

"That's true, Capt'n, but shootin' Mezkins is one thing. You're talkin' 'bout something else."

"We could make a fortune," Savage said.

"Or a trip to the gallows," Wes Smith said.

"That why you led us here, Capt'n?"

Magruder said. "To forge your bond with that son of a bitch?" He tilted his jaw at Lo Grande. "In blood."

Savage tilted his head toward the woman. "Figured to get her back, too."

Slowly Magruder rose. "Capt'n . . ." he began, but Savage had heard enough.

He lifted the Merwin Hulbert and shot the Ranger in the chest. Turning quickly, thumbing back the hammer, he tried to find Wes Smith behind the pungent white smoke, but another shot left his ears ringing before he could line up the young Ranger. Smith slammed over backward, spilling his chair, blood spurting from a purple hole in the center of his forehead as the light slowly left his eyes.

Doc Shaw stood, holding a Colt .45 in his right hand.

The woman on the floor shrieked.

Shaw gave Savage a quick glance before hurrying outside, raising his hands, one holding a smoking revolver. In a calming suggestion he yelled to the Rangers at the livery, "It's all right! Everything's all right!"

The woman kept screaming.

Savage looked at the two dead Rangers on the floor, considered Lo Grande a moment, then knelt by the whore. "Listen to me," he said.

She went right on with those damned howls.

Savage holstered the revolver. Spoke again. She didn't shut up, so he slapped her. Hard. The woman became quiet, looking at him with vacant eyes.

"That's a hard thing to see, ma'am. I'm taking you back to Texas, ma'am. Back to Terlingua." He helped her to her feet. "But you listen to me, ma'am. You ever speak a word of what you just saw, and I promise you you'll wish you were back with them hombres." He pointed at the smiling Lo Grande.

He left the woman standing, as he walked back to the table. The whore stood there, weaving, her eyes on the Rangers on the floor, but not really seeing the dead men, not really seeing anything.

"I guess that settles things," Savage said.

"Muy bien, mi capitán." Lo Grande spooned some grapefruit into his mouth.

"I'll take the woman and those bodies back." Savage picked up the revolver he had left on the table.

"You will be a hero in the eyes of all Tejanos." He spooned another slice of grapefruit.

"Maybe. But I don't reckon it would look right if I brung back just two dead Rangers and a whore." Turning, he thumbed back the hammer of the Merwin Hulbert, and shot off Leoncio's right ear. The black-bearded man screamed, dropping to his knees, putting his right hand over the bleeding, mangled cartilage. Before Lo Grande could swallow the grapefruit, Savage had turned, cocked the .44, and leveled the long barrel an inch from Lo Grande's head.

The woman was yelling again.

"¡No!" Lo Grande yelled, making frantic gestures at his men. *"¡Pare! ¡Pare! ¡No es nada! ¡Espere! ¡No importa!"* The men froze, guns halfway out of their waistbands, sashes, or holsters. The woman screamed. Leoncio toppled onto his side, writhing in pain, kicking, spreading blood across the sod floor.

The woman fell silent. Rangers poured into the doorway.

"It's all right," Savage said. "Isn't it, Lo Grande?"

"Es muy bien," Lo Grande said. For a Mexican, Savage thought, Juan Lo Grande looked mighty pale.

"Doc," Savage called out. "Demitrio. Load poor Magruder and Smith on their saddles. We'll take them home for burying. Bucky, fetch the woman. That's the whore from Terlingua. Taw, you take that one-earred greaser. He's our prisoner. That suit

61

you, Lo Grande?"

"*Sí,*" the bandit said.

"Then we'll be taking our leave. Don't try anything."

"*Buen Viaje.*" Lo Grande lifted his tumbler of tequila, but the glass shook in his hands. "*Hasta la vista, los rinches.*"

"*Adiós.*" Slowly, never lowering the Merwin Hulbert, Hec Savage backed to the door.

CHAPTER FIVE

For the past year, Hec Savage had called the presidio on the bluff overlooking the Rio Grande and the Chihuahua Trail home, but when the massive L-shaped adobe fort came into view, it didn't look inviting. It never did. It merely made Savage feel older than his forty-seven years.

He led his men, the Terlingua prostitute, and his prisoner off the dusty road and through the open gate into the adobe citadel. Squawking chickens and barking dogs ran across the compound as Savage wearily swung down from the saddle, handing the reins to a young Mexican boy.

A bald man in plaid trousers and a red bib-front shirt exited from a side building. He wiped the dirt off his spectacles with a yellow bandana before he made his way to Savage, nodding greetings as other Rangers passed. Suddenly he stopped, staring as Demitrio led a pair of bay geldings behind him, two bodies wrapped in canvas draped over the saddles.

"Who are they?" the man asked.

"Smith and Magruder, Lieutenant," Demitrio said without stopping.

"Damn." Shaking his head, Ranger Lieutenant Ray Wickes resumed his journey across the compound, glancing at the Terlingua whore and the Mexican outlaw, but focusing on Hec Savage.

They shook hands, though neither was glad to see the other. Wickes pointed his folded eyeglasses at the woman and prisoner. "You got the woman."

Savage nodded. He wasn't one to waste words answering an obvious question.

"What about the payroll?"

"No luck. But I reckon them miners would rather have their whore returned than any money."

"Who's the prisoner?"

"Calls himself Leoncio." Savage walked to the well, where a Mexican woman hurriedly hoisted a bucket. "One of Lo Grande's men."

"He need a doctor?"

"He's not getting one."

Wickes put on his eyeglasses. He had to walk fast to keep pace with Savage. "Smith and Magruder?" he asked.

"They bought it. But we put a hurt on Lo Grande."

They had reached the well. The woman offered Savage a ladle, but he shook his head, tossed off his hat, and dipped his hands into the cold water, splashing it across his face, running his fingers through his knotted hair. After he patted himself dry, he pointed at the woman who stood beside the corrals, not knowing what to do, or where to go.

"Eulalia," Savage told the Mexican woman, "the gal's name is Linda Kincaid." That much Savage had learned on the ride from San Pedro. "I'd be obliged if you'd see to her, give her some grub, maybe a dress or something. Fix her a bath. A hot bath. With some of that yucca soap you make that smells so nice. She's had a rough time."

"*Sí,*" the woman said, and took the bucket and ladle toward the Terlingua whore.

"You haven't polished off that bottle of good Manhattan rye, have you, Ray?" Savage asked. He picked up his hat, slapping it against his pants to rid it of the dust.

The lieutenant forced a smile. "Not yet."

El Fortín, or Fort Leaton, lay about five miles east of the town of Presidio. An old scalp hunter and trader named Ben Leaton

65

had built it in 1850 on the ruins of El Fortín de San José at La Junta, which the Spanish had founded in the early 1770s. Ben Leaton had built well. The long side stretched about 200 feet parallel to the Río Grande, the bottom of the "L" reaching about 140 feet against which the stockade for livestock had been constructed. The adobe walls, with fading whitewash, were at least eighteen inches thick, sometimes as thick as three-and-a-half feet. A parapet stretched atop the high walls, and two Rangers marched across, standing watch.

Most people considered Fort Leaton impregnable.

Old Ben Leaton didn't live there long. He died in 1851, and his widow was forced to sell it to John Burgess, who had held the mortgage. Burgess lived there until Bill Leaton, the old scalp hunter's son, killed him in 1875. The Burgess family finally abandoned the place in 1884, and Hec Savage had taken it over.

His office, a spartan affair with two desks, chairs, a case of rifles, and a few books, was near the main entrance to the fort. A map of Texas hung on the wall beside a wind-battered Lone Star flag. Ray Wickes reached between the stocks of a Winchester and a Sharps rifle, and retrieved the half-full bottle of Manhattan rye. While he filled two tumblers, Savage sat at his desk and shuffled through some papers.

Wickes handed Savage a glass, then sipped the whiskey and asked, "Exactly . . . well . . . where did you meet Lo Grande? The colonel . . . he really wants to know." Wickes gestured at the telegrams on the desk.

Savage finished about half the rye. He set the tumbler on the desk, scanned a line on one of the pieces of yellow paper, and tossed it into the wastebasket in the corner.

"My report'll say Cibolo Creek."

"Colonel Thomas will never believe that."

"I don't give a damn." Another telegram went into the trash.

Wickes pointed his tumbler at the papers. "Most of those are from Colonel Thomas. Wanting to know where you were. Demanding that you not cross into Mexico. Warning you that an engagement with the Rurales based in Ojinaga would lead to an international incident, something neither Austin nor Washington City would appreciate."

"Uh-huh." Savage gathered all the papers, even two rolled-up editions of the *Presidio County News,* the newspaper published in Fort Davis, and tossed them into the trash. "First of all, there are no Rurales in Ojinaga or San Pedro. Lo Grande's men massacred them."

"What?" Wickes spilled rye over his shirt.

Savage figured that would get the lieutenant's attention. Ojinaga lay just across the river from Presidio.

"Who'd you learn . . . ?" Wickes shook his head, the gravity of the situation slowly seeping through that bald head of his.

"Heard it from that prisoner. We'll keep the bastard here for a while. I'm not about to turn him over to the county sheriff or them miners in Terlingua. Not yet."

Wickes killed his rye, suppressed a cough, and said, "Maybe you should inform the commanding officer at Fort Davis. About Lo Grande and Ojinaga, I mean."

"Not the Army's concern. I'll keep an eye on things."

Wickes started to protest, but a knock on the door cut him off. Doc Shaw stuck his head through the doorway. "Begging the captain's pardon — hello, Mr. Wickes — but it's about that whore."

"Come on in, Doc. Pour yourself a whiskey."

Doc Shaw accepted the invite. As soon as he had killed a shot, he wiped his mouth, and said, "It's about Miss Kincaid, Captain."

"What about her?"

"Well, she don't want to go back to Terlingua."

Savage frowned.

"I don't blame her," Ray Wickes said.

Savage eyed his lieutenant with something between contempt and hatred.

"Where exactly does she want to go?"

"Houston."

"Why in hell would anyone want to go to that cesspool?" Savage finished his rye, and motioned to Doc Shaw, who held the bottle, for a refill. As the amber liquid poured into the tumbler, Doc Shaw explained.

"Well, Captain, she's got kin in Houston. She had a rough time with Lo Grande's men. You know that. Terlingua's just bad memories for her. She wants to start fresh. See if her folks will take her in. They live in Houston."

"This whore? She tell you that?"

"She told Eulalia. Eulalia told Demitrio. Demitrio told me."

Savage took a swallow of rye, then ran his rough fingers on the rim of the glass, considering.

"We could take her to Marathon," Wickes said. "Put her on an eastbound."

The problem, Savage knew, was that there was a telegraph office in Marathon. Doc

Shaw had to know that, as well. Savage certainly wasn't sure if the whore would keep quiet. That's why he wanted her in Terlingua, where the mail coach ran only once a week. It stopped at Fort Leaton, about sixty miles west, before heading north to Fort Davis and the San Antonio-El Paso road. Savage could inspect any outgoing mail, any letter Miss Linda Kincaid happened to write, any letter that looked threatening. Maybe he should have killed her, but, no Texas Ranger — no man — ever manhandled a petticoat. The sanctity of a woman, even a whore, even one from Terlingua, was something a man like Savage respected.

Yet if the woman reached Houston . . .

. . . She might talk. There might be a murder warrant issued for Hector Savage, and killing two holier-than-thou Rangers did not go over well in Austin. Well, Savage thought, he had only killed one. Doc Shaw had gunned down poor Wes Smith. Still, Colonel Thomas would hang Savage.

On the other hand . . .

"What did you say?" Savage killed his whiskey, and looked up at Wickes.

In a confused voice, Wickes answered, "I said we could take Miss Kincaid to Marathon. Let her catch the eastbound S.P. for

70

Houston."

Savage dipped into his outer coat pocket, rubbed the crucifix he had stolen off the Rurale lieutenant, found the makings, and began rolling a cigarette. "Wasn't Private Smith from Houston?" he asked.

"I'd have to check our records," Wickes said.

"Do it."

Wickes sat at the other desk, opened a drawer, pulled out a ledger, and began thumbing through the pages. "Yes. Smith enlisted in Houston in May of '83."

"Where was Magruder from?"

Wickes turned back two pages. "Alabama. Came to Texas in '67."

"No kin?"

"No, sir."

"Well, those two Rangers died in the line of duty. Died heroically." Savage struck a match against his thumb, fired up the cigarette. "They deserve a fitting sendoff. Lieutenant, I want you, Sergeant Chance, and Rangers Turpen and Babbitt to escort the bodies of Rangers Magruder and Smith to Marathon. The whore will go with y'all." He put the smoke on the ashtray, found paper and pencil, began writing out the orders. "You will proceed by train to Houston, deliver Miss Kincaid to her relatives, and see that Ranger Smith is given a proper funeral. Make sure the newspapers write about him and his funeral. I want his funeral to be the biggest thing to happen in Houston since . . . since I killed Duke Duncan there back in 1869.

"After that" — Savage paused long enough to take another drag on the smoke, and picked up the paper — "you will escort the body of Private Hamp Magruder to Austin, where he is to be buried in the state cemetery with full honors. If Colonel Thomas or that stupid governor make a fuss, tell them to go to hell. Magruder was an excellent man, spent many a year fighting for justice, and made the ultimate sacrifice. I think it is fitting and proper that he lie for eternity alongside Texans such as Ben McCullough and Albert Sidney Johnston."

He signed the order, folded it, and handed it to a reluctant Wickes.

"You think this is wise, Captain? I mean . . . with Lo Grande controlling Ojinaga?"

"I'll handle Lo Grande, Lieutenant. You handle the remains of your brave, late comrades. And that whore."

"But that'll leave you with just a dozen men."

"Fourteen." He took another pull on the cigarette. "Turpen and Babbitt are up on the parapet, right?"

"Yes, sir."

"Good. You will inform them of their orders. You will proceed with all due haste to the Southern Pacific depot at Marathon —" He frowned, and crushed out the cigarette. "Where is Sergeant Chance?"

"Dave was up in Murphyville, Captain," Wickes said. "A Mex carpenter informed him that Moses Albavera was in Fort Davis. He went after —"

"Who the hell is Moses Albavera?"

"He's in the book, Captain."

Sighing, Savage reached across the ashtray to the books, pulling out a worn copy of the 1882 *List of Fugitives from Justice.* It was outdated, but that was Austin for you.

"What county?" Savage asked.

"Galveston."

"Galveston. Jesus Christ!"

Savage found the page, scanned the list of names, and found the entry.

Albavera, Moses . . . First-degree murder (two counts); indicted July '77; Moorish, i.e., Negroid, about 6 feet 3 inches in height; 200 pounds; left-handed; fancy dresser; excellent marksman;

horseman. Killed Joseph and Chet Marin, brothers, at the Gulf Saloon & Gambling Parlor. Petty larceny (indicted July '77). Failed to pay hotel for five nights lodging. Horse theft (indicted July '77). Stole bay gelding & saddle, owned by Mr. Thad Taylor, Galveston. Horse recovered August '77 in Victoria. Saddle never located.

Slamming the book shut, Savage shook his head. "Why the hell would Sergeant Chance go after some colored boy who's wanted for killing two vermin in Galveston, hell, eight years ago, when there's plenty of outlaws west of the Pecos, and Juan Lo Grande's been raising hell?"

"He's wanted, Captain."

Six Rangers under Savage's command were too damned honest. Two of those were dead. Savage had concocted a plan to get rid of the other four, but Dave Chance had to light out after some fool Negro man-killer.

"He might be posted for another killing, Captain," Ray Wickes was saying. "I heard this Albavera fellow shot Prince Benton dead a few days ago up in Shafter."

Savage studied Wickes for a full minute, letting the words soak in, then burst out

74

laughing. As he filled his tumbler with more rye, he said, "Well, hell, that'll do, I reckon. If that darky doesn't kill Chance, Don Melitón surely will."

CHAPTER SIX

Moses Albavera suggested, "You might want to give me a gun."

Said Dave Chance, "I don't think so."

"Not even to protect myself from two dozen armed men?"

"That's my job."

Albavera swore, then spit.

The good sign was that Don Melitón Benton raised his right hand as he neared Chance and his prisoner, and the twenty-five vaqueros riding behind him reined in their lathered mounts. The bad sign was that the old man held a side hammer Allen & Wheelock pistol. On the other hand, that weapon was a single-shot, and Chance had always figured it would take something more powerful than a .22 to kill him. Of course, each of Don Melitón's vaqueros wore a brace of Navy Colts in their sashes, apparently all converted to centerfire, and carried Spencer carbines in their saddle scabbards. More than enough to finish off Chance and Albavera.

Chance studied the Schofield revolver as if it were a toy gun, and holstered it, putting his left hand on the saddle's cantle and hooking his left leg over the horn. He waited for the don to approach.

Nobody truly knew where Don Melitón Benton hailed from. Despite his dress — open-sided, concho-studded britches favored by Spanish noblemen, *calzoneras* they were called, and a suede jacket trimmed in red velvet with elaborate embroidery — he wasn't Mexican. An elegant mustache and neatly trimmed goatee, pure white, accented the bronzed face underneath a flat-crowned black hat secured underneath his chin by a horsehair braided stampede string.

Throughout West Texas and northern Chihuahua, stories were told that as a much younger man, he had fled Missouri — Chance always liked to believe the one that had Don Melitón, or Milton, as he had been called in earlier days, killing a man in a duel over a lady from Independence — into Mexico, where he had worked as a mule-skinner for a freighting outfit that ran from Meoqui to Ojinaga. By 1850, Milton Benton had married the daughter of a flour mill magnate in Meoqui, and taken over the freighting outfit. By 1855, he had expanded his runs to the Chihuahua and Santa Fe trails. Five years later, Benton left Meoqui with his wife, Francisca, and carved out a *rancho* in Texas's Chinati Mountains, some twenty-five miles north of the Río Grande. He bought land. Many stories said he learned the location of abundant springs from the Apaches.

His *rancho* along Cibolo Creek was more fortress than home, a hundred-square-foot adobe citadel with circular defense towers at the northern and southern corners in which visitors would always find armed guards. Other ranches he established in the Big Bend country were equally well protected.

His wife gave birth to a son, and Milton carved a kingdom in that patch of desert, trading at his *rancho,* raising longhorn cattle and sheep. Fruits grown in his orchards tasted spectacular, and nobody ever passed the chance to sample his peach brandy. By the end of the Civil War, nobody knew him as Milton Benton anymore. He was Don Melitón.

His accent hadn't changed, though. It remained pure Missouri.

"Reckon I'll take that b'hoy off your hands, pilgrim," he said.

"Reckon you won't, Don Melitón," Chance said.

"You know me?"

"I was at your *rancho* on Cibolo Creek this year, Independence Day, sir. Remember? You invited all of Captain Savage's Rangers from Fort Leaton." After shoving his mackinaw behind the butt of the Schofield, Chance tapped the badge pinned to his vest.

"You won't be invited back next Fourth of July. You son-of-a-bitchin' Rangers drank four kegs of peach brandy, another of pure Kentucky bourbon, and took two bottles of Manhattan rye."

"Yes, sir. It was quite the fandango. Captain Savage still has one bottle of the rye. Had, at least, last time I was down Presidio way."

"I want him." The old man pointed the barrel of the pistol at Albavera, but the .22 hadn't been cocked.

Yet.

"So does the county sheriff in Galveston."

"Galveston!" The old man practically spit.

"Yes, sir. He murdered a couple of brothers —"

Albavera interrupted, "It was a fair fight."

Chance kept on — "in a saloon there in the summer of '77. I'm bringing him in."

79

"For a reward, I take it," Don Melitón said.

"I don't know that there is a reward, sir."

"There is," Albavera said. "A hundred dollars."

"Not much money for a couple of brothers," Chance said.

"They weren't exactly pillars of the community," Albavera said.

"Shut your traps," Don Melitón snapped. "I don't care how many brothers this man killed in Galveston, or how many men he killed anywhere else. He killed my son. For that, I shall kill him."

Chance switched legs over the horn, stretched, and shook his head. "Don, sir, I don't think you'd have any trouble getting the attorney general to give Presidio County first crack at trying Moses Albavera. And knowing the folks out here, they'd have him swinging in a hurry."

"That's a sure bet," Albavera muttered.

Chance wished that big bastard would shut up.

"I'd prefer killing him myself," the don said.

"I don't blame you. But he gets a fair trial."

Albavera snorted with contempt.

"My wife has been dead ten years," the

old man said. "I'm not long for this world. I'd planned on leaving my empire to Prince. That man has taken away not only my son's life, but my legacy."

Albavera cried, "You were going to leave your fortune to that tinhorn? What he wouldn't have squandered away, he would have gambled away. You're better off alone, old man. Give your empire back to the poor bastards you stole it from. The Mexicans. The Apaches. Hell, give it to those brave riders you got backing your play. Give it to the great state of Texas."

Chance wouldn't bet on who was getting angrier with each word his prisoner spoke, the don or himself.

"Let me tell you about your son, old man," Albavera continued. "We were playing poker at Diego's Cantina in Shafter. He was losing. I was winning. This Mexican lady comes in off the street selling tamales. I bought one. He took one. I paid her. She asked your boy for some money. He took a bite, spit it out, told her it was terrible, and shoved the rest of the tamale in her face. Shoved real hard, too. She hit the floor, and I hit him. I admit, I hit your son harder than he hit the woman. He got up cussing me, calling me a 'swamp-running SOB,' and I hit him again. Told him my family was

Moors. I'm right proud of my heritage. He drew his revolver. I kicked it out of his hand and hit him again. Then I helped the lady up, gave her a dollar, and sent her on her way. I gathered my winnings, and started for the door. That's when I heard the revolver cock. I ducked, drew Miss Vickie, and spun. Your son's shot tugged at the collar of my coat." He tilted his head to the left, and Chance saw a hole in the buckskin coat's collar. "Mine hit him in the chest."

Chance let his leg down from the horn. His boots found the stirrups. His right hand found the butt of the Schofield.

"That's how it was, pardners," Albavera said. "You ask anybody in Shafter who was at Diego's Cantina, and they'll tell you that's what happened. Anyone who won't lie for you, Don Melitón."

Knowing Prince Benton, Chance believed Albavera's story, and, from the look on the old man's face, so did the don. Yet Chance knew the powerful merchant and rancher would not bend. The don looked again at Chance.

"I have no quarrel with you, Ranger."

"I've none with you, Don. Not yet."

"You say there is a hundred dollar reward for this man in Galveston?"

"I didn't say it." Chance's chin pointed

82

toward Albavera. "He did."

"I will pay you five hundred dollars. In gold."

Chance pushed up the brim of his hat. "When?"

The old man turned, barked an order, and one of the vaqueros rode up, reached into his saddlebag, pulled out two leather pouches, and tossed them into the dirt between the gray Andalusian and the sorrel gelding. The coins clinked when the pouches hit the dirt. Someone still standing in front of the saloon whistled. The vaquero backed his horse away from the don.

Chance studied the two pouches, looked at Don Melitón, then turned to Albavera. Taking a deep breath, he slowly exhaled, and sighed, shrugging at Albavera before he looked back at the old man. Chance reached into his vest pocket, pulled out a key, and tossed it to the dirt. "He's yours." Sliding from the Andalusian, he walked toward the money pouches.

"You greedy bastard," Albavera said.

Dismounting, Don Melitón barked an order at his riders, then walked toward the handcuffed prisoner, the single-shot pistol still in his hand, still uncocked. As Chance bent to pick up the gold pouches, the don swept up the key in his left hand without breaking stride. The old man made a beeline for the prisoner, never considering Chance, never seeing one of the pouches sail from Chance's hand until it was too late. The sack slammed into the don's crotch. Gasping, he dropped the side-hammer .22, grabbed his balls, and sank toward the dirt.

Chance drew the Smith & Wesson from his back, caught Don Melitón, turned him around, and pressed the barrel underneath the don's chin. "Move and I'll blow his head off!" Chance roared to the vaqueros.

Probably not, he thought. *Not with a .32, but Don Melitón would be dead, sure enough.*

Of course, so would Dave Chance and Moses Albavera after those vaqueros were finished. At least half of them had drawn Navy Colts or Spencer carbines. Those weapons were cocked and trained on Chance, but they'd have to shoot through their boss to kill him.

"What is it you wish us to do?" spoke the middle-aged vaquero who had carried the saddlebags full of gold.

"I want you to get the hell out of here," Chance said. "Ride back to Cibolo Creek, I'll take —"

"*¡Imbécil!*" the vaquero shouted, and Chance realized the question had been directed at Don Melitón.

The proud old man tried to straighten. Chance pressed the barrel deeper into the don's flesh, his finger tightening on the trigger. Don Melitón spoke in a voice muffled by pain, "Do as he says, Godofredo."

"Sí, *patrón.*" Disappointed, the vaquero shoved the Navy into his yellow sash, tugged on the reins, and led the other riders away from the two-story saloon. They turned south, and loped away.

From the doorway of the saloon, the woman gambler named Lottie said, "You got grit, mister."

"He's a damned fool," Moses Albavera said. "Did it ever occur to you, Ranger, that this old don might have just shot me out of the saddle before you could try to castrate him? Did it?"

"No." The Smith & Wesson felt like a cannon in his hand. He lowered the barrel, released his hold on Don Melitón, and shoved the the .32 behind his back. "It didn't."

The old man sank to his knees. Bent over, his hands on the ground, in terrible pain, he didn't utter a sound.

Chance picked up the single-shot .22, returned to the don, and helped the old man to his horse, a palomino with a good dosage of Arabian blood. He boosted the man into the saddle — Don Melitón hunched low, gripping the horn instead of the reins — before mounting the Andalusian.

"Let's go," he told Albavera.

"Which way?"

"Just to the Sender Brothers store."

"Don't know where it is, Ranger. You best lead the way."

"You lead," Chance said. "I'll tell you which way to go."

Albavera grinned. "You don't miss much, do you?"

"Not much."

The black man kicked the sorrel into a walk.

Thirty minutes later, Chance's saddlebags were filled with beef jerky, salt pork, a sack of Arbuckles' Ariosa Coffee, four airtights of peaches and one of condensed milk, not to mention extra ammunition for the arsenal he now carried, all paid for from a gold coin in one of Don Melitón's pouches. He figured the don owed him. Besides, Austin rarely paid his expenses in a timely fashion.

He left the old man tied to a chair in the back of the mercantile, ordered the clerk working the store to leave the don there for two hours before turning him loose. *Like hell,* Chance thought. *A powerful patrón like Don Melitón Benton.* If that weasel-faced clerk left the don tied up for ten minutes, Chance would be counting his blessings.

"All right, sir," Chance whispered into the don's ear. "If it had been my son killed, I'd likely feel as you do." He tapped the badge. "But I'm paid to uphold the law, and the law wants Moses Albavera in Galveston. I'm asking you to let the law handle it. Do like I say. You've got more pull than those Marin brothers ever had in Galveston. You can bring Albavera to trial here, and you know, as well as I do, that he'll hang." He wanted to say, but didn't, *No matter if your boy got what he deserved.* "I'm just doing my job. I'm leaving you here, and taking Albavera to El Paso. I'll turn him over to the deputy U.S. marshal there. Maybe you can buy a federal lawman. But you can't buy me."

He stood, threatened the clerk with jail time if he didn't keep the don tied up for two hours, and prodded Moses Albavera outside, onto the sorrel. Chance mounted the Andalusian.

"El Paso, eh?" The black man's head shook as he chuckled.

"I doubt if that old hard-rock believed it, either," Chance said. "But I had to try."

They rode north, but quickly turned

southeast.

"Murphyville?" Albavera asked.

Chance shook his head. "Too close. Marathon. We'll catch an S.P. there to Houston."

Albavera asked, "Reckon we'll get there?"

Replied Chance, "I doubt it."

CHAPTER SEVEN

There wasn't much to Marathon, Texas. Oh, it had a post office, behind the front desk at the two-story hotel, but only one saloon — and it was only a tent.

The town had been founded a few years earlier when the Galveston, Harrisburg and San Antonio Railway crew, laying track east from El Paso for the Southern Pacific, reached those wind-blown plains surrounded by mountain vistas, although a few cattle ranchers and sheep men had settled in the area some time before. Albion E. Shepard, an ex-sea captain who had surveyed for the S.P., established his Iron Mountain sheep ranch in the spring of 1882. When he applied for a post office, he recommended the name Marathon. Seems the area reminded him of the plains of his native Greece.

By 1884, thanks to the railroad, Marathon had become a key shipping point in West

Texas, but the town probably had fewer than seventy-five permanent residents. Of course, if you asked Grace Profit, the only permanent residents were those buried in Boot Hill or in the boneyard behind the Catholic church on the other side of the S.P. tracks. She hadn't been convinced Marathon would really last.

That's why her saloon, which she had set up when the railroad first reached that point, remained a canvas structure — not stone or adobe — held up with mesquite posts, and held together by Grace Profit's stubbornness.

She had turned thirty-seven last month. Her face was bronzed, weathered by years working canvas saloons at railroad hell-on-wheels towns across Texas, Kansas, and New Mexico Territory, but most men — so she had often been told — found her stunningly beautiful. Her hair — blond, shoulder length — was tied up in a blue silk bandana. She wore hand-sewn Congress gaiters she had ordered from Bloomingdale's, a beaded brown cashmere jersey over her chemise — too fancy to be cooking in, but the railroad men liked it — a navy blue skirt, and a ruffled apron trimmed with lace. Since she was outside, she had donned the heavy gray double-breasted range coat her ex-husband had owned.

It was about the only thing that two-timing cad had left her, but it kept her warm on winter nights, and she wouldn't trade it to have that son of a bitch back.

Her eyes were like sapphires. That's what most men noticed about her. They made men overlook the crow's feet, few strands of gray hairs, and her leathery skin, although she needed spectacles to read these days. She had a brand-new book, *The Adventures of Huckleberry Finn* by Mark Twain, on the bureau by her bed in the hotel, the latest copy of *Lippincott's Magazine,* and a month-old edition of the *Tucson Citizen* an east-bound traveler had left behind that she couldn't wait to read.

Whenever she decided to close up the saloon.

She stood outside, grilling mutton over a mesquite-wood fire, watching the setting sun turn those crystal skies into a palette of orange, gold, red, yellow. The wind had died down, and the temperature had risen into the low forties, though it would surely plummet as soon as the sun finished sinking behind those mountains and mesas.

From the west, on the road from Mur-phyville, came a buckboard, escorted by a pair of riders on dark-colored horses. She studied them a moment, then turned her attention to the mutton, forked the meat over, the aroma pleasant, the sound of the grease dripping onto the coals reminding her that she hadn't eaten since breakfast. It had been a busy day at the saloon. The railroaders, having received their pay, had gotten good and drunk, and now they were hungry. Likely, those men in the wagon would be hungry, too, and good and drunk before midnight came.

She looked up again, and lowered the fork to her side.

The driver of the buckboard was a man, but beside him, wrapped in a blanket, rode a woman.

They drove past the depot, where one of the men wheeled his horse, and dismounted.

Grace glanced at the mutton, then called out to a man in red sleeve garters who stood inside the tent saloon, making whiskey. "Horatius?"

"Yes, ma'am?"

"Cut up this mutton. Put it on plates. Deliver it to the S.P. men."

"Yes, ma'am."

"Make sure they pay you before they eat."

"Yes, ma'am."

He stepped through the opening, and Grace handed him the fork. Pulling up the collar of her range coat, she thought about stepping out toward the road to see who those strangers were, but decided business came first. She needed to finish making that whiskey while Horatius fed the railroad men.

The swamp-root she served at Profit's House was her own blend. Grain alcohol aged in a porcelain-lined preserving kettle for ten days with burnt sugar and two tablespoons of iodine, colored with four five-cent plugs of Star Navy Chewing Tobacco, then poured through a milk strainer to cut down on the number of tobacco flakes a patron might swallow, and blended with water from the three-hundred-foot-deep well behind the depot. Two parts whiskey, one part water.

You had to do it that way, she reasoned. Anyone who drank that wretched water straight was bound to get really sick, maybe die.

She shed the coat. A couple of cast iron stoves kept the tent quite warm. Hanging from posts and from a hemp rope beneath the canvas top, coal oil-burning lanterns kept the saloon well lit.

Horatius served mutton to the railroaders, while Grace mixed the whiskey and water, funneling the finished product into brown clay jugs, which, when full, she corked and set on the mesquite table behind the bar. The front canvas flap opened, and two men walked inside, one of them escorting the woman to a table, the other headed straight for the bar. Before he was halfway across the room, the flap parted again, and the third man entered, slapping dust off his hat. Apparently, he had finished whatever business he had at the depot. He looked around before taking a seat across from the woman.

Leaning against the bar, the newcomer rubbed a gloved hand across heavy beard stubble, and set his derby hat on the bar. Grace picked up a relatively clean tumbler, a fresh jug, and walked to him. She poured a shot and slid it in front of him.

A badge cut from a peso was pinned on the bib of his red shirt.

"On the house, Ranger."

The man looked up. "Thanks." He downed the shot, and his eyes immediately watered. "Maybe." He coughed. "Maybe I thanked you too soon."

Grace smiled, and refilled his tumbler.

He didn't look like a Texas Ranger. Too old. Too bald. He wore plaid trousers, a red bib-front shirt, a yellow bandana, well-worn brown boots, and old Spurs. A russet gun-belt with a Colt holstered butt forward hung on his left hip. He wore eyeglasses that highlighted his brown eyes, but Grace figured he needed the glasses to see both near and far. She only needed hers to read.

"I've met some Rangers up here," Grace said, tucking a strand of blond hair back underneath her silk bandana. "Captain Savage," she said, trying to conceal her bitterness. "Dave Chance. Wes Smith. But I don't think I've ever had the pleasure of your company."

"Reckon not, ma'am. I don't think I've been north of the Chalk Mountains since I was posted to Captain Savage's battalion two years back. Name's Wickes, ma'am. Ray Wickes. I'm a lieutenant with Company E. Based down at Fort Leaton near Presidio."

"Grace Profit," she told him.

"Pleasure." He lifted the glass, but merely wet his lips with the potent brew. "I know Dave Chance. He's a good man. You haven't heard from him of late by chance?"

She shook her head. "Why?"

"He went after a man-killer named Albavera. The darky killed Prince Benton down in Shafter."

She'd had the displeasure of meeting Prince Benton two or three times. She'd shed no tears over his passing.

"But I'm afraid I'm bearing bad news,

95

Missus Profit" — he sipped the whiskey again — "about Wes Smith."

"Oh?"

"Yes, ma'am. I regret to inform you that he's dead. Got killed when Captain Savage attacked Lo Grande's camp. That's why we come here. To Marathon."

That saddened her. She had met Wes Smith only once, but he had seemed a nice lad. Too young, really, to be a Ranger.

The lieutenant pointed to the woman and the other two Rangers sitting silently at a table near the door flap. "Catching the train. Got to get that woman to her kin in Houston. And we're escorting Private Smith and another slain Ranger, Hamp Magruder, for proper burials. They're packed in charcoal in coffins in the back of the wagon, though, cold as it has been, I don't reckon they'll ripen too much." He fished a coin from his pocket, slapped it on the bar, and asked for the jug and two more glasses.

She obliged him.

"Well, ma'am," Wickes said, "I best get this liquor to Turp and Babbitt. They've worked up a powerful thirst."

Before he could don his derby and head to the table, Grace asked, "Who's the woman?"

"Just a whore from Terlingua. She got

taken by Juan Lo Grande's men. We rescued
her down at San Ped— at Cibolo Creek, I
mean, near Don Melitón's *rancho*."

Grace had heard enough. "Jesus, Wickes,"
she snapped, ducking underneath the
roughhewn cottonwood plank that served
as the Profit House bar. The Ranger lieutenant looked astonished as she moved past
him, dodged Horatius, who was hurrying to
the bar, and ignored a few catcalls from the
railroaders as she made her way to the table.

The two Rangers leaped up, sweeping off
their hats, but Grace ignored them, pulled
up a chair, and gripped the woman's right
hand. Her eyes were vacant, her face ashen.
She looked petrified.

"Miss . . ." Grace began, and quickly
turned to one of the stupid Rangers.
"What's her name?"

"I forgot," the one with the drooping
brown mustache said.

"It's Linda," said the one with no chin.
"Linda something-or-other."

"Kincaid," Ray Wickes said. "Linda Kincaid. You know her?"

"No, Lieutenant, I don't. But I know
enough that a woman who's been through
what she has doesn't need to be sitting in
this saloon while you three drink whiskey
that'll blind you if you're not careful."

The woman's dress was torn, stained with blood, most of the buttons removed. Grace could even see the woman's left breast.

"Christ, she's still wearing these clothes. Did anyone ever think to give her a bath?"

"Yes, ma'am," Ray Wickes said. "Our captain, Hec Savage, he asked this Mex woman to give her a bath, and a dress, but, well, the Mex woman said she didn't have a dress to spare, and the woman started screaming, saying she didn't want to take a bath, that she'd never get clean again." He finished the whiskey.

The one with the drooping mustache snorted. "Don't that beat all, coming from a whore?"

Grace ran her fingers through the woman's greasy hair, and shook her head.

"Lieutenant Wickes is right, ma'am," No Chin said. "Maybe she would have snapped out of it. Maybe we could have found her some man's clothes that might have fit, but Captain Savage ordered us to bring her here."

"Ordered us to proceed with all due haste," the lieutenant added, bobbing his head. "We had to do it."

"She'll be all right," the chinless one said. "Once she gets back to Houston."

"She said that's where she wanted to go,"

Wickes said. "Got kin in Houston."

" 'Course, she said that before she started screaming," Drooping Mustache said.

"I think her mind's gone," No Chin added.

"When's the train get here?" Wickes asked.

"Man at the depot said noon tomorrow," No Chin answered. "But he told me to bring you these." He pulled out a handful of telegrams from the pocket of his mackinaw.

Grace helped Linda Kincaid to her feet, steered her toward the doorway.

"Ma'am," Lieutenant Wickes asked. "Where you going?"

"She's not waiting with you till noon, Lieutenant," Grace snapped. "She'll be in my room. Horatius! I'm gone till tomorrow afternoon."

The Iron Mountain Inn was pretty nice. The rooms were large, if spartan. Clean. Comfortable. Kind of permanent, Grace always figured. Until the town died, and the owners either pulled the timbers apart and carted them off to the next town, or left the place behind to rot in the wind and dust.

Linda Kincaid sat naked in a large bathtub of black tin, trimmed with blue and gilt stripes, a wooden bottom and handles.

Grace sat beside her on a bench outside the tub, rubbing her back with Turkish bath soap, careful not to press too hard against the cuts and black bruises. The woman had said nothing, hadn't protested the hot water, hadn't made a noise as Grace undressed her and put her in a tub of steaming water. She just sat there, eyes barely blinking.

"I can't go on."

At first, Grace thought she had imagined it, but as she absently lowered the bar of soap, she saw Linda Kincaid's mouth trembling, and tears finally leaking from the corner of her hollow eyes.

"What's that, honey?" Grace asked.

She shut her eyes, and began shivering. "Can't go to Houston. Captain Savage will kill my mother."

That Ranger had been right. The woman's mind was gone.

"Captain Savage wouldn't do that. He's a Ranger."

"He killed those men."

Grace nodded. "Yes, I'm sure he did. He killed Lo Grande's men to save you."

"Not them. Them!" Her chin pointed toward the window.

Grace considered that a moment, unsure. Then, she asked, "Those two Rangers? In the buckboard?"

"Killed them in San Pedro. Killed one of them, at least. Another Ranger killed the other one. In a cantina there. Down in Mexico. Told me if I ever told anyone what he had done, he'd kill me." Her eyes opened. Her stare sent a chill racing down Grace's spine. "I guess . . . now . . . he'll kill you."

CHAPTER EIGHT

The two men hid behind a fortress of reddish black lava rocks, the boulders high enough to shield their horses from anyone who happened through the tight little cañon. Moses Albavera squatted in front of a small fire, a skillet in his manacled hands, while Dave Chance rubbed down the unsaddled horses. A coffee can sat on a flat rock over the coals. Chance had gathered dried wood that wouldn't smoke. He made Albavera do the cooking.

Albavera asked, "You think we're clear of that old don?"

"Nope," the Ranger answered.

The Ranger didn't talk much — unlike Albavera, who loved to gab. They probably hadn't spoken a dozen words since they'd loped out of Fort Davis. Albavera didn't even know the Ranger's name. He looked to be in his thirties, same as Albavera, with dirty, sand-colored hair that touched his shoulders, a weather-tanned face covered with at least a week's stubble of beard, broad shoulders, and narrow hips. His hazel eyes didn't miss much. He had long fingers meant to play a piano, perhaps, or work a rifle or short gun.

Marathon lay about sixty miles southeast of Fort Davis. The Andalusian and the sorrel could have covered that distance in a day, though the horses wouldn't be worth spit for three or four days, maybe never, after such a hard run. Or they could have made forty miles, gotten an early start the next morning, and loped into the cattle- and sheep-shipping point by noon. Twenty miles would have been easy.

Instead, they had covered, maybe, twelve.

Albavera had expected them to ride hard that day, put as much distance as they could between them and Don Melitón Benton and his vaqueros, but the long-haired Ranger had been cautious. He hadn't put the horses in anything faster than a canter, and those lopes had lasted only a few minutes. Some bone-jarring trots lasted a little longer when they had to cross the plains. Yet even when they traveled through open country, the Ranger played it safe, never kicking up too much dust, staying close to the growths of cactus, or dipping into the ravines and arroyos.

Mostly, they had kept their horses at a walk over rough country, the iron shoes of their mounts clopping on hard rock, through narrow canyons, around the sides of mesas, bouncing in a zigzag pattern from mesa to ridge, arroyo to canyon. The Ranger never allowed himself or Albavera to skyline, never allowed Albavera to get too close to him. When they reached a high point, the Ranger rested the horses while surveying their back trail.

Smart gent, that Ranger. Staying out of view, making it tougher for Don Melitón to track them by riding over hard rocks, keeping Albavera at a distance.

Hell, Albavera begrudgingly admired the man. He'd hate to have to kill him, yet he knew killing the Ranger was his only chance of staying alive.

"Way I see it, old Benton, when he realizes he can't really track us, he'll have to send some of his men toward El Paso. Just in case you weren't lying to him. Then he'll think about Murphyville, and point some of his men in that direction, it being the closest S.P. stop. But he'll also think you might have hauled my ass off to Fort Stockton to get some help from the Army there. He owns the C.O. at Fort Davis, so he'll have to consider it. Maybe he'll think — having seen my Andalusian and your sorrel — with horseflesh like that, maybe we'd just take the San Antonio–El Paso road. Some of those vaqueros would have to lope down that pike. And finally, he'd have to think about Marathon. So he'd order a few riders there. All of them under orders to send a galloper back for the others as soon as they found us."

The Ranger said, "What makes you think he can't track us?"

With a chuckle, Albavera turned his attention to the supper he was frying. He tilted the cast iron skillet, letting the pieces of salt pork slide in their grease. "I ever tell you what happened betwixt me and the Marin brothers?"

"I don't care." Chance moved from the sorrel to the Andalusian.

"Joe Marin, he was the youngest, was working a crooked faro layout at the Gulf Saloon," Albavera said, pleased for the chance to talk. "I saw how crooked the game was, him milking this mate from a sloop that had sailed into the port, and coppered a bet. You know how easy it is to cheat at faro, don't you?"

Chance didn't answer.

"Marin saw what I was doing. Didn't like

it a whit, but he was either going to have to pay me five hundred dollars, or pay the mate seven-fifty. You're smart enough, even for a Ranger, to see what he did."

Chance didn't appear to be interested, but Albavera kept right on talking.

"So I took my winnings, headed for the bar, and ran into Chet Marin, who was a beer-jerker at the Gulf. Chet had seen what I had done, and he didn't like it any better than Joe had. I asked for a glass of wine, and he said, 'Why don't you take your ass somewhere else?'

"Well, this being Texas, I looked at the flies gathered around the bar, and realized I wasn't likely to get a glass of wine, and it would probably be in my best interest to take my Moorish ass somewhere else. So I did. Planned to, anyhow."

Chance moved to the other side of the Andalusian.

"But not before I went back to the faro layout and told the mate how he was being cheated. Joe Marin was using 'sand-tell' cards and a screw box. You know faro, I take it. Easiest game in the world for a dealer to cheat at."

"Dealers aren't the only ones who cheat," Chance said.

Albavera smiled. Apparently, the Ranger

was listening. He also had an easy way with horses. That Andalusian didn't let just anybody get close to him. Albavera had been surprised — well, disappointed, actually — that the stallion had not bucked the Ranger off.

"That's true," Albavera said. "Very true. Not that I've ever cheated as a dealer or player, mind you. But Joe Marin, he had no qualms, and he was pretty good at it. You got to have an easy touch to work a screw box, have a feel for those cards. I'll give Joe Marin that much. He was a really good cheat, maybe the best I've ever caught, and I bet that screw box of his, silver plated and engraved, likely cost him five hundred dollars. 'Course, he likely made back that money and then some after a couple days in a place like the Gulf. All he had to do was press a little button with his left finger, and it would widen or narrow the slot from which he was skinning cards. Narrow slit would give him one card, wide slit would let him pull two as one. He had sanded the faces on the high cards, the backs on the low cards. Easy as pie. I showed the mate that. Joe turned mighty pale. Well, it turned out that mate had half his crew from the sloop in the Gulf Saloon. The fight was just commencing when I left." He slid the skillet back, and looked at Chance. "How am I supposed to turn this pork over without a knife or a fork?"

"Use your fingers."

"I might burn them."

"You have gloves."

"A fork would be easier."

"You're not getting a fork, Albavera."

His black head shook. He reached into the back pocket of his pants to fish out a pair of deerskin gloves, blackened from use. "Well, don't blame me if your salt pork's burned to a crisp."

"Charcoal's good for your teeth."

Albavera sniggered. "Where was I?"

"I don't care."

"Oh, yeah. I was leaving the Gulf Saloon. Chet Marin came out through the doors, grabbed my shoulder, and jerked me around. I put my fist through his face, and he went flying through the doors, back toward the melee. That's a good French word, melee. Comes from Latin. I bet you didn't know that, did you, Ranger?"

"I don't care."

Albavera flipped the meat over, the grease staining the tips of his gloves, and burning his fingertips anyway. "Chet came out again, swinging an Arkansas toothpick at my gut that he'd pulled from his boot. It was a pretty good fight for a while. He ripped open my vest and shirtfront, cut me good across the stomach. Little deeper and I wouldn't be your chef this evening. Then he charged me. I grabbed his hand, twisted that knife, pushed him against the wall of the saloon, and stuck that blade into his brisket." Shaking his head, Albavera chuckled. "You should have seen the look on his face as that son of a bitch soiled his britches and dropped onto the boardwalk in a lake of his own blood.

"Well, I was bleeding a mite myself. Had to lean against the wood column for support, trying to catch my breath. Then Joe Marin comes through those batwing doors, sees his brother lying there, palms a pepperbox pistol, calls me a filthy name, takes a shot. Mind you, my back was to Joe. He could have killed me. Probably would have if that mate hadn't busted him up mighty fine. I was lucky. Sort of.

"Now, here's the deal with Galveston. It's civilized. Men can't go in the city limits armed with revolvers. I didn't own Miss Vickie back then, just had an old cap-and-ball Remington, and I'd left it at the constable's office, being a man who respected and obeyed the law. I read an account a while later in the *Galveston Daily News* I happened to get, after they'd indicted me on two counts of murder. They say I shot first. How could I? I didn't have a gun. That's not how it happened."

The grease was popping, the salt pork making Albavera's mouth water. He hadn't realized how hungry he was. The Ranger had left the horses, and stood a few rods from the fire, staring at Albavera, waiting for him to finish his story.

"His first shot grazed my left arm, and I was on him. We got into a struggle, and I did young Joe pretty much the same way I'd done Chet, only he got a bullet in his gut, instead of a knife. Joe made a deathbed statement that I'd murdered him and his brother both, the liar. I read that in the *Daily News,* too, but I tell you it was self-defense. I left them both dying on the boardwalk, grabbed the first horse I could find, and lit a shuck."

He slid the salt pork around some more. "Now, Ranger, doesn't that sound like self-defense to you?"

"Why'd you run?"

"In Galveston? You think I'd stand a chance killing two white men? I've never shot down anyone in cold blood. The Marin brothers. Bill Carter. You don't know about him, but it was either me or him, too. Prince

Benton. Everyone I've ever killed I had to kill. You believe me?"

"I don't care."

Albavera shook his head. "You're a hard man, Ranger. What's your name, anyhow? I know it ain't polite, asking a man his name, but, well, what would you expect from a heartless murderer such as I?"

"Chance. David Marion Chance, sergeant, Company E, Texas Rangers. Dave for short."

"Well, Chance, you better come get this salt pork before it's burned to a crisp."

Chance smiled, stepped toward the fire, pointing at the coffeepot on the rock. "Want me to open that can of milk —"

He never finished the question. Grinning, eyes fixed on the fire, Moses Albavera had struck out as fast as a rattlesnake. Lifting the skillet in his right hand, he flipped the salt pork, but mostly the ton of hot grease the meat had produced, at Chance's face.

Chance stepped back and to his left quickly, bringing his left forearm up to protect his face and eyes as he turned his head. Most of the grease caught his arm and vest, although a piece of hot pork slapped the side of his face. He whirled, trying to clear the Schofield's long barrel from the holster.

Albavera leaped over the fire, manacles

clinking as he slashed the skillet, cutting through the air.

Chance stumbled, and went down. That likely saved his life. The blackened frying pan weighed close to eight pounds. Had it connected with his face, it would have crushed his skull.

The skillet swooshed over his head, clipping the crown of his hat. The momentum of the swing sent Albavera spinning, and he tripped over a rock. The skillet slipped from his grip, crashing against the lava boulder.

The horses snorted, and stomped their hoofs.

Chance rolled over, freeing the Schofield from the holster with his right hand. He was thumbing back the hammer when Albavera leaped onto him, pinning the Ranger's hand in the sand with his knee. Albavera, his face an ugly grimace, leaned forward, bringing the chains that held his wrists against Chance's throat. He pressed down with all his might.

His right hand pinned, the Smith & Wesson behind his back, impossible to reach, Chance shot his left hand forward, past the chain, and went right to Albavera's throat. He locked tight, and squeezed.

Their eyes met, locked, masked in determination.

112

It seemed just a matter of who'd slip into unconsciousness first.

CHAPTER NINE

The cold front had passed on, bringing the temperatures to something more reasonable, something one would likely expect from a burnt-over patch of brutally harsh desert. The wind hadn't stopped, of course. The wind seldom died down in Texas.

Hec Savage led his Rangers through a forest of ocotillo, the arms of the cacti stretching out, swaying, like tentacles from a navy of giant sea monsters. The Santiago Mountains rose to the east, the Del Norte range was ahead. The sky was clear, pale, and endless. Toward the Rangers came a lone rider, heading south. Savage had been watching him for the past twenty minutes, but showed little concern. One man against ten Rangers? Ten of Savage's Rangers, for that matter.

Suddenly, Savage reined in the gray, lifting his right hand, bringing his men to a halt behind him. Ahead, the rider spurred his brown horse into a lope. Lowering his hand, Savage pushed back the tail of his coat, and gripped the horn.

At first, he let out a long sigh. Then, he muttered an oath.

"Ain't that . . . ?" Doc Shaw began.

"Yeah." Savage spit tobacco juice onto a pile of coyote dung.

The rider slowed his gelding, and walked the last few rods, smiling pleasantly, greeting the Rangers. The wind carried the dust to the southeast, away from Savage and his men.

After he shifted the chaw of tobacco to his other cheek, Savage said, "Wickes, what the hell are you doing here?"

The smile on Lieutenant Ray Wickes's face vanished. "Well —" he started.

"I ordered you, Turp and Babbitt — wrote those orders out, mind you — to escort the bodies of your fallen comrades for fitting burials back east. Didn't I?"

"Yes, sir."

"Yet here you are. Twenty-five miles from Marathon."

"Yes, Captain. But —"

"Where are Turp and Babbitt?"

"Oh." Wickes's gelding fought the bit. He pulled back on the rein, and spoke to the horse, shifting his weight in the saddle.

"They got on the eastbound S.P. all right. I gave them the orders you wrote me, told them what to do. They'll make sure Magruder and Smith are buried properly. Just like you wanted, Captain."

"My orders said for you to go with them, Lieutenant."

"I know that, sir. But you once told me orders aren't written in stone. Some are meant to be broken."

"Orders from Austin. Not mine."

"But there were a passel of wires to you, Captain. From the colonel in Austin. I thought I should bring those to you. Colonel Thomas is in a snit."

"Bugger the colonel!" Savage thumbed out the chaw, and hurled it across the desert floor.

In the silence that followed, Ray Wickes wet his lips with his tongue. A gust of wind almost took his hat off. He had to grab the crown with his right hand, and that spooked the gelding more. When Wickes had his horse under control again, he turned in the saddle, opened one of the bags strapped behind the cantle, reached inside, and withdrew a slip of yellow paper.

"Captain," he said. "This telegraph was waiting at the Marathon depot." The lieutenant lowered his head, and read:

UNDER NO CONDITIONS WILL YOU PURSUE LO GRANDE ACROSS THE RIO GRANDE STOP KEEP CLOSE TO MARATHON AND MURPHYVILLE STOP TOO MUCH AT STAKE STOP ADVISE IF YOU NEED ADDITIONAL MEN STOP

"It's signed Colonel Thomas. There are more wires, too."

"Hand me that one."

Wickes eased the gelding closer to Savage and the gray. The Ranger captain snatched the paper from Wickes's fingers, and folded the telegraph's edge. Next, he fished out a pack of Bull Durham, sprinkling an even measure of tobacco flakes onto the paper. Once he had pulled the drawstring shut with his teeth, he shoved the tobacco pouch back into his coat pocket, and casually rolled the telegraph into a cigarette. After licking it, he stuck it in his mouth. Doc Shaw eased his chestnut closer, struck a lucifer against the butt of his Colt, and brought the match closer as Savage leaned over to light the smoke. Staring at Wickes, Savage sat ramrod straight in the saddle, took a deep drag, held the smoke for a moment, then exhaled.

"That's what that pettifogging colonel's messages mean to me," Savage told Wickes.

117

"That's what I think of his damned orders."

"But —"

"I intend to stay close to Marathon and Murphyville. Why the hell do you think I've left Fort Leaton?"

"Well, yes, sir. Of course, sir. But . . . well . . . Colonel Thomas's instructions about men. You lost Magruder and Smith. I didn't think you'd want to send all of us with their bodies. I mean, Turpen and Babbitt could handle the job. I thought you might need me."

With a snigger, Savage removed the smoke from his lips. "Need you?" He shook his head.

"You heard from Sergeant Chance?" Doc Shaw suddenly asked.

The smile vanished from Savage's face. Suddenly, he looked interested.

Wickes shook his head. "The woman who runs the saloon —"

"Grace Profit?" Savage interrupted.

"Yes, sir. She hadn't seen him in a while. Asked about him, though."

"She ask about me?" Savage winked. The cigarette, even though the paper tasted funny, had put him relatively at ease.

"No, sir. Well, she told me she'd met you." He shook his head sadly. "She'd met Wes Smith, too. Nice woman. But the whiskey she serves . . ." He let out a haggard breath. "She took that whore."

Savage stiffened, his calm feeling abruptly halted. He gripped the saddle horn again, and leaned forward. "What?"

"Took that whore. Miss Kincaid. We were sitting in that tent she calls a saloon, and she grabbed the woman, took her to the hotel. She, Miss Profit again, or is it Missus? I don't know. Anyhow, that's where she lives. In the hotel. She took the whore to her room. Said it wasn't right for Miss Kincaid to stay with us. Not after all she'd been through. She was right about that. Turpen told me and Babbitt, after those two women had gone, told us we should have done that, or at least suggested it. Guess we weren't thinking straight. Grace Profit said she'd take care of the woman, give her a bath, give her a new dress."

"I told Eulalia to fix that Kincaid woman a bath. Told her to give her a dress."

"I know that, Captain," Wickes said. "But Eulalia didn't do it. Maybe that whore didn't want one. She was acting fairly crazy when we got her to Fort Leaton. But she was real calm, gentle, when Grace Profit led her out of that tent."

Savage flicked the cigarette into the air. He'd have a few words with Eulalia when he returned to Fort Leaton.

"Well, that's all right, I reckon," Savage said, feeling a little better. "I'll thank Grace personally when we get to Marathon."

Doc Shaw cleared his throat. "You did put that whore on the train, Lieutenant? Didn't you?"

"We meant to. . . ."

Savage gripped the horn tighter, and felt the blood rushing to his head. He heard the stupid oaf talking, but couldn't quite believe what that asinine Ray Wickes was saying.

"Figured we'd just fetch Miss Kincaid when the train came the next day. About ten minutes before it was due, I sent Babbitt to the hotel, but Grace Profit met him at the door to the hotel. She said Linda Kincaid had changed her mind, that she wasn't going anywhere with the likes of us. Babbitt came back and told me, and I went to the inn. She, Miz Profit that is, told me the same thing. I told her I had orders. Pulled them out of my pocket. She said she didn't give a damn. I asked her if Miss Kincaid planned on returning to Terlingua. Said I was riding back that way myself and could escort her. She said, no, Linda was staying with her. For the time being. You reckon Miz Profit wants a whore for her saloon?"

Savage eased back in the saddle, rested

his hand on the butt of the Merwin Hulbert.

Wickes kept talking.

"I told Miz Profit that I'd need to hear that from Miss Kincaid, and, just like that, I heard a voice, looked up, and there was Miss Kincaid, leaning against the balustrade, telling me, in a real soft voice, that everything was all right, she had changed her mind, didn't want to put her mother in harm's way. I don't know what she meant by that. She was wearing a robe. Her hair was wet. She'd taken a bath that night and again that morning. Looked a whole lot better than she had. She wished me luck. That was more than she'd said to Turp, Babbitt, and me on the whole ride up there.

"Anyway, like you said, orders aren't written in stone, and we couldn't force Miss Kincaid back to Houston. The train pulled up, I saw that the two coffins were loaded, shook hands with Turp and Babbitt, and watched the train pull off. I left the buckboard and Turp's horse at the livery, and mounted Cimarron here." He patted the horse's neck, but the gelding didn't appear to like being touched. "I gathered all those telegrams, and rode back to find you. Now, about those telegraphs Colonel Thomas had sent . . ."

He turned again, reached behind him for the open leather bag.

Savage drew the .44 and shot him. The bullet caught Wickes low in his right side, just above the waistline. It tore a wide path through his intestines, lodging just underneath his belly button. Gut-shot, Ray Wickes was a dead man. But not yet.

He let out a yell of surprise, and sank low. As the bullet's impact turned him around, his right hand latched onto the saddle horn, and his left grabbed the brown gelding's mane, keeping him in the saddle. The horse, which had been acting skittish on the journey south, bolted. Wickes's hat flew off. The horse galloped across the desert floor, leaped over an arroyo, weaving a path among the ocotillo.

"Stop that son of a bitch!" Savage fired again, knowing he had missed.

His first shot had spooked the other horses, even the gray. Savage had to fight to get his own horse under control after the second shot. So did his men. Nobody had expected Savage to shoot. Even Doc Shaw's mouth hung open.

"He's getting away!" Savage screamed, and raked the sides of the gray with his spurs. He extended the Merwin Hulbert, and pulled the trigger, but the gray was leaping, spoiling his aim. The horse jumped the arroyo, but stumbled on the far side, and Savage dropped the .44. Kicking free of the stirrups, he sailed over the gray's head, landing with a thud, trying, futilely, not to lose the reins.

He scrambled to his feet, saw the gray galloping after the brown, then turn and run southwest. The brown, with Wickes still in the saddle, raised dust toward Elephant Mountain. Savage drew his other .44, started to cock, but stopped and shoved the revolver back in the holster. Wickes and the gelding were out of pistol range. That damned horse flew like Pegasus.

"Get him!" Savage thundered, watching Doc Shaw lead the men across the desert. Demitrio went after Savage's gray, now loping in the general direction of Fort Leaton. Bucky Bragg, a Ranger who Savage knew faced the gallows if he ever returned to Arkansas, rode up, slid from the saddle, and offered Savage the reins to his bay.

Savage grabbed the reins, and leaped into the saddle. "Find my .44," he ordered, and spurred the bay. He put the reins in his mouth, clamped down on them with his teeth, reached across his stomach, and jerked the revolver from the left-side holster. Wickes was still out of range, and about three of the Rangers pursuing the dying man were in Savage's line of fire. Savage pulled the trigger anyway.

The brown gelding turned northwest. The Rangers pursued — except Doc Shaw, who reined up as Savage galloped past him. Savage looked back. The wind whipped his hat off his head. Shaw was pulling a rifle from its scabbard.

Savage jerked the reins out of his mouth. "Kill the horse!" Savage yelled back to Shaw. "Or kill the man. Just stop him." He turned back, leaned forward, urging the bay to run faster by pounding its hindquarters with the .44's barrel. He wasn't making up much ground. If anything, that damned brown horse seemed to be lengthening the distance.

Likely, Doc Shaw was the only chance Savage had of stopping Wickes. Oh, Wickes was dead. Of that, Savage had no doubt. A man with a bullet in his gut would die hard, but if Wickes happened to run into somebody, tell what had happened, well, that might end all of Savage's plans, his dreams, his empire.

Savage chanced a look behind him. Doc Shaw had dropped the reins to his horse, was kneeling, the rifle in his arms.

Shaw's weapon was brand-spanking new.

John M. Browning had mailed a copy of his latest design to the Texas Rangers, and Colonel Thomas had shipped it down to Fort Leaton with the great state of Texas's appreciation. Savage had, in turn, given it to Doc Shaw, the best rifle shot in Company E. It was a Winchester High Wall, a single shot in .45-120 caliber, thirty-inch octagon-barrel with straight grip, an unbelievably strong falling block action, and tremendous range. Doc Shaw had taken the long brass telescope that had been on his old .45-70 Remington Rolling Block, and put it on his new toy. He had sighted in that rifle, too, and dropped a horse thief from his saddle at six hundred yards. Savage guessed that Wickes was a good eight hundred yards from Shaw.

He heard the muffled report of the Winchester. Looked. Wickes and the brown never broke stride. Savage swore. Doc Shaw had missed.

Yet almost as soon as the curse had left Savage's lips, Ray Wickes slipped from the saddle, and fell into the dust. The brown kept running, but Savage didn't care.

By the time Savage reached the others, they had rolled Ray Wickes's dead body on the ground, marveling at the bullet hole that had hit Wickes in his temple and blown out the left side of his head. One Ranger pocketed the dead man's watch. Another removed the badge and tossed the star up to Savage, who caught it, slid it into his pocket beside the crucifix he had taken off the Rurale lieutenant a few days ago.

"Doc Shaw sure can shoot," Ranger Eliot Thompson said.

"He can," Savage agreed.

"What about the horse?" Ranger Joe Newton asked.

"Let it go. Horse can't talk. We've spent enough time here. We need to get to Marathon. See to that whore. Let's ride back. Pick up Bucky and Demitrio, my hat, my horse, and my other .44."

"Should we bury him?" Thompson pointed at the corpse.

"Wolves and ravens will take care of Lieutenant Wickes," Savage said. He turned the bay around, and loped away.

CHAPTER TEN

The chain bit into Dave Chance's neck, drawing blood. His brain screamed for air, but Moses Albavera appeared to be getting stronger, not weaker, despite the fact that Chance's left hand gripped the black man's throat like a vise. He struggled to free his right hand, but Albavera's knee wouldn't budge. Chance kept his left hand locked just beneath Albavera's Adam's apple, and managed to turn his head, feeling the rugged chain rip deeper into his flesh.

He was closer to the fire than he realized. The coffeepot sat on the rock. He wondered . . . could he reach it?

Immediately, he released his grip on Albavera's throat. The black man seemed surprised, but instinctively took a deep breath, relaxing his grip just a bit. Chance's arm shot out, grabbed the enamel pot. Once blue, burned black from years of use, the pot was scalding. It burned his fingers, his palm, but Chance didn't care. He lifted the pot, and flung it.

Albavera let out a savage oath, but didn't scream, ducking as the hot coffee splashed against his shoulder and neck. He fell off. Chance barely heard the clanging of the manacles, the pot clanging on the dirt. He was too busy filling his lungs with oxygen. He tried to lift the Schofield, but his right hand wouldn't work, numbed from the pressure of Albavera's knee. Chance grabbed the .45 with his left hand, and brought the revolver up.

Albavera had stumbled and was sitting up, his back against a lava boulder. He reached for something and stood.

Chance cocked the Schofield and aimed as best he could, though he had never been much good at shooting left-handed. He pulled the trigger. The .45 bucked savagely in his hand.

In the close confines of their boulder den, the pistol's report sounded like a cannon, causing Chance's ears to ring painfully. Yet he heard the whine of the bullet ricocheting, and felt the slug sail over his head, barely missing him. Through the smoke, he saw the bullet had knocked Albavera back on his haunches, slamming something black against the boulder to the prisoner's right.

The cast iron frying pan.

Albavera had lifted the heavy skillet, used it as a shield, and saved his life. The Schofield's bullet had slammed into the center of the pan, ricocheted off — damned near killing Chance in the process — knocking the skillet out of Albavera's hand, landing him back on his butt.

Flexing the fingers on his right hand, Chance felt the blood flowing down his throat and neck, but his hand remained asleep. He tried cocking the Schofield with his left hand. Albavera was on his feet, running toward the horses. Chance aimed, but held his fire, not wanting to hit the horses, which were stomping and rearing.

"Stop!" Chance's voice sounded muffled by the ringing in his ears, like it was coming from within a deep well. He took a step.

He had removed saddles and blankets from both mounts, but had left the bridles on. He hadn't bothered hobbling the horses, figuring they might need to vamoose pretty damned quick if Don Melitón's men found them. He'd considered keeping the horses saddled, but decided they didn't need to stand around all night with that extra weight. Those saddles weighed close to forty pounds apiece. As Albavera grabbed the reins to the Andalusian, Chance wished he had hobbled the sorrel and the stallion, or at least haltered them.

Albavera flew onto the back of the gray Andalusian with ease, yelling something. Chance couldn't make out what he said, but the horse turned, and leaped over the saddles. The black man looked like he had been born on horseback. With a grimace on his face, he leaned over the horse's side, Indian style, to keep Chance from hitting him. Guessing, Chance figured, that a man like him wouldn't want to shoot a horse.

He didn't — not kill nor wound a horse like that.

But he would.

Yet as Albavera leaned, his hat, miraculously still on his head, flew off. Chance looked surprised, but not as stunned as Albavera, who, instead of leaning onto the stallion's side, pitched off, and fell into the dirt. As the Andalusian loped away, past Chance, he heard the shot.

The second round carved a furrow across Chance's left side. He dived back toward the fire, landing hard, saw the Andalusian split two riders loping into the little canyon levering fresh rounds into their Winchesters as they rode. Vaqueros. Don Melitón's men. But only two of them.

He could feel his right hand again, and

quickly changed hands holding the Schofield. Cocking it with his left hand, he rose to his knee. One of the riders wheeled his horse, and dropped the reins. Smoke and flame belched from the Winchester, the bullet tugging at Chance's collar. Chance squeezed the trigger, dived to his left, and came up ready to fire again.

The horse, a palomino, loped out of the maze of lava rocks. The vaquero lay spread-eagle on the ground, a Winchester at his boots, something by his head. The skillet.

Another shot boomed. Chance ran in a crouch, stopped, and dived out of the way of another running horse, also riderless. Stepping out of the dust, he aimed the Schofield at Moses Albavera.

The black man stood behind the saddles, the sawed-off Springfield rifle in his hands, smoke serpentining out of the short barrel. A few rods in front of the saddles lay the other vaquero, his head a gory mess. Behind Albavera stood the sorrel, sidestepping, snorting, but not running.

Spotting Chance, Albavera straightened, and glanced down at the rifle in his hands.

"You're empty," Chance said, not lowering the Schofield.

"Don't I know it."

Both men sounded terribly hoarse.

Albavera dropped the rifle onto the saddle-bags, leaned against a boulder, and started massaging his throat. Chance walked slowly, pressing his left hand against his bloody side. His throat felt raw, pained, as if he had swallowed a ton of torrid sand. His eyes burned. He didn't bother a glance at the dead vaquero. He wasn't about to take his eyes off a man like Moses Albavera. He had made that mistake too many times already.

The black man lowered his hand from his throat with a smile. "Where'd you get a grip like that?"

When Chance didn't answer, Albavera spoke again. "You damn near crushed my windpipe."

"I swung a sixteen-pound sledgehammer for the Texas and Pacific for six years," Chance said. He remembered that too well. Swinging that sledge in the heat of July, laying track from Longview to Dallas. He'd felt like a kid when he started. Hell, he had been a kid, but he built a lot of muscle over those years. Figured he'd lay track all the way to San Diego. That was the T&P's plan, to build a transcontinental railroad in the south, but the railroad never got out of Texas. Back in '81, T&P crews had met the Southern Pacific in Sierra Blanca, about a hundred or so miles east of El Paso. By then, Chance had left the railroad and was riding for the Texas Rangers. Course, it had been the T&P that had gotten him the job with Captain Savage.

"How far will that Andalusian of yours run?" Chance asked.

"He's stopped." Albavera pointed. "Already loping back."

Chance kept his eyes on the black man, but he heard the hooves of a horse.

"All right," Chance said. "I'll saddle the horses. You bury those two men."

"Bury them? With what?"

"Your hands."

Albavera shook his head. "They wouldn't have buried us."

Chance didn't reply.

"Well, what happens after I bury those two?"

"We'll ride out."

"What about supper?"

"You threw supper away. You want to pick up those pieces of salt pork, go ahead."

"Horses will be worn out."

"I imagine they will be. But" — he gestured at the closest dead man — "I don't want to get trapped here by Don Melitón."

Albavera shook his head. "You don't have to worry about that."

"Those dead vaqueros say different."

"Those aren't vaqueros, Sergeant Chance."

The Andalusian trotted right on past Chance, and walked straight to Albavera, nuzzling his chest, pushing him back. He laughed, grabbed the bridle, and rubbed his hand on the gray's neck. "See for yourself," the black man said.

Chance risked it. The rider was a Mexican, all right, with a huge sugarloaf sombrero, the brim splattered with blood. He couldn't recognize the face, wouldn't have even been able to call it a face, not after the impact of that .45-70 slug. Chance moved closer, keeping Albavera is his sights, and knelt beside the dead man.

It wasn't one of Don Melitón's riders. He remembered the don's vaqueros had been armed with Spencers; the dead men carried Winchesters. Chance studied the man closer. He wore gray britches, Apache moccasins, and a canvas jacket over a muslin shirt. A dagger was sheathed in a yellow sash, two bandoliers of .44-40 cartridges were strapped over his chest, and a couple of gory scalps were affixed to the bandoliers. Probably Apache hair.

Tugging at the man's jacket, Chance pulled a leather pouch from the inside pocket, and dumped it onto the ground between the dead man's legs. A rosary. A few pesos. A rabbit's foot. And a half dozen Morgan dollars. He picked up one of the silver coins, hardly a scratch on any of them, and checked the date. Freshly minted. Undoubtedly stolen. He gathered the dollars, slipped them into his vest pocket. Something else was stuck in the sash. Chance pulled out a pewter flask. Liquid sloshed inside, and he unscrewed the lid, sniffed.

Tequila.

He closed the lid, and shoved the flask into his waistband.

Carefully, rapidly, Chance looked over at the man he had killed, saw the sinking sunlight reflecting off the conchos that lined the sides of his *calzoneras.* That's what had made Chance mistake him for a vaquero. That and the Mexican saddle and old sombrero. But he also had a bandolier, although his was strapped across his waist, and he wore the gray jacket of one of Porfirio Díaz's Rural Guards.

"Rurales," Chance said, rising. "What are two Rurales doing this far north of the border?"

Albavera stepped from behind the gray stallion. "Not Rurales. Likely bandits in Rurale uniforms."

"Most of the Rurales I've run across are bandits."

"Spoken like a true Texan." Albavera laughed.

Chance ran his finger over his jacket, and found the bullet hole in the collar. "We match."

"Not quite," Albavera said. "Prince Benton's bullet went through my left collar, not right. Besides, my coat's a lot more expensive than that rat-chewed mackinaw of yours."

"Why do you think they hit us?"

"Heard our ruction, most likely. Figured we'd make easy pickings. You want some water?" He picked up a canteen.

"Yeah." Chance holstered the revolver, and stepped toward Albavera.

"So, how'd you go from swinging a sixteen-pound sledgehammer to wearing a peso star?" Albavera asked after Chance had taken a long pull from the canteen.

As he asked he noticed a few things about the Ranger:

1. Chance kept his right hand on the butt of the Schofield revolver holstered high on his hip.
2. He kept his distance from Albavera, and never took his eyes off him.

Rarely even blinked.

3. His throat and the side of his neck were raw, bleeding, from where Albavera had tried to choke him to death, and his side was bleeding from a bullet wound, but the Ranger didn't seem in any pain. Unlike Albavera, whose hands still rang from having that skillet shot out of his hands, and whose throat felt raw. It had hurt just to swallow the mouthful of water from the canteen. Of course, he wasn't about to admit any of that.

4. The white Ranger didn't wipe the spout of the canteen after Albavera, a black man, had drunk from it.

The latter impressed him the most. Maybe Chance was too damned tired. Or maybe . . . oh, yeah. Albavera grinned. Chance would have had to take his right hand off that .45's butt to wipe the canteen.

"Ever hear of the Constantine gang?" Chance asked.

"Can't say I have."

"They were a band of brothers along the Arkansas-Texas border. Three of them. They tried to rob a Texas and Pacific that was bound to Texarkana."

Albavera grinned again. He took the canteen back, but before he drank, he said, "And you just happened to be on board."

Chance nodded. "Work detail. I was in the smoking car. Playing poker with the boys."

"When it was all said and done, the Constantine gang was no more. That it?"

"Something like that. I shot Will dead. Put a bullet in Greg's shoulder. He lived long enough to hang. Mickey McGee, an Irishman I worked with, crushed Robert's head with a sledgehammer before Robert could shoot me."

"All that . . . just to protect the railroad?" Albavera drank.

"Railroad hell," Chance said. "Those bastards aimed to rob us."

He caught the canteen when Albavera pitched it back to him. Used both hands. Albavera figured he had missed his best shot to try that Ranger, but, hell, he was too tired anyway. Chance drank again, and once more he didn't wipe the canteen. He shook the canteen, then poured some onto his hand, patted down the scrapes on his neck, wincing, and at last poured some onto his side. That must have burned like a branding iron.

"You all right?" Albavera asked.

"Just a scratch."

"Oh, I'd think it's deeper than a scratch, Ranger." He reached into his vest, and pulled out a silk handkerchief. "Here. You best draw this through it. You could disinfect that wound with some of the whiskey in that flask." He pointed at the pewter container.

"It's tequila," Chance said. He pulled the flask from his waist, opened it, and poured enough to wet the handkerchief.

"Here." Albavera rose. Chance had the Schofield halfway out of the holster, but the black man didn't seem to notice it. He took the handkerchief in his left hand, shoved the tail of the mackinaw aside, pushed up Chance's vest and shirt, and placed the tequila-sodded piece of silk against the dark line seeping blood.

"Son of a bitch!" Chance bellowed. His boots tapped out a little dance.

Albavera chuckled. He stepped back, dropping his manacled hands.

Chance still held the flask. He pushed the Schofield back into his holster, lifted the container, took a pull, swallowed, and tossed the flask to Albavera, who finished off the liquor.

"Guess I should get to burying those two banditos," Albavera said, and walked to the one he had killed.

Behind him, he heard Chance say, "I'll help you."

CHAPTER ELEVEN

A rooster crowed. A dog barked. The sun broke free of clouds hanging low in the eastern horizon, bathing the riders in warming beams as Hec Savage and his Rangers made their way down what passed for a main street in the ramshackle village of Marathon. They rode straight to the tent saloon, the canvas flapping in the wind. The entrance was tied shut, the saloon empty.

Hec Savage nodded at Doc Shaw, who eased from his saddle, wrapping the reins around the hitching rail, which he ducked underneath. Shaw pulled a knife from his jacket pocket, unfolded the blade, and sliced through the canvas ties, although it would have been just as easy to untie them. He slipped inside the saloon. A moment later, he reappeared, shaking his head.

Savage had expected as much.

He turned his horse, and headed toward the Iron Mountain Inn. A blue roan stood in front of the two-story structure, lathered with sweat, ground-reined, shotgun in the scabbard, about half a dozen quail hanging from a string wrapped over the scattergun's stock. As Savage pulled up his mount, a man stepped out of the front door, pulled off a bowler, and wiped sweat from his brow. It was too damned cold to be sweating.

The man came to a stop when he saw the Rangers.

"Morning, Horatius." Savage gripped the saddle horn, and leaned forward, kicking his boots free of the stirrup, stretching his legs. He smiled.

"Captain." The old barkeep sounded nervous.

Behind Savage, the other Rangers reined up their mounts.

Savage jerked his thumb toward the quail hanging from the roan. "Pretty good hunting for this time of year. Thought I heard some shots." He tilted his head toward the eastern clouds. "But the boys said it was likely thunder. Reckon they were wrong."

The barkeep set his bowler back atop his head. Shuffled his feet. Stared past Savage at the Rangers behind him.

"Where's the whore?" Savage straightened in his saddle.

"What whore?" The beer-jerker had found

his voice. Nervous, but at least he had spoken.

"You know damned well who I mean, Horatius." He pushed back his coattail, and rested his right hand on the butt of the nearest .44. "The one from Terlingua. Linda Kincaid. The one I ordered that son-of-a-bitching Ray Wickes to put on the eastbound Southern Pacific. The one your boss took from my men."

"I don't know —"

"You do know, mister. Don't play me for a fool. You saw our dust, and lit a shuck for here. Look at how lathered your horse is, how sweaty you are. You rode right here to warn that —"

Suddenly looking past Horatius, Savage brought his right hand off the Merwin Hulbert to the brim of his hat, which he swept off his head, and bowed slightly as Grace Profit stepped onto the warped boardwalk that ran in front of the hotel. She kept her left hand tight against the top of the range coat she had slipped on over her chemise. Her legs and feet were bare.

"Morning, Grace." Savage returned his hat, grinning.

"Captain Savage," she said.

"You're up early," he said.

She shrugged. "You and your boys were

143

loud enough to wake the dead. If you and the boys are thirsty, I'll have Horatius open up the saloon."

The barkeep started down the boardwalk, but stopped when Savage barked out, "Not yet."

The captain's hand returned to the revolver's butt.

"I'll take Linda Kincaid, Grace," he said.

"She's gone." Her eyes, normally a rich, deep blue, looked pale, cold, hard. And bloodshot.

Savage grinned.

"We put her on the westbound," Grace said.

"Then you don't mind us searching your room."

The words weren't out of Savage's mouth when two men slid from their saddles, and barged past Grace, a blond-mustached man shoving her aside so hard, Grace had to let go of the coat and grip a wooden column to keep from falling down.

"Cutter!" Savage shouted.

The blond Ranger turned in the doorway.

"Apologize to the lady, Cutter."

Cutter swept his battered porkpie hat off his head. "Sorry, ma'am," he said before heading inside.

Savage shook his head. "Sorry, Grace. It's

hard to get good men anymore."

She pulled the range coat back over her chemise, her lips tight, wanting to say something, yet not daring to.

Savage passed the time by reaching into his coat pocket and pulling out the cross he had taken off the Rurale. He admired it for a moment, then shoved it back, and came out with his sack of Bull Durham. He kept his eyes on Grace as he spread the flakes onto the paper, and deftly rolled the cigarette, licking it, sticking it in his mouth, finding a lucifer and striking it against the revolver's butt.

From inside came the chimes of spurs and pounding of boots on stairs. A moment later, Taw Cutter and Joe Newton stepped back onto the boardwalk. Cutter held a blanket in his arms.

"She wasn't up there, Captain," Newton said, "but somebody had been sleeping on her sofa." Cutter held up the blanket.

"That would be me," Grace said.

"Bed had been slept in, too."

"So I got up to read, got comfortable on the sofa, pulled up a blanket. You know how I love to read, Hec."

"You're the best-read woman between Austin and Tucson, I warrant." Savage pulled deeply on the cigarette.

"Yeah." Cutter dropped the blanket at his feet, and held up a badly torn, bloodstained dress. "But I also found this in her trash can."

Savage flicked the cigarette toward Grace. "What about that, Grace?" he asked.

"What of it? You know that woman was here. I never denied that. I gave her one of my dresses, took that filth off her. Which is more than you did, Hec Savage." She looked past him. "More than any of you bastards thought to do."

Joe Newton dropped his eyes. Even Savage's shoulders slouched. Only Taw Cutter chuckled.

"I asked my maid to . . ." Savage shook his head. "Hell, it don't matter. Where is she, Grace?"

"I told you. I put her on the westbound."

He smiled a cold, chilling smile, and shook his head. "No, Grace." He tilted his head toward the rising sun. "See that black smoke off in the distance. That's the westbound. Making good time. Lieutenant Wickes told me he put the boys, living and dead, on the eastbound yesterday at noon. Then he left that whore with you. Westbound ain't due until today, and there she is. Right on time, for once." Shaking his head, he let out a sigh. "You used to be a

146

much better liar, Grace."

She stepped to the edge of the boardwalk, looking past Savage at the men in the saddles. She wet her lips. "Where is Lieutenant Wickes?"

No one answered.

Savage turned in the saddle, looked up and down the street. Marathon was coming to life. A Mexican peon led a burro loaded with firewood down the street, sombrero in his hand, walking nervously toward the gathering of men. Across the street. a merchant stood in front of the mercantile, holding a ring of keys in his trembling left hand. Another Mexican, a woman in a muslin dress, stood in the doorway of her jacal, kneading dough. In the tents beyond the hotel, railroad hands were brewing coffee and frying bacon. Slowly, Savage's eyes turned back to Grace. Without looking away from her, he asked, "Doc, how far you make that train?"

"Couple miles, I reckon."

Savage nodded. "You want to give up that whore, Grace?"

"She went on the westbound," she said.

"Not yet, she ain't."

"It was a special run."

He smiled. "Nice try, ma'am. I'm afraid I got to shut down your saloon, Grace."

"For what?"

"Serving bad whiskey."

"Same whiskey I've been serving here for better than three years."

"Yeah." He drew the .44 and shot the bartender in the left leg, just above his kneecap.

Grace staggered back, bringing both hands to her open mouth, as Horatius grabbed his leg, screaming, and toppled off the boardwalk and into the dust. His horse danced away, started to run, but Doc Shaw grabbed the reins and held the blue roan tight. The railroad workers bolted out of their tents, rounding the corner, a couple of them wielding sledgehammers and one thumbing back the hammer of an old cap-and-ball Navy Colt. Rangers Eliot Thompson and Bucky Bragg wheeled their horses, Thompson pulling out a Remington revolver while Bragg tapped his peso star and said, "Stand easy, boys. We're the law."

"Go back to your breakfast, gents," Hec Savage said, still staring at Grace Profit.

On the ground, Horatius reached for the boardwalk, missed, fell back into the sand, dragged himself up, and put both hands on his bleeding leg. Tears streamed down his sand-covered face, his eyes tight with pain, but he managed to spit out a few curses at

Savage before he let out a little whimper, and fell back on his side.

Lowering her hands, summoning up her resolve, Grace started for the beer-jerker, but Savage stopped her. "I'll take care of him, Grace." He nodded at Cutter and Newton. "Take him behind the depot." Finally, Savage holstered the Merwin Hulbert. "Put his legs on the rail."

Grace stared, incredulous. "You can't be serious, Hec."

"Oh, I am, Grace. Indeed I am." He kicked his horse back a few steps, tugged on the reins, and led the way to the depot.

Horatius wailed in agony when the two Rangers grabbed him with rough hands, and dragged him through the dirt, off the road, across the empty lot toward the railroad tracks. Grace hurried off the boardwalk, screaming for them to stop, but they kept right on. She whirled, seeking help from the railroad men, but the last of them hung his head, and walked back to the tents. Across the street, Rodney Kipperman, who ran the mercantile, hurriedly opened the door, slammed it shut, and pulled down the shade. Even the Mexican woman had returned inside the jacal, and the old man with the load of wood stood, mouth open, crossing himself.

"Damn you, Savage," Grace cried, but had to step out of the way of Doc Savage as he led the other Rangers after the captain. "You can't do this. What kind of men are you?"

The last two Rangers pulled the mounts of Newton and Cutter behind them. One of them had taken the dead quail and was wrapping the string around his saddle horn.

She remembered Horatius's shotgun. He had let her shoot it a couple of times, a double-barrel made in London, so light, she doubted it weighed more than five pounds. Likely loaded with only birdshot, it wouldn't kill anyone unless she got really close, and really lucky, but it was all she could think of. She turned, took a step, stopped. Behind her Horatius yelled, cursed, and cried.

The William Moore & Grey 12-gauge lay in the street, the blue roan a few rods away. The Damascus barrels lay beside the boardwalk, the stock near the watering trough. She hadn't even heard the Rangers bust it apart.

Upstairs, if those Rangers who had searched her room hadn't found it, she had a .38-caliber Colt Lightning, which would kill a man. She bolted onto the boardwalk, grabbed the doorknob, when the westbound's whistle let out a shrill scream. She stepped back, saw the thick black smoke from the locomotive, knowing she'd never reach that pistol in time. Instead, she turned, leaped off the boardwalk, ran across the lot in her bare feet, tails of her range coat whipping behind her, leaping over patches of prickly pear, stubbing her toe on a rock. She knew she was crying. She didn't care.

"Savage! Savage! No!" she yelled. She stumbled near the depot's platform, letting the sight sink in, still not certain she believed it, then charged down the slight embankment toward the tracks, only to be stopped by Doc Shaw's hands. She fought him, but he gripped her around the waist, held her tight, and pulled her into the shade, up onto the platform.

Kneeling, Cutter and Newton held Horatius at his shoulders, pinning him to the dirt, both legs on the railroad tracks, his right one soaked with blood, his left kicking frantically. The bartender frothed like a rabid dog, his eyes wide. The two Rangers kept glancing down the tracks, inching away from the rails, making sure they wouldn't get hit when the big Baldwin locomotive pulled up to the depot.

"Savage! Hec! Don't!" She looked for the captain, found him on his gray horse, telling a couple of his men to ride out a ways toward the oncoming train.

"Let that engineer see your badges," Savage ordered them. "Don't show him any guns, just your badges. That way he'll know we're not holdup men, just lawmen doing our job."

"Your job?" Grace stamped at Doc Shaw's feet, but the Ranger merely chuckled. "You crazy son of a bitch," she snapped.

Savage turned his horse, and nudged the gray to the edge of the depot's platform. "Hell, Grace, I'm doing Horatius a favor. If my bullet hit bone, that leg of his'll have to come off. Wheels of that train will do the job a lot faster, cleaner, than some old hack with a surgical saw."

The screams of the locomotive drowned out Grace's curse and Horatius's screams.

She turned, saw the engine, its headlamp staring like Cyclops. Whitish gray smoke poured from the stack. She could hear the rattling, the hissing, could make out the number on the front of the train so clearly — 421. The engineer leaned out the window, his face blackened with soot, then disappeared. Grace heard the brakes squeal, and saw the sparks fly.

"Captain!" It was Doc Shaw's voice.

Grace closed her eyes, felt the bile rising

up her throat.

"Get him out of there!"

She felt the warmth as the Baldwin engine slid past her in a cacophony of noise, heard the last belch of steam, felt her whole body go limp. Only Doc Shaw's grip kept her from collapsing in a heap.

The engineer scrambled out of the cab. "What the hell was you doin'?"

"Getting information," Savage said, swinging down from the saddle, oblivious to the surprised eyes staring at him from the windows of the passenger cars. The conductor ran alongside the rails, demanding to know what was going on. Savage ignored him, and swept the hat off his head, bowing slightly.

Grace opened her eyes to see Linda Kincaid step onto the platform, her lips trembling, her face ashen.

"Miss Kincaid," Savage said.

The whore's fingers clenched into fists.

Around the front of the locomotive came Cutter and Newton.

"Where's the barkeep?" Bragg asked.

Cutter hooked his thumb. "Back yonder. Passed out. Messed his britches." He winked at Grace. "But don't worry, ma'am. He's still got both his legs. I mean, limbs, ma'am. For the time being."

"Fetch that roan of his," Savage ordered. "No sidesaddle, Miss Kincaid, but it'll get you down to Presidio."

Grace found her voice. "Why are you taking her?"

"She's a witness, Grace." Savage donned his hat. "I'll need her to testify when we catch old Juan Lo Grande. But till then, I figure it's best to keep her in, what do you call it? Oh, yeah, protective custody. Bragg, fetch a few jugs of Grace's brew for the journey south. Then burn down that saloon. I told you, Grace, I gotta shut you down."

CHAPTER TWELVE

Chance and Albavera circled around Marathon, coming in from the east instead of the west, not taking any chances, not doing anything that would play into the hands of Don Melitón and his vaqueros. When they reached the eastern outskirts of town, Chance reined in the Andalusian, and told Albavera to stop.

Pressing the Winchester Centennial against the saddle, Chance stood in the stirrups and studied the street, the buildings, even the shrubs and cactus, before he sank back down, letting out a haggard breath.

"I guess we won't be cutting the trail dust with some of that forty-rod Grace Profit serves, eh, Sergeant Chance?" Albavera asked.

They had a clear view. The wind carried wisps of smoke into the darkening skies. Where once Grace's canvas tent stood, they saw only scorched earth, ashes, and smoldering ruin.

Raising the Winchester, Chance pointed the barrel down the street, ready. The stallion stamped its forefoot and shook its head, but Chance gave the reins a slight pull. He wasn't ready to go yet. He kept searching the streets for people. Marathon rolled up its streets at night, but it wasn't yet dark. The railroaders weren't in their tents. Hell, the tents were gone. There was nobody to be found on the town's main street.

The black man leaned forward, the chains of the iron bracelets jangling in the evening air. "Don Melitón's handiwork, I warrant."

"Maybe." Chance thumbed back the hammer on the big .45-70. "I don't see his men, though." He pointed his chin at the corral on the southern side of the street. "No horses in the livery yonder. Nothing. Nobody."

"You wouldn't," Albavera said. "Wouldn't see any of that old reprobate's killers, not if they're worth a flip. Yonder's your good residents of Marathon, though." Albavera pointed, and Chance followed the long, thick finger, seeing the Catholic church on a little rise across the Southern Pacific rails on the northwestern edge of town. The big door to the church was open. So was the gate to the little cemetery behind the adobe building. A crowd, by Marathon's standards, had gathered among the ocotillo crosses and warped cottonwood tombstones.

"Looks like a burying." Albavera swept off his hat and bowed mockingly. "Should we pay our last respects?"

Not bothering with a reply, Chance watched the crowd at the graveyard for only a moment. People at a funeral posed no threat to him. Quickly, he turned his gaze back down the street, examining each building, every window, the alleys, everything, one more time.

Albavera asked, "You think that old don's waiting to ambush us?"

"It's crossed my mind."

"Why not take these cuffs off me? Give me a gun? I can help. And I can shoot."

"I don't think so."

"I thought we was friends."

"I don't think so."

"After all we've been through?"

Chance didn't answer. Thinking, he ran his tongue across his dry lips. He would have bet a month's wages Don Melitón would have had at least two riders there, waiting to ambush him, or to at least find him and the man-killer, before riding out to lead the old man and the rest of his gunmen back into the city.

Albavera was talking again, but all Chance heard was, "You know I'm innocent."

"I don't care."

Albavera chuckled. "Well, let's ride on into town. Hell, those folks might as well stay put at that graveyard. Chances are, if Don Melitón's around, they'll be burying you and me before sundown." He kicked the sorrel into a walk, sitting erect in the saddle. With a muffled curse, Chance spurred the Andalusian.

They rode toward the sinking sun, the clopping hooves sounding incredibly loud. The wind picked up, and Chance caught a movement toward the tracks. He looked up, saw the thin strand of a telegraph wire slapping against the pole next to the depot.

Albavera had noticed it, too. Little escaped that man's eyes. "Guess you can't wire your boss in Austin to let him know you've captured the notorious Moses Albavera, or give the reporters in Galveston a chance to meet us at the station . . . if any of them remember me, or the Marin brothers."

Chance gripped the Centennial a little tighter, risking a look at Grace Profit's saloon as they rode past.

Nothing but ashes, smoke still snaking its way from black and gray mounds, a few charred jugs, broken from the heat. He detected no sign of any attempt to put the fire out, but water was scarce, and the residents had likely let the flames consume the canvas structure — the place undoubtedly went up fast — and concentrated instead on wetting down the sides and roofs of the hotel and mercantile. He couldn't fault them for that, and, neither, he figured, would Grace Profit. Both she and Chance had seen entire towns go up in flames.

"Wonder what caused the fire," Albavera said.

Chance was bothered more by the cut telegraph wire.

"I sure hope Miz Grace wasn't hurt," the black gunman said.

"Me, too," Chance whispered. He looked ahead at the Iron Mountain Inn, to an upstairs window. Grace's room. No light. No movement. He felt worried, hoping, praying it wasn't Grace they were burying on that hilltop cemetery.

They halted at the depot. A CLOSED sign hung on the door, but the schedule, written in chalk on a blackboard, stood between the door and the clerk's window. Being closest to the depot, Albavera leaned forward and read it. He turned to Chance with a grin. "Eastbound's due noon on Sunday. Gives us a while to rest. Too bad Miz Grace's saloon burned down."

"You know Grace, eh?" Chance said.

Albavera grinned. "Yeah, but I don't think I know her as well as you do, Ranger." He chuckled.

Chance frowned. He tilted his head down the street, and Albavera let the sorrel walk toward the Iron Mountain Inn. Both men seemed startled when the door swung open. Albavera pulled back on the reins, leaning to his right, ready to leap from the saddle; Chance lifted the Centennial, dropping the reins over the stallion's neck. A Mexican woman backed out the door, setting a keg of water and a mop on the boardwalk. Cleaning lady. Chance and Albavera relaxed, whistling simultaneously. Chance lowered the heavy rifle, and the Andalusian snorted.

Turning quickly, the woman, a petite lady with silver-streaked black hair, grabbed a crucifix that dangled between her breasts. As Chance reached for his hat brim, she whispered, *"Los rinches. Los rinches."*

And took off running.

"You have a way with the ladies, my friend," Albavera said.

They watched her run, lifting the hem of her skirt, across the dusty street, into a tiny jacal. She shouted something, and a burly

160

Mexican exited, staring at Chance, then at Albavera. He walked around the side of the hut, and came back with a pitchfork, taking long strides toward the two riders.

Chance didn't like it, but he lowered the hammer on the Winchester, and slid from the saddle, keeping the barrel of the heavy rifle pointed at the ground. He let the reins drop to the ground, and pushed up his hat brim, smiling, starting out with a friendly, *"Buenas tardes, ami—"*

"Damn!" Chance leaped away to avoid the prongs of the pitchfork the black-haired, barrel-chested Mexican thrust at him. He let go of the Winchester, lost his balance, and fell on his buttocks. Shaking his head, he looked up. First he saw Albavera in the saddle, eyes bright, howling, and heard his mocking laughter. A second later, he saw the Mexican.

And the pitchfork.

"Now wait . . ." Chance rolled to his right, felt the tool swish past his ear. He shot to his feet, came up with his hands extended, palms outward, placating. "Listen, mister, I —"

He ducked again. Instinctively, his hand reached for the butt of the Schofield, but he didn't want to kill the peon. He tapped the peso badge pinned on his vest.

The Mexican looked massive. Hands like hams gripped the pitchfork's handle. His muscles strained against the homespun cloth of his shirtsleeves. The front of the shirt was unbuttoned, revealing a strong, hairy chest. He wore sandals and ragged pants. His eyes were dark, malevolent. Dirt was caked on his face, in his hair. His brow knotted. *"El rinche,"* he said.

"That's right. I'm a Ranger. Now . . . Crap!"

A prong caught the left sleeve of Chance's mackinaw. He barely pulled free.

Albavera kept laughing.

The pitchfork came slashing again. Chance rolled underneath the Andalusian, came up on the other side. The horse bolted a few rods away. He backed against the sorrel, quickly ducked, fearing Albavera might join the fight, but the prisoner kept cackling.

Chance felt something running down his left arm, realizing the pitchfork had caught more than just his jacket sleeve. He backed away, found the Schofield's butt, and kept his hand there.

"Hombre," Chance said, shaking his head. *"Por favor."*

"Hijo de la puta." The Mexican spat, and lunged the pitchfork at Chance's gut. *"Pendejo."*

162

Chance leaped back, jerking the big .45 free of the holster. He gave his prisoner a moment's consideration.

"He doesn't seem to like you much, Ranger Chance," Albavera said. He still sat on the sorrel, eyes bemused. He seemed to have completely forgotten about Don Melitón. For that matter, so had Chance.

"How about some help?" Chance asked. "I don't want to have to kill this guy."

"I don't care," Albavera said.

"I thought we were friends. All we've been through."

Chance dodged the pitchfork again. "You're making a big mistake, amigo. I'm" — he ducked the prongs again — "a lawman." He sidestepped another thrust. "I'm a Texas Ranger, señor."

"He knows that," Albavera said.

"Let's talk" — he dodged again — "this over."

"Maybe he don't speak English," Albavera said.

"Then he's out of luck." Chance had grown weary of that damned pitchfork, of everything. Those prongs were getting closer. His left arm had started throbbing. He brought the Schofield up, and eared back the hammer.

The Mexican woman screamed from the

jacal, but the man didn't seem to notice the weapon in Chance's hand. He drew the pitchfork back, prepared to send it toward Chance's torso again.

"*¡Miguel!*" a woman's voice called from across the street. "*¡Para ya!*"

Holding the pitchfork raised, the big Mexican slowly turned his head, and stared at Grace Profit standing in the middle of the street. Chance kept the Schofield aimed at the man's paunch, but he slowly relaxed, trying to steady his breathing, his heartbeat.

"It's all right, Miguel." Grace walked slowly, smiling. Behind her came others, the crowd from the funeral, dressed in black, or at least wearing black sleeve garters or scarves. Grace wore a double-breasted twill jacket trimmed in navy blue over a gray blouse and a black box-plaited skirt. A mourning bonnet, trimmed with crepe loops and black ribbon strings, set atop her blond hair. Even from that distance, Chance saw how red her eyes were, knew she'd been crying. He couldn't blame her for that. Hell, her saloon was nothing but ashes.

She spoke quietly in Spanish, and the Mexican lowered the pitchfork. Giving Chance a final, cold stare, he walked back to the jacal, his wife meeting him at the door. He leaned the tool against the adobe wall, and he and his wife went inside.

"You all right, Dave?" Grace said.

He started to holster the Schofield, but turned, ducked, and brought the .45 up quickly. The gunshot echoed, and a mound of dirt leaped up toward Albavera's hands, inches above the Winchester Centennial laying in the street. Chance hadn't even noticed the man dismount the sorrel.

"Leave the rifle put." Chance cocked the revolver.

Albavera straightened, letting his manacled hands drop by his waist. "Just trying to help, Ranger."

"You can help me by keeping your hands off that rifle."

"All right."

"You want to help, take the horses to the corral. Water and grain them."

Albavera nodded, grabbed the reins to the sorrel, and led it across the street, tipping his hat as he passed Grace. He gathered the reins to the Andalusian, and walked to what passed for a livery stable in Marathon.

Chance lowered the hammer, holstered the .45, and hurried to pick up the Winchester. Turning back toward Albavera he called out, "And Moses, don't try to ride off."

Albavera let out another laugh, and led the horses into the corral.

"Dave?" Grace's voice was calm, soothing.

Chance moved the Winchester to his left hand, and lowered it. He pressed his right against his aching, bleeding left arm, and, slowly looked at the woman in black. "What the hell is going on here?"

"I'll tell you, Dave," she said, "over a drink. God knows, I need one tonight."

CHAPTER THIRTEEN

She never drank the whiskey she served in her saloons. Grace Profit wasn't that daring, or stupid. From the top drawer of her bureau, she pulled a bottle of Jameson Irish Whiskey, and filled three glasses, handing one to Dave Chance, another to his prisoner, and picking up the fullest for herself. She sat on the couch, and Chance sat in a rocking chair. Moses Albavera, his hands still manacled, leaned against the wall, taking occasional glances out the window.

"How close are you to your captain?" she asked.

"You mean Captain Savage?" Chance sipped the whiskey. "He saved my life four years ago."

She ran a finger across the rim of the glass, not certain if she should continue.

"What happened to your saloon, ma'am?" It was the black man who asked the question. She looked across the room, and studied him for a moment, her eyes falling from his rugged face to the iron bracelets. Ray Wickes had said Chance was chasing a black man who had killed Prince Benton. That would explain a lot.

"Captain Hector Savage burned it down." She lifted the glass, took a swallow, and stared at Chance. "Had it burned, anyway."

The Ranger set his glass by his boots, crossed his legs, and ran his right hand over the growth of beard stubble on his face. Trying to form a decent question, she figured, but all he said was, "Why?"

She let out a little snort, and finished the Jameson. "Spite. Meanness. Oh, he said it was for serving bad whiskey, but it wasn't so bad he stopped his men stealing a few jugs before they doused the tent walls and bar with it and set my place of business ablaze. It's the same damned brew he's been drinking since I set up here more than three years ago. He shot my bartender, too."

"Horatius?" Chance asked.

"Yeah."

"Did he — ?"

"Horatius didn't have a gun, Dave. Savage shot him because he's a son of a bitch." She felt the blood rushing, and decided she had better refill her glass. She went to the bureau, poured herself four fingers, and walked across the room, topping off the glasses held by Chance and Albavera.

"Is he dead?" Chance asked.

Albavera thanked her, and looked out the window.

Corking the bottle, Grace said, "If you're looking for Don Melitón's men, you don't have to worry. Savage shot down two of the old man's vaqueros before riding out of town. He rode out with a woman, Dave. No, he didn't kill Horatius, but only by God's grace. Shot him in the thigh, just above his knee, but the bullet didn't hit bone. We were burying the don's men when you two rode into town." She was talking too fast, felt her hands shaking and took a drink. "Horatius is down the hall. You don't believe me, maybe you'll believe him."

The bartender lay atop the sheets and quilt, sweating like a cowhand in August, grimacing while Grace changed the blood-soaked bandage that covered a grisly wound in his thigh that had been cauterized by packing the bullet hole with gunpowder and touching it off with a match. Chance wondered if Grace Profit had served as doctor, the nearest sawbones being the post surgeon at Fort Davis. Whoever it was had done a remarkable job. If infection didn't set in, Horatius would likely live. Albavera lifted the bartender's head as gently as possible, considering the iron cuffs on his wrists, and let him finish off the whiskey in his glass. The barman coughed, gave a little nod, and Albavera lowered his head back onto a pillow.

"After he shot you," Chance asked, "he burned the saloon?"

"Yeah." Horatius grimaced. "Well, first he had his men drag me to the railroad tracks. They put my legs over the rails. Held me down. Westbound was coming. They wanted me to tell them where we'd hid that woman from Terlingua. Criminy, I didn't know."

Albavera wiped the barkeep's sweaty forehead with a towel.

"Like I told you, I'd been out hunting, saw the dust they was raising. Coming from the south, I figured it had to be Rangers. I hit the saddle, galloped back to town, ran upstairs to warn Grace and Miss Kincaid, then I come down and, well, there was the captain and, I don't know, ten men."

"And Don Melitón's men?" Chance asked.

"I don't know. I'd passed out by then."

Grace tied off the bandage, looked up at Chance. "Savage had set fire to the saloon. Those two vaqueros rode up, saw Horatius lying on the street, heard me screaming, cussing. I guess they thought I needed help — hell, I did — and they loped down the street. One of them yelled a warning, told Savage to stop. The other drew a rifle. They were shot dead out of the saddles."

"Likely they didn't see the badges, thought they were outlaws," Horatius said.

"They are outlaws," Grace said icily. "Savage's men are killers, vermin." She stopped. "Well, not you, Dave. But the men he had with him today. And even if the vaqueros saw those badges . . ." She shook her head, started to rein in her tongue, but couldn't. "Look at that badge on your lapel, Dave. It's cut out of a peso. You can't blame any Mexican in South Texas or West Texas for hating you Rangers. *Los rinches* is not a term of endearment, of respect. They fear you. And with good reason. You've never shown them any respect, the Mexicans, I mean. Hec Savage has been riding rough-shod over those people since he came here a decade ago."

"Grace," Chance began, "that's not —" He stopped. It was true. "You sure those two *vaqueros* were Don Melitón's?"

"Rail M brand. The Rangers rode off with their horses."

"Mine, too," Horatius said. "They put that Terlingua woman on him."

171

"Maybe you could arrest Captain Hec Savage for horse theft," Moses Albavera said, chuckling.

"Shut up," Chance said.

"You rest, Horatius." Grace rose from the bed. "If you need anything, just shout. I'll be right down the hall." She nodded toward the door.

They were creatures of habit. Grace was back on the couch, Chance in the rocking chair, and Moses Albavera pressed his back against the wall, looking out the window. Their glasses contained the last of the Irish whiskey.

"The captain had to have a reason," Chance began.

"Don't make excuses for him, Dave," Grace said. "He's not the same person he was when he first came out here. Not that he ever was a gentleman, from what I hear."

"This wasn't a gentle place, Grace." He swallowed some whiskey. "Still isn't."

"He's changed. And you know it."

Chance couldn't argue that point. Besides, a good chunk of those Rangers the captain had recruited over the past few years likely were better suited in prison stripes in Huntsville, not wearing a peso star like the one he was fingering on his vest. At least a couple of them — Bragg, Cutter — were wanted, but Captain Savage had said he didn't care what a man had done in the past, providing he wasn't wanted by the law in Texas. When Grace had called Savage's men outlaws, she wasn't stretching the truth.

Savage had also been hitting the bottle fairly hard, always on the prod. Yet Chance had shrugged it off as pressure. It wasn't easy commanding a group of Rangers along the Mexican border, and that bandit Juan Lo Grande didn't make things any easier. So when Savage had gotten word of Lo Grande's raid on Terlingua, he had ridden off after him, but hadn't taken Chance.

"I need you here," the captain had said.

"Yeah, but . . ." There weren't many men around who could argue with Captain Hector Savage.

"Need a man here I can trust, a man I know can get the job done . . . if something were to happen to me."

"Nothing can happen to you, Captain," Chance had said.

"I don't want anything to happen to you either, Dave. Remember Fort Stockton."

It wasn't like he'd ever forget what had happened at the Bad Water Saloon in that parasite town that sprang up because of the military post. And it wasn't like Hec Savage would ever let Chance forget. If he could single out one of Savage's annoying faults, it was his habit to draw Fort Stockton like a six-shooter.

"Anyway," Savage had said, as if he realized he'd struck a little too close to the quick with his sergeant, "I'd rather have you running this deal than Ray Wickes."

Wickes.

Grace was speaking of him, asking Chance what he thought of the lieutenant.

Chance shrugged. "He's a good man." *Better suited behind a desk in Austin than in the saddle in Presidio County.*

"Do you trust him?"

Chance finished the whiskey. "With my watch, sure. With my life . . . ?" He shrugged.

"What about Wes Smith?"

He nodded. "He can handle a gun for a kid. Sure, I trust Wes."

"He's dead. And" — she had to reach for the name, but she caught it — "Magruder."

The words slammed Chance like a mule's hoof. He couldn't believe what Grace was saying.

"This is what Linda Kincaid, the woman from Terlingua, the one Lo Grande's vermin had kidnapped, told me. She said Captain

174

Savage killed them in a cantina in San Pedro, where he was meeting Juan Lo Grande."

"Killed who?" Chance asked.

"Smith and Magruder." She watched Chance's brow knot, his face pale. "He killed one of them, I mean. Someone else, another Ranger, killed the other. That's why Lieutenant Wickes came here. He put two coffins on the eastbound with two other Rangers. Escorts."

"Was Doc Shaw one of them?" he asked.

"No."

"Figures." Chance's thoughts whirled. Shaw had probably killed the second Ranger, if he could believe what Grace was telling him. Savage was capable of a lot of things, but murdering two of his own men? The woman, Linda Kincaid, must have been mistaken. She had been brutalized by Lo Grande's bandits. Sure, that was it. She was just confused.

But why had Savage shot that bartender? Why had he taken Linda Kincaid back to Fort Leaton? Why had he really burned down Grace's saloon? Why would he have sent two Rangers back east as a sort of honor guard, with Lo Grande still playing hell on the border, short-handed as Company E was?

Chance wished Grace had another bottle of Jameson. Hell, even some of that Taos Lightning she served at the saloon would have helped his nerves.

"I can't remember their names."

"Turpen and Babbitt," Chance said.

"Maybe." She finished her whiskey. "I can't say for sure."

She didn't have to. He knew. Turpen, Babbitt, Wickes, and Chance had been left behind when the captain went off after Lo Grande and the Terlingua raiders. He would have trusted Turp and Babbitt with his watch or his life. They were good men. Damned good. So was Magruder.

"What was the woman doing here?" Albavera asked.

Grace and Chance gave him a surprised look. Grace cleared her throat, and answered. "The captain had sent her to catch the train back to Houston. That's where her folks live."

"But she witnessed the murder of those two Rangers?"

"Yes. That's what she told me."

"Then why didn't Captain Savage just kill her, too?"

"I guess he has principles."

Chance shot out, "But he took her back with him."

She nodded. "Said it was for her own protection."

"Changed his mind." Albavera finished his whiskey. "Got smarter. Smart, too, cutting the telegraph wire. He kinda cut you off, eh, Sergeant Chance?"

"Not really. Telegraph wire can be fixed."

"He did more than cut that wire here in town," Grace said. "I heard him order a couple of his men to ride in both directions. 'Pull an Apache trick on the wires,' is what he said. You know what that means?"

"Yeah." Chance frowned. "Cut the wire. Splice it with a rubber band. Tie it back to the pole. Takes a really good eye to spot it. The railroad crews'll likely spend a few days just trying to find the cut." He turned to Grace. "Where are the railroaders?"

"Murphyville, most likely," she said. "After the Rangers burned down my saloon, Savage told the railroaders they might as well head down the track to Murphyville to do their drinking. That was before they cut the wire. Savage also had one of those men send out a wire to the S.P. offices in Houston and El Paso saying the lines were down because of the weather, and that they'd likely be down for five days."

Chance considered that. "Five days."

"They could send a wire to El Paso from

Murphyville," Albavera said.

"They won't," Grace said. "The captain paid them to keep quiet."

"Five days," Chance repeated.

"That's what the lady —" Albavera turned quickly, staring out the window. Chance heard the clopping of hooves then, and slowly drew the Smith & Wesson from behind his back. Keeping away from the window, he maneuvered his way to the wall, and stood across from Albavera. The rhythmic noise drew closer, then stopped.

Albavera looked out the window, turned to Chance. "One horse. No rider."

The coal-oil lamp hanging from the wooden column cast dim yellow light on the weary brown gelding that stood in the street, head hanging down, a Cheyenne saddle hanging off-center on the right, both reins missing from the headstall.

Chance, Albavera, and Grace had come down the stairs, and through the back door — the same door Grace had sent Linda Kincaid through, to hide in the church, when Horatius had told them he thought Savage's Rangers were riding into Marathon. Albavera had volunteered to stay in Grace's room, but Chance wasn't about to leave him alone.

Hugging the side wall tightly, Chance brought the Winchester Centennial to his shoulder, and looked down the street to the west, then east. Not that he could see much, dark as it was. He waited. The horse snorted.

A minute passed . . . then five . . . then fifteen. Neither Grace nor Albavera ever sounded impatient, just stood behind him, waiting.

Finally, Chance decided he could wait till dawn, or check that brown horse now. So with a slight whispered curse, he stepped away from the wall, up the boardwalk, down the steps, and walked into the street, speaking softly to the gelding, stepping lightly, shooting quick glances up and down the darkened street. Albavera and Grace were a few steps behind him.

He shoved the stock of the Winchester under his arm, and pressed a hand against the horse's neck. Rubbing it in a counterclockwise motion, he tried to soothe the horse, though the way it looked and felt, it was too tired to run away.

"Easy, boy," he said, and moved to the saddle. "Easy. You know me, boy. We'll take good care of you."

He ran his hand down the saddle. The streets were dark, true, but the lanterns from the Iron Mountain Inn provided enough light for him to see the brown stains on the saddle. Dried, but still a bit tacky. Blood. A lot of it.

He looked over the horse's back, saw Grace and Albavera standing there.

"It's Ray Wickes's horse," Chance said.

CHAPTER FOURTEEN

"What's that they say about Texas weather?" asked Albavera. "If you don't like it, stick around for a minute, and it'll change."

"Texas weather." Chance had taken off his mackinaw, and was tying it atop his bedroll behind the cantle of his saddle. "Arkansas weather. Kansas weather. Colorado weather. New Mexico weather. Every damned state says the same damned thing about the same damned weather."

The weather had warmed considerably, probably pushing the mercury up to the sixty-degree mark, a far jump from the twenties and forties. Not hot, not as hellish as it would get in the summer, but that sun baked you like an oven. Even the wind felt warm. Chance finished securing his coat, and turned back. Removing his hat, he wiped the dust off his forehead, and stared south. A dust devil blew across the path about twenty yards away. The sky was pale and cloudless, the sun a white glare directly over their heads.

"Feels more like April than November," Albavera said. "You take these bracelets off, I'll take off my coat, too."

"Those bracelets stay on," Chance said. "So does your coat."

"But I'm hot. This buckskin is heavy, too."

"I don't care."

Albavera shook his head. "You've been in a grouchy mood since we left Marathon."

Without a word, Chance nudged the gray stallion into a walk, putting his hat back on his head, wetting his cracked lips. Albavera rode alongside him, pulling Ray Wickes's brown horse behind him. They rode in silence, but only briefly, for Albavera found it difficult to keep his trap shut.

"I still don't know why we're riding south."

"Told you." Chance tilted his head toward the brown gelding. "That's the lieutenant's horse. Wickes might need help."

"If Wickes needs anything, it's burying. You see all that blood on that saddle?"

"Then we'll bury him."

"If we find him. That's a big if." He shuddered. "This country gives me the creeps."

Chance knew the feeling. Mountains rose in the distance, clouded by a haze caused by the wind-blown sand. There were no trees, just cactus, an occasion shrub, and mostly rocks and ridges. Albavera went right on talking.

"That wind will scar you with sand, blind you if you aren't careful. Rattlesnakes and scorpions will bite you. Plants will poke you, if not poison you. You'll be baking like bread in an oven one minute, then a blue norther will leave you covered with sleet, freezing your ass off. Even the water here will kill you if you're not careful."

"Yep. It would make a good hell."

"It is hell." Albavera had to hold his hat on as a sudden gust of wind sprayed the man and horses with sand. He spit, and wiped his tongue on the sleeve of his duster.

"All right," Chance said. "I have an excuse. The Rangers sent me out here. This is where I happen to work. I'm just following orders. But what brings you to this hell?"

"Well, on this particular morning, to this particular hell, you've brought me here, Ranger Chance. I still haven't figured out why."

"Would you have preferred being left behind in Marathon? So when Don Melitón returned, he could hang you?"

"No. For one, I don't think that old codger would have hanged me. Shot me, sure. Maybe buried me up to my head near an ant bed, or staked me out in the sun. On the other hand, I'm not certain the don would come to Marathon. Your captain killed his two men, and the old man likely thinks they're still alive, waiting to see if we show up. Yeah, you could have left me in Marathon. I would have been safe. Only there isn't anything to drink in that town now. Thanks to your captain."

No, Chance thought. Albavera was wrong. Secrets were hard to keep from Don Melitón. Hec Savage had made a mistake sending that railroad crew to Murphyville. Those men might not wire any explanation to the Southern Pacific offices in El Paso, but they'd definitely tell somebody in some Murphyville bucket of blood what had happened to those two vaqueros Savage's men had killed, and the don's men would have returned, likely in force. Instead of correcting Albavera, however, Chance said, "That wasn't my meaning. What brought you to this country?"

"Money."

Chance nodded. They rode.

He didn't need to hear anymore, but Albavera made sure he did.

"First, I planned on betting on some boxing match they were having in El Paso.

Then, I figured there was a bunch of hard-rock miners in Shafter worth visiting."

"Instead you ran into Prince Benton."

"Bad luck. You play enough cards, you learn. Sometimes luck's with you. Sometimes she's against you. I didn't take it personal."

"Don Melitón did."

"Well. I also figured this country could swallow you up. Be easy for a man to disappear."

"A lot of people have."

"Maybe your lieutenant."

Chance shrugged. "Maybe. But you didn't. After you killed Prince Benton, you could have hidden out." He pointed at the mountains off to the northwest. "There in the Del Nortes." Pointed at the rises in the southeast. "Or there in the Tinajas." Pointed directly south. "Or down in the Santiagos, the Chalk range, the Chisos. Hell, you could have swum the Rio Grande and hidden out in Mexico. Instead, you found a poker game in Fort Davis. Acted like you wanted to get caught."

A grin stretched across Albavera's chiseled face. "Did I really act like I wanted to get caught, Ranger Chance? Seems to me you played hell getting these bracelets on me."

185

Chance had to laugh at that. "Point taken," he said.

The black man shook his head. "You misunderstood me, Sergeant. After I killed that bastard Prince Benton, I wasn't about to hide. You know as well as I do that nobody could hide from Don Melitón Benton. He'd come, and come to kill. I was waiting for him in Fort Davis. You just happened to get there first."

"Why did you need country to hide out in?" Chance asked. "You were surprised when I arrested you for killing the Marin brothers. Seemed stunned to think anyone remembered those murders."

"It was self-defense," Albavera corrected.

"Oh, yeah. Right."

"Like I told you. You knew about the Marins. And Prince Benton. But there was —"

"Bill Carter." Chance's head bobbed.

"That's right. You got a good memory, Ranger. Bill Carter. The one you didn't know about — which was self-defense, too."

"Of course." Chance's voice was placating.

The tone didn't appear to annoy Moses Albavera. "After I killed the Marin fools, I drifted. Piedras Negras. San Carlos. Spent some time in Mexico, then came back to

186

Texas. Didn't stop, mind you. Just passing through. To Kansas. Colorado — Denver, Leadville, Lake City — gambling. Betting on horses. Poker. Keno. Faro. Finally, I drifted back to Texas. Figured you Texans have short memories, and the Marin brothers would be long forgotten. Hit The Flat, Jacksboro, Fort Worth. Luck was running with me.

"Finally, I was told there was to be a big boxing match in El Paso, and I figured there was money to be had there, so I boarded a stagecoach in Jacksboro and headed for El Paso. Well, everything was going along just dandy till we got to Fort Stockton."

"Stockton?"

"Yeah. You know that town?"

Involuntarily, Chance raised his right hand, ran his fingers around his throat. "Yeah," he said in a dry whisper. "I know Fort Stockton."

"A miserable blight in a miserable country. Alas, the stage had busted an axle, so I was stuck. Decided to pass my time at the Bad Springs Saloon."

"Bad Water," Chance corrected. "Bad Water Saloon."

"Indeed, you're right, Ranger Chance. You do have a great memory. Well, I went inside, bellied up to the bar — how I love that term, bellied up to the bar." Chuckling, he shook his head. "Then this woman comes up to me. I buy her a drink. She's a whore. I know that. Hell, everybody in the Bad Springs, I mean, Bad Water Saloon knew that. She didn't care if I was Moorish. I didn't care that she was white."

"But somebody did."

"You know Fort Stockton. You know how it was."

"I can imagine."

Albavera shook his head. "All we were doing was drinking what passes for whiskey in that groggery. I didn't touch her. Certainly didn't kiss her. We were just drinking, passing time, laughing at a joke now and then."

"And Bill Carter took exception."

"He damned near took my head off with a meat cleaver. If Loretta, that was the whore's name, hadn't screamed her head off, I wouldn't have my head now."

"So you killed Bill Carter."

"Had to. Shot him in the stomach with Miss Vickie, and he still came at me. I had to smash in his skull, and as soon as he hit the floor, Loretta was saying, 'Oh, my God, you've killed Bill Carter. You best light out of here.' She didn't have to tell me twice. I could see the Bad Springs — Water — Saloon was filled to the brim with friends of

188

Bill Carter. But they looked struck dumb. One of them whispered, 'I didn't think Bill Carter could get killed.' Another added, 'Specially by no darky.' I told them to keep their hands on the table and their feet on the floor, and kept them covered with Miss Vickie. Fools were too stupid to realize it's a single-shot rifle, and I hadn't reloaded. Backed through those batwing doors —"

"And stole this stallion." Chance smiled at Albavera.

"You don't miss much, Ranger Chance."

"I'm alive."

"Well, I never made it to El Paso. Decided I might hide out in this Big Bend Country, and I did for a while. But this country . . ." Shuddering, he shook his head. "I'm not a man who enjoys solitude. I need people. I need noise. The sound of chips on a felt cloth. The shuffling of paste-cards. The clinking of glasses. The laughter of whores. I figured I might as well try my luck in Shafter."

"Where you killed Prince Benton. You seem to run into a lot of trouble in saloons, Moses. You might want to stay out of those places."

"That I can't do, Ranger Chance. Those saloons, those gambling parlors, they're like a home to me. Besides, a lovely little whore

189

in Shafter — black lady, me figuring people wouldn't get riled at me for talking and drinking with her — told me that I didn't have to worry about being posted for killing Bill Carter, not if he got killed in Fort Stockton."

"There's some truth to that. Fort Stockton's —"

Chance stopped the Andalusian. Albavera reined up the sorrel and followed Chance's gaze southeast. At first, he saw nothing, but then found about six or seven birds circling overhead. They seemed to have silver wings, but both men knew those birds were really black or brown.

"Like I said, your lieutenant doesn't need help. He needs burying."

"Let's find out." Chance's spurs raked the stallion's side, and the gray took off in an easy lope across the desert floor.

A huge turkey buzzard, better than two and a half feet long, lifted its red, featherless head, which seemed so tiny compared to the rest of the bird's body. A piece of gut hung from the hooked ivory beak, before the bird shook its head, swallowed the entrails, and, staring at the two riders, hissed. Other carrion kept right on feeding, waddling around, occasionally looking up, grunting.

Sounding like pigs, not birds.

They were hideous creatures in a horrible scene. Gray, dead eyes. Pale legs, clawed feet, red heads, dark feathers. Feasting on what once had been a man.

Catching the odor of blood and death, the horses danced nervously. The buzzards showed no fear.

The Andalusian turned in a circle as Chance drew the Schofield and fired once, twice, three times, the reports echoing, sending the birds noisily flapping into the sky. Few traveled more than twenty yards before lighting on the boulders, waiting for the riders to leave them to their find.

After holstering the Schofield, Chance swung from the saddle, drew the Winchester from the scabbard, and handed the reins to Albavera.

"Wait here," he said.

"That's what I planned on doing," Albavera said.

"If you try to ride off, I'll kill you."

"If I go anywhere" — Albavera looked away — "it'll be to that bush yonder. To throw up." He covered his mouth. The gunman looked sick.

Chance took a few steps, stopped, spit, and pulled his bandana over his mouth and nose. His eyes watered. Bile rose from his stomach, but he kept it down. He made it ten more feet, then leaned the Winchester against a rock. He lifted the bandana just enough to spit, almost spraying a boulder with vomit, but somehow managed to hold everything together.

Lucky, he tried to tell himself. Spring or summer, even early fall, ants would have been with the turkey buzzards, beetles, too. He studied the ground. Coyotes had already been there. Bits of clothing had caught in the rocks and yucca, or had been snagged on prickly pear. The ground around the dead man was stained brown from dried blood.

He had reached the body. What was left of a body, anyway.

The chest cavity had been ripped apart. So had the shirt, but Chance could tell it had been red flannel with a bib front. The shirt along the side hadn't been torn apart by the scavengers. He pulled a piece of cloth off the sticky mess of bloody flesh and bone, and put his finger through a hole, a hole no animal had made. He looked at the cloth carefully. The cloth was dried with blood, but he could make out powder burns.

Chance looked around. He didn't see a badge, but spotted a pair of glasses, one lens missing and the other broken, laying crumpled beside the man's eyeless head.

He couldn't identify the man. He had no features left, but Chance knew that turkey buzzards and coyotes weren't the only animals responsible. They had ripped through his flesh, eaten his eyes, pulled out his tongue, but a bullet had slammed into his left temple, and blown out the back of his head.

The man had been shot twice. In the side. In the head. The side wound had been first. Had to be, Chance figured, from all that blood he had found on Ray Wickes's saddle.

A shadow crossed Chance's face. He looked up and found Albavera standing over him. Chance shot a quick glance, and saw the three horses hobbled, the Winchester Centennial lying where he had left it. He stared at the black gunman. "Thought you were going to be sick."

"I decided I'd better buck up," he said. "Be a man. See if you need any —" He made the mistake of looking at the corpse. "Oh, hell."

"Yeah."

"Is that your lieutenant?"

"Yeah."

"Shot in the head, wasn't he?"

"Yeah." Chance pointed to the corpse.

"Took another bullet in his side. That one caught him at fairly close range. There are powder burns on the cloth."

"Reckon those two bandidos who jumped us did it?"

"No. For one thing, those powder burns on his shirt — Close range, like I said. Ray Wickes was green in a lot of ways, but he wasn't stupid. He wouldn't let a stranger get close to him. No, most likely, he knew who shot him. The first time. And that head shot? That pair of bandidos had Winchester carbines, .44-40 calibers. The bullet that blew off the lieutenant's head came from a much more powerful rifle."

Chance couldn't get the image of Doc Shaw and that new High Wall rifle out of his mind.

"I'm sorry," Albavera said, sounding like he meant it.

"Fetch the lieutenant's bedroll," Chance said. "We'll wrap him in it. Take him back to Marathon, bury him in that church cemetery."

"That boneyard's getting crowded of late."

Chance rose. "It'll get a lot more crowded, too, before I'm finished."

CHAPTER FIFTEEN

The spade bit deeper into the sandy soil only to slam into a buried rock that left Moses Albavera shaking his ringing hands. Letting the tool fall, he leaned back against the mound of dirt, and examined his hands. "It would be a lot easier for me to dig this grave," he told Chance, "if these bracelets came off."

"They stay on." With a grunt, Chance drove a pickax into the ground.

"My hands are getting blistered."

"I don't care."

The two men stood alone in the cemetery behind the Catholic church of Marathon. Chance swung the pick again, leaned the tool against the wall of dirt, and knelt, prying out a rock with his hands. He tossed the stone, and pushed back his hat. The morning was cool, the sun behind a wall of clouds. He rose, found the canteen, and drank.

"It doesn't seem right, if you ask me," Albavera said. "Those two Rangers your captain killed, get sent off on a train with a pair of guards to get a fine funeral, and this lieutenant of yours gets buried here alongside a couple of dead vaqueros."

Chance didn't answer. He just drank.

"Did Lieutenant Wickes have any kin?"

That time, Albavera got a response. "He wasn't married." Chance tossed the canteen to his prisoner, who caught it with his cuffed hands. "That's all I know."

"His saddlebag wasn't fastened. I noticed that when I got his bedroll. I secured the bag. He might have some personal property, name of his next of kin, something like that."

"He might." Chance hadn't thought to check. "I'll write or telegraph Colonel Thomas in Austin. If Wickes had any kin, and they want his body, they can dig him up, replant him in the family plot."

"Poor bastard. He doesn't even get a coffin, just his bedroll."

"Wood's scarce around here."

"You're either the hardest rock I ever met, Ranger Chance, or the cheapest son of a bitch there is."

Albavera got another response, one that pleased him. Dave Chance looked at him, and grinned.

Albavera drank, corked the canteen, set it aside, grabbed the shovel, and resumed digging.

Two hours later, when they had finished the grave, they lowered the remains of Ray Wickes into the hole, using ropes, and went inside the church to fetch the priest. They were at the door, the priest walking outside with a rosary and Bible, when Albavera cleared his throat, and pointed down the hill toward the town.

Coming up from the road that led to Presidio loped six riders.

"They're not Mexican," Albavera said.

"They're Rangers," Chance said. He turned to the priest, handing him a few coins. "Padre, sorry, but we can't stay for the funeral. Like I said, Ray Wickes was Catholic, a good man, loyal to Texas, and died in the line of duty. Say something like that." He turned to Albavera. "Let's go."

"You're kidding."

"No, I'm not."

As they walked down the rocky path from the church, Albavera snapped his fingers. "You knew they'd come back."

Chance didn't answer.

Shaking his head, Albavera went on talking. "I tried to figure out why we were digging this grave. You could have paid the padre or some peons to do it. We could have been riding east, to deliver me to the authorities in Galveston, or riding south, to find that whore, find your Captain Savage. Instead, we spent most of the morning digging a grave. At first, I figured you're just too damned cheap to pay for a grave, or the state of Texas is too cheap. But, no, that wasn't it. We were here waiting."

Chance shifted the Winchester Centennial under his armpit. Actually, he hadn't minded digging the grave. It gave him time to think, sort things out, figure out what the hell was going on. And it reminded him of those years swinging a sledge for the railroad.

"How'd you know they'd come back?" Albavera asked.

They had reached the flats, and started walking toward the empty lot where the railroaders had once pitched their tents before Savage had sent them packing off to Murphyville.

"Savage couldn't afford to leave Grace behind," Chance answered at last.

"So what do you plan on doing?"

Chance levered a round into the heavy rifle. He kept on walking.

"You are seriously loco, Ranger Chance."

They rounded the corner. Six horses stood

in front of the Iron Mountain Inn. Two riders remained in the saddles. Another stood in the shade, leaning against the wall near the front door. All three put their hands on the butts of their revolvers, but just watched as Chance and Albavera made their way down the dusty, practically deserted street.

"Hello, Sergeant." One of the mounted Rangers smiled. He didn't take his hand away from the revolver.

"Cutter," Chance said, stopping at the edge of the boardwalk. He nodded at the other Ranger on horseback. "Joe." Climbing onto the boardwalk, he greeted Bucky Bragg, who had pushed back that big sugar-loaf sombrero he wore. He had taken it off a dead Mexican bandit he had killed two years back.

"Who's your prisoner?" Joe Newton called from his horse.

"Moses Albavera."

"Ain't he the one that killed Prince Benton?" Taw Cutter asked.

"And Chet and Joe Marin in Galveston," Moses Albavera answered. "And Bill Carter at the Bad Springs Saloon in Fort Stockton."

"Bad Water Saloon," Chance corrected. He kept the barrel of the Winchester pointed at the ground, but his finger remained inside

199

the trigger guard, his thumb on the cocked hammer. "Captain Savage inside?"

"He is." Bragg pulled open the door.

At a square table in the middle of the hotel's parlor, Captain Hec Savage sat in a rocking chair, head bent. His hat rested crown down beside his right arm on the roughhewn table, next to one of his Merwin Hulbert .44's. He was scribbling furiously on a piece of stationery. A cigarette burned in a nearby ashtray. Across from him sat Grace Profit, who turned and watched as Moses Albavera and Dave Chance came inside. The door slammed shut after them, and Savage looked up, smiling.

On the second-story landing stood Doc Shaw, the High Wall rifle cradled in his arms. Behind the registration desk waited Eliot Thompson, who was carving off tobacco from a plug of Star Navy with a folding knife. Chance positioned himself between the door and the front window, directly in line with Hec Savage, but out of view of any Rangers out front.

Lowering the pencil, Savage reached for the cigarette, took a long pull, then blew a smoke ring toward the ceiling. "Hello, Sergeant," he said after a moment. "I see you caught your man."

"I did."

"Don Melitón didn't give you any trouble?"

"None to speak of. He might come after you, though. Killing two of his men."

"A regrettable incident." Savage crushed out the smoke in the ash tray. "But I think the old man will be hunting you before he comes after me." He looked at the prisoner, sizing him up, nodding. "So you're Moses Albavera."

"That's right."

"Moorish?"

"That's right."

Savage returned to the note he was writing, on his third page now. "You can't wait for the train here, Sergeant. Don Melitón might return. I don't hold out much hope that those railroaders I sent to Murphyville will keep quiet about what happened here. You should proceed to Strawbridge — Sanderson, I mean. All these towns changing their names because of the railroad confuses me. Travel to Sanderson. Wait for the Southern Pacific there. I don't think Don Melitón will think you'd ride that far. You will board the eastbound train when it arrives, and deliver your prisoner to the authorities in Galveston."

Sanderson was a little less than sixty miles

due east of Marathon. It had the reputation of a wild railroad town, with no law.

"Is that an order, Captain?" Chance asked.

Savage's hand moved wildly as he signed his name. "It is, Sergeant. I have another important duty for you, too." He kept writing. Four pages now.

Chance studied Doc Shaw and Eliot Thompson, then looked briefly at Grace.

"Where's Demitrio Ahern?"

"Back at Fort Leaton," Savage answered. "I left him with four men at our headquarters. Mainly to keep an eye out for Juan Lo Grande."

"And Linda Kincaid?"

Setting the pencil aside, the captain pushed back his chair, tilted it on its back legs, and rocked a moment, considering his sergeant. "O'Brien and the others returned her to Fort Leaton. To keep her safe. She's what we call a material witness."

"Wouldn't she have been safer in Austin or Houston?"

Savage nodded. "She didn't want to go. Isn't that right, Grace?"

Grace's head bobbed slightly.

Chance asked, "You'll be taking Grace, too?"

"It's for her own good, Sergeant." He looked at the last page he had written, then folded the papers together, and held them in his left hand between his forefinger and middle finger. "Before you deliver your prisoner, Sergeant, you shall take this message personally to Colonel Thomas in Austin. That's an order, Sergeant Chance."

"Is that your resignation or confession?" Chance asked.

Savage shifted uncomfortably in his chair. He flung the letter to the edge of the table.

"My demands, Sergeant," he said, regaining his composure, smiling again. "I guess you could call this our articles of secession. The boys and I have decided to form our own province out here."

"Savage, Texas." Eliot Thompson laughed.

"No, not Texas. Not anymore. It's the kingdom of Savage," Doc Shaw hailed down from the balustrade.

Grace eyed the captain with a look of bewilderment. Moses Albavera blinked, then tried something. "Captain, this new country you're founding. Would you have any use for a good man like me?"

"No niggers allowed in Savage," Eliot Thompson said, and spit out a mouthful of tobacco juice that missed the cuspidor and splattered on the wooden floor.

"If you're so good, how come your hands are cuffed?" Savage asked.

Grinning, Albavera shrugged.

"Grace," Savage said, "let's take our leave."

"She stays," Chance said.

"That I'm afraid she can't do, Sergeant." Savage put on his hat, and reached for the .44, keeping his eyes trained on Chance as he slowly picked up the revolver, and slid it into the holster on his right hip. "She's a material witness, too. And, as you well know having just dug a new grave, Marathon is not safe for anyone these days."

"That's what I want to know, Captain," Chance said. "Which one of you killed Ray Wickes?"

A long silence filled the hotel lobby. Finally, Savage shook his head, and let out a little chuckle. "Well, Dave, I guess Doc Shaw and I both had a hand in it. I shot him first. Doc finished him. But you knew that already, didn't you, Sergeant?"

"I just wanted to hear you say it," Chance said tightly.

"I've said it. Anything else you want to know?"

"Yeah. Hamp Magruder and young Wes Smith. Who killed them?"

"I shot Magruder," Savage answered. "Doc killed Smith. Now here's a question for you, Sergeant. Which one of us will kill you?"

"You won't ever know, Captain, because you'll be dead before I hit the ground."

Savage looked down. "Floor, Dave. Not ground. I'll be dead before you hit the floor. This hotel is pretty fancy, for Marathon." He looked up, smiling. "But not today, Sergeant." The captain rose, walked around the table, pulled Grace Profit gently to her feet. "You don't want Grace to get hurt, and if I don't return to Fort Leaton, the whore from Terlingua dies. Besides, you wouldn't kill me. You owe me, Dave. Or have you forgotten Fort Stockton?"

Chance fell quiet.

Grace looked at him, felt Savage's hand squeeze her shoulder. "It's all right, Dave," she said. "I'll be fine. Captain Savage believes in the sanctity of womanhood."

"That's right." He shoved her forward, and followed her closely, picking up the note on the table's edge as he walked by. The door opened, and Grace walked outside. Savage stopped and held out the note.

"It's delivered to Austin. You catch the train in Sanderson. Savvy?"

Reluctantly, Chance took the note. "That's the way you want it."

"No, Dave, not really. I wanted you and

Ray Wickes escorting Smith and Magruder, and Miss Kincaid, on the eastbound. That's what I wanted. But Ray was stupid, and the whore got cold feet. And you" — he shook his head — "were always just too damned dedicated to this job. Had to go off after that . . . Moor. I didn't want to see you hurt, Dave. Damned sure didn't want to see you dead. Take the train. Hand the note personally to Colonel Thomas. Hell, you'll probably get invited to discuss my demands with Governor Ireland, too. And don't come back, Dave. Don't make me kill you."

Savage backed out, and off the boardwalk, grabbed the reins to his gray, and swung into the saddle. Chance watched Bucky Bragg help Grace Profit into the saddle of his horse, then Bragg mounted the Andalusian. Quickly, Chance looked at the round corral where he had left their horses. Sure enough, the sorrel and Wickes's brown were still grazing. Hearing the footsteps, Chance stepped aside to let Doc Shaw and Eliot Thompson walk out and mount their horses.

Slowly, Chance eased down the hammer on the Winchester Centennial.

"Just follow your orders, Sergeant." Savage tipped his hat, then raked his spurs over the gray, and led the Rangers and Grace Profit down the main street, turning south, kicking up clouds of dust.

"That low-dealing bastard." Moses Albavera pushed his way past Chance and stepped off the boardwalk, raising clenched fists in his manacled hands, shaking them at the dust the wind was blowing away. "You son of a bitch! You swine!" He whirled, ripped off his hat, and slammed it onto the warped boards. "Sergeant Chance, I want to swear out a complaint. Your high and mighty Texas Rangers just stole my damned horse."

CHAPTER SIXTEEN

Whereas we, the undersigned men of Company E, Frontier Battalion, Texas Rangers, having risked our lives innumerable times for better than a decade, and having been ignored, mistreated, and maligned by the stupidity of our duly elected leaders and commanding officers in Austin, having been underpaid, shot at, wounded, and having been forced to bury our dead, having been abused by the damned Mexicans that dominate this territory, below and above the Rio Grande, we hereby declare that the encroachments of Mexican banditti and Austin politics make us fully justified in withdrawing from the state of Texas and forming our own union, appropriately named Savage, effective immediately.

Whenever any form of government becomes destructive of the ends for which it was established, it is the right of the people to alter or abolish it, and to institute a new government.

Thus said your country's founding fathers. Thus says Captain Hector M. Savage, captain, Company E, commanding, hereby known as President Savage, the first commander in chief of our new province.

The newly christened empire of Savage shall be defined as being the land currently west of the Pecos River in what has been heretofore called the state of Texas to the current boundary with New Mexico Territory to the north and the current boundary with the nation, loosely defined, of Mexico to the south, bordered there by the Rio Grande Del Norte, following the course of said river to approximately 10 miles northwest near the village of Pilares in Chihuahua, Mexico, proceeding thereupon at a north by northeast direction through Van Horn's Well and Hurd's Pass, proceeding east of the Salt Lakes region until it intersects with the Pecos River again at the border of New Mexico Territory.

To wit: the current counties in the state of Texas known as Reeves, Pecos, and Presidio.

This new country of Savage is open to trade with the state of Texas and the countries of Mexico and the United States of America. The railroads running through this country called Savage may continue to do so unimpeded pending a security deposit of $100,000, which can be delivered to President Hector M. Savage at Fort Leaton, outside of Presidio, which will serve as our new nation's capital. Stagecoach travel may also continue without delay, pending a security deposit in the amount of $25,000, which can be delivered to President Hector M. Savage at Fort Leaton, outside of Presidio, capital of Savage. The military commanders at the United States Army outposts of Fort Stockton and Fort Davis are ordered to lower their flags and withdraw all military personnel east across the Pecos River into Texas or west across the Reeves and Presidio county lines and into the current Texas county of El Paso. The State of Texas must also pay Savage $200,000 because we say so. It is right, and a fair — below fair, actually — price to pay for all we have been through since being assigned to this country in 1874.

Failure to make these payments in a timely manner will lead to the deaths of hostages being held at Fort Leaton. These hostages include Leonard J. Childress, mayor of Sanderson, Texas; Leviticus Hendry, state representative and barber from Presidio, Texas; Father Miguel de la Vega, priest at the Our Lady Of Guadalupe Catholic Church in Presidio, Texas; Linda Kincaid, whore from Terlingua, Texas; Nelson J. Bookbinder, captain, and three of his enlisted men, troopers Sam Jennison, Ricardo Milano and Hans Kruger, 3rd United States Cavalry, formerly stationed at Fort Davis but captured by Company E, Texas Rangers at La Mota Mountain; and Grace Profit, formerly a saloon owner in the town of Marathon, Texas.

Acceptance of these demands, as well as a deposit of ten percent of the aforementioned duties payable from the Southern Pacific, Wells Fargo Company and other stagecoach companies, and the state of Texas, should be sent to President Hector M. Savage at Fort Leaton, capital of Savage, no later than the seventeenth hour of Sunday, the twenty-ninth of November, in the Year of Our Lord Eighteen and Eighty-five.

Justly affirmed,
Hector M. Savage
Jasper J. "Doc" Shaw
Bucky Bragg

Taw Cutter
Eliot Thompson
Joe Newton
Tom O'Brien
Demitrio Ahern
Oliver Drago
Steve Coffman
Bill Barr
P.G. Foner
J.K. Scheidner
Harry Jones
Munge McSween

All of the signatures were in Hec Savage's handwriting.

After rereading the note, making sure he understood everything Savage had written, had ordered, Chance handed the papers to Albavera. As the black man began reading, sniggering and shaking his head, Chance stepped onto the street, and made a beeline for the corral, ignoring the mercantile owner, Rodney Kipperman, who kept asking, "What's going on here, Ranger?"

Once he had leaned the Winchester against the post, Chance ducked underneath the rails, grabbed his bridle, and caught up the sorrel. The mercantile owner gave up, let out a sign of exasperation, and went inside his store.

Silently, Chance slipped the headstall onto the gelding, and led the horse to the gate, then threw on blanket and saddle. He was cinching up the saddle when Moses Albavera entered the corral.

"Your captain is crazy as a loon." Albavera shook his head. "Secession. That went over really good the last time you stupid white-ass Southerners tried it. Christ Almighty. What was that his man told me? 'No niggers allowed in Savage'? I suppose they'll kick all the Mexicans out of this new kingdom, too. They're all insane."

"The captain's a lot of things" — Chance pulled on the horn, satisfied, and stepped away from the sorrel — "but crazy isn't one of them."

"You might belong in Bedlam yourself. Hell." Albavera waved the note in his hand. "Did you read that? He wants to form his own little country out of three Texas counties. He and those Rangers declared their independence, but I don't think that's the will of the people, especially the Mexicans your captain doesn't regard too highly. What do you think Don Melitón'll say to that?"

"You want to ask him?" Savage grabbed another bridle hanging on the fence.

With a snort, Albavera shook his head, and picked up the blanket and saddle to the

213

late Lieutenant Wickes's horse, carrying them after the sergeant.

"All right," Albavera said when he had set down the saddle and blanket beside the brown horse. "What do you think your captain's doing?"

"I don't know."

"Some kind of political statement?"

Chance handed the reins to Albavera, and grabbed the blanket, set it on the brown's back, made sure it was straight, then heaved the saddle onto the horse. He shook his head. "No. Captain never was much for politics." He tossed a stirrup over the saddle, reached down and grabbed the girth.

"I guess I can see that." He looked at the note again, shaking his head. "His language isn't exactly that of Jefferson or Lincoln. You plan on doing like he says?"

"Some of it."

"He did order you."

"Uh-huh. But the captain always said orders were made to be ignored. Besides, I have my own notions."

"Well, what do you think the governor, the army, and the citizens will do when they hear about Captain Savage's demands?"

Chance pulled the latigo tight, tucked the end in the slit, then reached inside his vest pocket and withdrew a key. "Savage says payment must be made by the twenty-ninth. That's four days." He leaned against the saddle, staring off toward the south, watching the dust rise into the skies. He pictured Grace Profit, and wondered if she knew Savage was threatening her life. What was it Grace had said? Captain Savage believes in the sanctity of womanhood. Yeah, sure he does. He said he'd kill Grace and the prostitute from Terlingua, even a priest. Even soldiers of the U.S. Army.

Chance let out a haggard breath. He spoke in a whisper. "Or he'll start killing the hostages he has at Fort Leaton."

Albavera shook his head. "And you say he's not crazy?"

Four days — until 5:00 P.M. Sunday the 29th. Chance looked up. The sun was directly overhead. Actually, three and a half days. He let out a muffled curse, and faced Albavera, fingering the small key he held in his right hand. "No way the Southern Pacific, the stagecoach company, or the state could make that deadline."

"And the Army? Don't forget, Savage says they have to vamoose, too."

"Generally the Army wouldn't stick its nose in this fight. It's a civil matter. But Savage made it a military affair by taking some soldiers hostage. The Army will have to react, with or without a request from the governor. As soon as they find out what Savage has demanded, what he's doing, troops will head down to Fort Leaton to get those boys of theirs back."

Albavera swore and spit. "That might get Grace Profit killed."

"Maybe." Chance studied the key, then looked again at his prisoner.

"Well, do you plan on going to Sanderson, catching the train, and delivering this note" — Albavera waved the note in his fingers — "to your Ranger boss or Governor Ireland?"

Chance stepped away from the horse, and in front of Moses Albavera, who looked stunned as Chance took one of his hands in his own, and slid the key into the handcuff's lock. "Eastbound's not due till Sunday," Chance said. "It's four hundred miles from here to Austin. I couldn't get to Austin by Savage's deadline if I tried. Certainly couldn't get word to Savage of Colonel Thomas's and the governor's response by then."

"You could telegraph Austin from Sanderson. Wait for a reply. Providing Savage hasn't cut those wires, too."

Chance looked up, face-to-face, eye-to-eye with Albavera, his key still in the lock. Would Captain Savage have had the telegraph lines east of Sanderson cut, too? Had he ordered Chance to Sanderson knowing that? He looked down, turned the key. No, Savage wouldn't send him on some forlorn hope. He needed Austin to know what he planned to do.

What he *said* he planned to do.

"That's right," Chance said. "That's all I can do. Savage knows this. When Colonel Thomas gets that telegraph, he'll blow his top. Likely send a company of Rangers, and plenty of Southern Pacific railroad detectives on a special train. They'll storm Fort Leaton, with or without the Army's help. Texas and the Rangers won't make any deals. Not with Captain Savage. Not when they hear this."

The iron manacles dropped to the dirt.

"The Army'll help," Albavera said. "I don't hold most of those soldier boys in high regard, not when it comes to poker, faro or anything else like that, but they aren't yellow. Those Army boys will want Savage's hair."

"That's right. Savage knows that as well."

Albavera began rubbing his wrists. He stepped back, studying Chance, not quite sure what to make of all that. "You think you know your captain pretty well, eh?"

"I don't think. I've ridden with Captain

Savage for seven years. He calculates everything. He knows what Colonel Thomas will do, knows what the Army will do. And he's not crazy enough to think he could actually form his own little country and kick out the United States Army. He knows the S.P. will never agree to his toll charges, or whatever the hell he called it in that stupid letter he wrote. Nor will the stagecoach companies that run along the old Butterfield trail. He's not crazy."

"He sure fooled me."

Chance handed the reins to the brown gelding to Albavera. "I'm riding to Fort Stockton. I'll tell the commanding officer there what has happened."

"Isn't Fort Davis closer?"

"Yeah. A little. But I don't want to meet up with Don Melitón or his men. I'll tell the commander at Fort Stockton, and he'll send a galloper to Fort Davis. Both posts will send a lot of troops south to Fort Leaton."

"Am I going with you?"

"No. I want you to ride to Sanderson. Send that wire to Colonel Thomas in Austin."

With a wry grin, Albavera asked, "What makes you think I'll do that? This isn't my fight."

"Sure it is. 'No niggers allowed in Savage.' Remember?"

The grin turned upside down into an angry scowl. Albavera's eyes hardened. "Yeah," he said, barely audible. "I'm not likely to forget that." Louder. "You trust me?"

"I don't have a choice. I have to alert the Army. And I have to get word to Austin. I can't do both."

"Suppose I go to Sanderson. Suppose I send your telegraph. Then what?"

"I don't care."

Albavera chuckled. He rubbed the brown's neck. "Do I get to keep this fine little gelding?"

"I'll give you a bill of sale if you want. Won't be legal, but I'll do it."

"Not what I'd call a fair trade, Ranger Chance. Your captain stole my Andalusian."

"It wasn't your horse. You stole that stallion at Fort Stockton. That's why I can't send you there. But Sanderson . . . It's just a short ride south to Mexico — after you send that telegraph."

He took Savage's note, and shoved it in his vest pocket. "I'll need this to show the C.O. at Fort Stockton. You need me to write down Savage's demands for you to give the telegrapher?"

"I got a good memory, too, Ranger Chance. I can remember."

"William E. Thomas, colonel, Texas Rangers, Austin."

"Got it."

Chance pulled the Smith & Wesson from his back, offering it butt forward to Albavera, who stared at the small pistol.

"Like Captain Savage said, Don Melitón won't think to have his men there. That's a bit off his range, anyhow. But Savage knows I'll have to go to Sanderson to send that wire. No choice in the matter. He cut the wires here. Closest telegraph office is Sanderson. He wants me to send that wire. He knows I won't take the train. Knows there's not enough time, that I'll have to wait for a reply from Austin. But after I send that telegraph, he'll want me — or whoever sends that telegraph — dead."

"Why would he want you dead? If he wanted you dead, he could have killed you today."

Chance shook his head. "He needed me to send that telegraph. Needed me to deliver a message. But once that's done, he'll want me dead."

"Why?"

Chance grinned. "He knows me. Knows what I'll do. Same as I know him."

"So he'll have a couple of his Ranger boys waiting for you — or rather, me — in Sanderson?"

"Just one. He only has fourteen men. He can't afford to spare more than one. For whatever it is he's planning."

"Which is?"

Chance shook his head. "I don't know."

With a heavy sigh, Albavera took the double-action .32 and stuck it in the pocket of his buckskin jacket. "This isn't a fair trade, either. This little popgun . . . I'm not sure it would kill a fly. Now, with Miss Vickie, when I hit somebody, that body stayed down."

"Bill Carter didn't. Remember?"

Albavera laughed. "Damn, Ranger, you and your memory. But do you remember Fort Stockton?"

Rubbing his throat, Chance nodded. "Yeah," he said, his voice lacking any emotion. He walked to the gate, opened it.

Albavera leaped into the saddle. "You think this horse'll get me to Sanderson?"

"He'll have to." Chance led the sorrel out, grabbed the Winchester, shoved it into the scabbard.

"Good luck, Ranger Chance," Albavera yelled as he loped out of the corral, and hit the road that ran east, parallel to the railroad tracks.

"Good luck," Chance said, and thought to add, "Moses."

CHAPTER SEVENTEEN

They didn't head to Presidio.

Two miles south of Marathon, once Hec Savage was certain they weren't being followed, a tall, barrel-chested Ranger with a sugarloaf sombrero, left the group, and took off at a high lope east. He rode that strong gray Andalusian stallion, the horse Dave Chance had been riding.

The only place he could be going, Grace Profit figured, was Sanderson. The same town where Chance was to catch the train, and then deliver Savage's demands personally to the Ranger colonel in the state capital.

Two other riders, one named Eliot and the other called Taw, cut out a short while later. They rode northeast. Back to Marathon? Grace wasn't sure.

That pared the group down to three — Savage, Doc Shaw, and a third Ranger called Newton — and for a moment, Grace wondered if she might risk an escape, but decided against it. She couldn't get away, and besides, Linda Kincaid might need her.

After another mile, Savage turned his gray horse off the road and led his command west, then northwest, through the Del Norte mountains, and across the desert flats. No sound, except the clopping of hooves and the rustling of the wind. Savage put his gray into a hard trot, and they followed, Grace cringing, gripping the horn, trying to stand in the stirrups and lessen the jarring her spine took. The bay horse she rode was hell on her back.

At least she wasn't riding a sidesaddle. Shortly after they had left Marathon, Savage had apologized that he had no sidesaddle to offer her, but Grace didn't mind. Hell, she hadn't ridden sidesaddle since she was fourteen. She was a pretty good rider, but, damn, she hated a trot, and the bay had no easy gait.

They rode most of the afternoon, trotting and bouncing in the saddles, until Grace thought she'd either fall off the bay, or throw up from all the torment her stomach, let alone her back, kept taking. They'd slow down, walk their horses for ten or fifteen minutes, and start trotting again.

She lost track of time. They kept riding.

For November, the day had turned warm. The clouds had moved off, the sun burning her face, neck, and hands. She hadn't thought to wear a hat — hadn't expected to be going for a long ride — and no one had offered her his headgear, not even a bandana to turn into a bonnet.

By mid-afternoon, the top of her head felt like a burned hotcake.

They slowed their horses again, letting them walk across the stone-filled prairie. To the north, she could see the southern edge of the Glass Mountains, and wondered if that's where Captain Savage was taking her. Or beyond there. To . . . Murphyville?

Her horse stopped. A moment later, she heard its urine spraying the rocks.

Doc Shaw rode point, Hec Savage having spurred his gray to check their back trail. She heard a horse loping behind her, and Savage called out, "How you faring, Grace?"

He reined in beside her, holding out a canteen. She wasn't too proud to accept. Smiling, he watched as she drank greedily. She would have kept right on drinking had he not taken the canteen from her worn hands. "Best go easy on that, girl." He corked the canteen, and wrapped the strap around his saddle horn. "I've been meaning to apologize for torching your saloon." He pulled off his hat, and wiped his brow. "Had to do it."

"For serving bad whiskey," she said.

"Nah. You know better than that, Grace. Your whiskey had nothing to do with it. Besides, I think it's pretty good hooch. But I had to let everyone know I mean business."

"After ten or twelve years, Hec, I think everyone in West Texas knows you mean business."

He laughed. Leaning over, he slapped the bay's rump. The horses started walking again. "What would you say if I offered to buy you a new saloon? One without canvas walls. Maybe a fancy mahogany back-bar. You could serve the finest whiskey and wines, good beer, even sell some expensive cigars. What would you think of that, Grace?"

"You gonna buy that on what you make as a Ranger?"

He shook his head.

"Then maybe that hundred thousand you're extorting from the Southern Pacific."

He studied her, curious.

"I was sitting at that table, Hec, when you were writing your letter. I can read upside down. Even someone with as lousy penmanship as you."

He looked ahead. "Likely, you wonder where we're going."

She brushed her hair off her face. "I figure you're taking me wherever your men took Linda Kincaid. I mean, you're following the same trail they did." She pointed at a pile of horse apples near a broken stem of a long-dead ocotillo.

Savage reached into his coat pocket and pulled out the makings. "You missed your calling, Grace. You should have been a scout instead of a peddler of forty-rod whiskey."

Actually, that had been a guess. Oh, she had seen the dung here and there, and the occasional print of a horseshoe, but she wasn't certain Linda Kincaid had come that way. She remembered the note Savage had written, his articles of secession or whatever he had called them. He had said Kincaid, and others, were being held in Fort Leaton. But they weren't going to Fort Leaton. She wanted to ask if those soldiers, that priest, and the others were prisoners down near the Rio Grande, but decided she had better not press her luck. She had been serving whiskey in saloons long enough to know when a person wanted to talk, and when a fellow just wanted to drink.

Savage had talked himself out.

A match flared. Cupping his hands, Savage

lit the cigarette he held tightly between his lips. He rode silently beside her until he had finished the smoke, then pitched it to the ground. He told Grace, "We'd best cover some territory," and spurred the gray into another backbreaking trot.

They were climbing in elevation, heading toward Cathedral Mountain, a limestone ridge, almost like a flat-topped mesa, except for the chimney, or cathedral-like point that shot out on one edge. Rising close to two thousand feet over the flats, it sloped down toward the foothills that surrounded the peak.

The grass had thickened, and Grace could make out the live oak, piñon, and juniper. Her horse, along with the others, snorted, and picked up the pace. They smelled water.

Before crossing Calamity Creek, they stopped to let the horses drink their fill. The water flowed richly, cooly, and turned the desert into an oasis. That far north, fed from streams and its headwaters near the dead volcano called Paisano, the creek ran year-round. Farther south the stream became intermittent as it wound its way deeper into the Big Bend, through the Santiagos, eventually flowing, when there was water, into the Rio Grande.

Willows, soapberry, and cottonwoods grew along the banks. Birds sang. Floating overhead, a red-tailed hawk watched the travelers with suspicion. Across the rocks that lined the far bank of the creek scurried a lizard. Cliffs rose above the creek, offering shade.

Rugged country, but lovely.

Grace tried to find her bearings. They were a few miles south of Murphyville. On Don Melitón Benton's range. Still, she couldn't figure out where Savage was taking her.

When the horses had slaked their thirst, Savage kicked his gray into a walk, and the others followed, traveling along the creek, northwest, through the canyons, toward Cathedral Mountain.

A few minutes later, she saw the turkey buzzards circling overhead. Ewes and rams scattered, and at first Grace figured the buzzards were after a dead sheep, but after they had gone another mile, she realized her mistake.

The sheepherder, a white-bearded Mexican in muslin rags, lay on a flat boulder stained by a lake of dried blood, his eyes staring sightlessly at the buzzards overhead. The front of his shirt was also stained with blood that had seeped from three bullet wounds in his chest.

A dog lay beside a cairn of rocks, having bled out from a belly wound. Beyond that, she spied a young boy, barely in his teens, shot in the back, apparently as he tried to run away.

Sheep scattered, running frantically toward the rocks, their bleating sounding like a fingernail being scraped across a blackboard.

The Rangers rode on silently, barely glancing at the corpses, ignoring the pitiful cries of the sheep. Grace had trouble holding down the water in her stomach.

When they reached a clearing, they turned away from Calamity Creek, and Grace saw the compound — several buildings and a couple corrals. A couple men, sitting in the shade, rose from their chairs, rifles held in the crooks of their arms.

La Oveja.

She knew the place. Oh, she'd never been there, but she had heard of Don Melitón Benton's sheep-raising operation in the Glass Mountains. It did not resemble any sheepherder's camp. It was more fortress than home, built for protection and comfort. A five-foot-high stone fence with a big wooden gate surrounded the perimeter. Cottonwoods and Mexican walnuts, even without any leaves at that time of year, offered shade.

Beyond were the corrals, a few lean-tos, and an adobe barn. A two-seater privy, a smokehouse, and two wells built over natural springs were closer to the house. A couple adobe buildings reminded Grace of those old dogtrot cabins she had seen far east of there. They were joined by cottonwood vigas that stretched from roof to roof, and cast lines of shadows on the flat rocks that formed a porch. The buildings were square, except for a circular *torreón* that rose a good eighteen feet at the corner of the eastern building. As they rode toward the corrals, a man stuck his head from the opening in the top of that watchtower, calling out, *"Hola, mi capitán."*

Savage wearily dismounted, pulling a shotgun from the saddle scabbard, handing the reins to one of those men who had been sitting in a rocking chair. He looked up at the man in the torreón.

"Demitrio," he said, "you damned fool. I told you not to draw any attention. Those buzzards are sure to do that."

"¿Por qué?" The Ranger looked at the sky. "But we have done nothing. I did not notice those birds."

"Nothing?" Savage spit. "A dead old man,

231

a dead kid, a dead dog. That sound like nothing to you?"

"But . . ."

Savage stepped toward the nearest well, his attention turned toward a figure walking out of the west-facing adobe building. Thumbing back both hammers on the shotgun, Savage muttered an oath underneath his breath.

"Amigo," a black-mustached Mexican said, grinning widely, revealing four gold-capped teeth. "It is good to see you, no? Do not blame your *rinches* for those poor souls I sent to their maker. Your hombres trusted that old man and his grandson to tend sheep, and not run to Don Melitón. Me? I decided dead men mind their manners a lot better than living ones. Besides, it seemed to me that they would make good witnesses against you and your men, and me and mine."

He looked younger than she had expected. He had slicked-back black hair that touched his shoulders, and a waxed mustache, with piercing dark eyes and a bronzed face. He wore an unbuttoned, red silk shirt, revealing a silver crucifix hanging against a muscular chest. His fancy black boots had silver spurs with giant rowels, and his black *calzoneras* were trimmed with gold French braid and studded with silver conchos down the sides. A brace of ivory-handled Colts were stuck in a yellow sash around his waist. Grace knew who he was before Savage said his name.

"Lo Grande," Savage said icily, "I told you to stay put in Ojinaga."

"*Sí. Es verdad.* But you know Juan Lo Grande. 'No,' I tell myself, 'it is not right. It is not right to let you and your *rinches* take all the risks. It is not what good partners do.' As Shakespeare wrote in *Julius Caesar,* 'I love the name of honor more than I fear death.' On my honor, I could not let you take all the risks, señor." Laughing, he snapped his fingers, and several men, brandishing repeating and bolt-action rifles, appeared in the doorways to both buildings, in the entrance to the barn, around the corners of the lean-tos, and one alongside Demitrio Ahern in the torreón.

"So I bring many hombres with me," Lo Grande said. "We share in the risks. We share in the spoils. Equally, amigo. And I thank you. *Mil gracias, mi capitán.* It was so good of you to bring that puta from Terlingua to this place. I missed her so. *Adelante,* amigos. Adelante. Come in. Come in. There is much wine, and plenty of mutton, and frijoles. You must be tired from your long journey."

He brought a cigar to his mouth, but lowered it, spotting Grace Profit for the first time. Quickly, he swept the sombrero off his head, and bowed slightly. He spoke to Hec Savage, but his eyes never left Grace Profit.

"But where are my manners? You bring another woman here? Ah, Capitán Savage, you are a true friend. She is more woman than that frail, bony *puta* from Terlingua. Much more woman. It will be good to make her acquaintance."

He walked closer, bowed, straightened and, like a great thespian, recited a line from *Antony and Cleopatra* with not a trace of his Spanish accent.

" 'Age cannot wither her, nor custom stale
Her infinite variety; other women cloy
The appetites they feed; but she makes hungry
Where most she satisfies.' "

He smiled again, his eyes lecherous. *"Buenas tardes, señorita. Yo soy Juan Lo Grande. El gusto es mío."*

CHAPTER EIGHTEEN

Fifteen miles from Sanderson, the brown gelding collapsed. Kicking free of the stirrups, Moses Albavera managed to leap clear, hitting the ground hard, somersaulting, and landing on his buttocks. He caught his breath, found his hat, and stumbled over to the dying horse.

"That's all right, fella," he said, stroking the lathered head. "You done fine. Just fine." Hell, he had expected the horse to die five miles back.

Slowly, he drew the Smith & Wesson .32 from his coat pocket, and pressed the muzzle against the horse's head. With a heavy sigh, he pulled the gun back, broke open the barrel, and looked at the cylinder. Four rounds. That brilliant Sergeant Chance apparently felt the need to keep the chamber under the hammer empty. He hadn't thought to give Albavera any extra ammunition, either.

The horse snorted, as if begging for a bullet.

"I don't want you to suffer, boy," Albavera said as he snapped the barrel back in place. "But I might need that bullet." After returning the .32 to his pocket, he slid back, and unfastened the saddlebag. Telegrams, mostly. A book. A couple of blank warrants. A tin cup, plate, and spoon.

Grunting, exhausted, he tugged until he had pried the other bag from underneath the dying horse, dragged it over, and unfastened the flap. Inside, he found a pair of socks, an extra shirt, and a pouch containing a couple of Ranger badges. Likely belonging to those two dead guys Savage had sent east for burial. Wickes must have forgotten about those. He looked at the badges cut from pesos, and, bemused, pinned one on his vest before continuing his search. Another pair of socks, desperately needing darning. Finally, wrapped inside a silk bandana, he discovered a sheathed knife.

And a flask. He unscrewed it, sniffed, smiled, and dropped it into the other pocket of his coat. "You were a good man, Lieutenant Wickes."

Albavera unsheathed the knife, and ran his thumb gently across the sharp blade.

"Adiós, caballo," he said, and brought the knife to the brown's throat.

The sun low behind him, Albavera stumbled, dropping the saddle and bridle he carried. He tilted his head forward, sucking in air. He tugged the saddlebags he had draped over his shoulder, and let them collapse on the road. Chest heaving, he drew the flask from his pocket, unscrewed the lid, and polished off the last of the Scotch.

He had no idea how far he had traveled since slitting the brown's throat, but knew Sanderson wasn't that much closer. Lugging along a forty-pound saddle, he wasn't covering much ground, but he might need that saddle.

Albavera chased down the whiskey with a slug of water from the canteen, ran his tongue over his cracked lips, and stared down a road that led to nowhere, forever. He let out a weary sigh.

That's when he heard the noise.

A low rolling sound, metallic, with a steady squeaking. He couldn't place the noise, but it was coming closer. Climbing to his feet, leaving the saddle and bags in the road, he stared off into the distance, letting his gaze move north of the road, to the railroad tracks. Through a pass in the buttes, he saw something.

Albavera blinked. Swallowed. Squinted his eyes.

"Hell," he said, and hurried back, grabbing the saddle, bridle, and saddlebags. He dragged them off the road, over creosote, as he climbed the embankment to the edge of the railroad tracks. He dropped the tack at his feet, whipped off his hat, and began waving it over his head.

"Hey!" His voice was barely audible. He tried again. "Hey!"

Two men worked the hand pump on a railroad handcart. The one facing Albavera, a burly man in a bowler, let go of the pump, and pointed. The man with his back to Albavera slowly turned, and tipped back his slouch hat. Briefly, the men stared as the cart rolled down the tracks. Bowler said something, and Slouch Hat turned back. They furiously worked the pump, increasing speed.

"Stop!" Albavera yelled.

They pumped harder.

"Dumb bastards." Albavera tossed the saddle, bags and bridle onto the track, and drew the .32.

Bowler let go of the pump and bent over, reaching for a rifle on the cart floor.

With his left hand, Albavera tugged on his

vest, showing off the peso badge. "Stop, you damned fools. I'm a Texas Ranger."

The man lifted the rifle.

Albavera put a bullet in the stock. Bowler's rifle went flying off one side of the cart. He yelped and fell off the other.

Slouch Hat turned, and lifted his hands. He stood there, eyes wide, with his hands held high.

"The brake, you idiot! Stop that damned cart!"

The man knelt, reached to the side, pulled up the arm, and the cart began grinding to a halt, coming to a stop about ten feet in front of the saddle.

"What the hell's the matter with you?" Albavera said. Without waiting for an answer, he grabbed the saddle and tack, and heaved them onto the front of the cart. Stepping aside he watched Bowler walking down the tracks, rubbing his left shoulder, the knees of his duck trousers torn.

"You all right?"

Bowler answered with a lame nod. "We thought you was gonna rob us."

"Do I look like Jesse James?" Albavera climbed onto the cart. "Does this look like a Rock Island express?"

"Well, you don't look like no Texas Ranger we ever seen, neither."

Albavera grinned. "Where y'all headed?"

"Wire's down somewhere near Marathon. We was going to fix it."

"Work for the Southern Pacific?"

"Uh-huh."

Bowler leaned against the side of the cart, still rubbing his shoulder. "Fellas sent a wire saying the bloody line was down because of the weather. But there ain't been no weather, least not in Sanderson, and it shouldn't take no five days to put that wire back up."

Nodding at Bowler's comment, Slouch Hat added, "The superintendent sent us. Told us, 'Make damned sure that wire is up before Saturday.' "

"Something big's coming on the east-bound," Bowler said. "So we need to be on our way."

Albavera looked at the box of tools on the cart's floor. "That'll have to wait. I need you to get me back to Sanderson."

"But —" Slouch Hat began.

"No buts." Albavera tapped the badge, enjoying himself. "I'm the law."

The method of transportation befitted a man of Moses Albavera's stature. Not riding a horse to death. Not carrying a heavy saddle across a desolate patch of nothingness. But sitting on the back of a cart, smoking a cigar, letting a couple Irishmen do all the work. Even the squeaking of that hand pump sounded musical to Albavera's ears.

They'd be in Sanderson shortly after dark. At least, that was Bowler's prediction. Albavera could send his telegraph then.

"Many saloons in Sanderson?" Albavera asked.

"Six," Slouch Hat answered with a grunt.

"Gambling?"

"In every saloon."

"But you gotta tell our super that you made us come back. He'll be madder than a hornet."

"I'll tell him." He pitched the cigar onto the tracks, and leaned back, careful to avoid the hand pump. He looked up at Bowler. "You said something big was coming on the eastbound."

Bowler brought the pump down, then up. "Yeah."

"What?"

He shrugged. "Just what we hear. They don't tell us much."

Added Slouch Hat, "But O'Rourke, he's our superintendent, he said make sure we had that downed line fixed before Saturday."

Albavera ran his hand across his mouth, then remembered the telegraphs inside the saddlebags. He opened one, saw the socks, realized it was the wrong bag. Opening the other, he pulled out one telegraph and scanned it. Just orders not to pursue Juan Lo Grande across the border. He found another.

CAPT SAVAGE STOP REPORT IMMEDI-
ATELY TO ME STOP COL THOMAS

He tossed it into the desert and found another. He had to read it again. Whistling, he folded the yellow paper, and tucked it inside his vest pocket. Slouch Hat was grunting, panting. Albavera brought his feet up, and rose, feeling the cooling air against his face.

"You're worn to a frazzle, mister," Albavera told Slouch Hat. "Let me spell you. We need to get to Sanderson fast."

Night enveloped them long before they crossed the bridge over the dry creek, and came into town. Sanderson, née Straw-bridge, had been established when the Texas and New Orleans Railroad reached the site a few years earlier. Six well-lighted saloons, and several less busy, less lit buildings dotted one side of the railroad tracks. The depot and a handful of buildings, including a big adobe barn or warehouse lined the other. Beside the barn were a dozen empty freight wagons.

The place looked like hell, and Albavera didn't think it would appear much better in daylight.

Someone clawed on a banjo inside one of the saloons. Light shone through the windows, and Albavera could see several horses tethered to the hitching rails. The town was dead, except for those six grog shops.

He had thought he might play a little poker in one of those dens, have a whiskey or two, before lighting across the border and disappearing again. The telegraph he had read changed his plans. He knew he wouldn't go to Mexico. Knew he'd ride back west, and try to find Chance, who needed all the help he could get.

Yet Albavera couldn't quite figure out why the hell he had decided on such a foolish option. It wasn't a sure bet. It was sheer folly.

Bowler pulled up the brake lever, and the cart slowed. A man in a sack suit stormed out of the depot, and turned up the two lamps hanging on the wall. Hands on hips, chewing on a corncob pipe, he walked to the side of the platform.

"The wire's still down west of here, Keegan!" the man said. "O'Rourke told you two —"

He stopped, and withdrew the pipe, as Albavera stepped up. He towered over the man in the sack suit.

"Need to send a telegraph," Albavera said.

"Office is closed."

Albavera showed him the badge. "It's important."

The man stared, first at the badge, then up into Albavera's eyes. "Since when do the Texas Rangers hire —"

Suddenly staring down the barrel of the Smith & Wesson .32, Sack Suit shut up. He swallowed, nodded, and turned toward the depot building. "Soon as this wire's sent," Albavera said, "I'll need a" — a whinny drew his attention to the saloon directly across the tracks — "horse." He stared, but it was too dark to tell for sure. The horse whinnied again. Yep, that was the gray Andalusian, all right.

"Inside," Albavera said. "And be damned quick."

A drunk with a coarse white beard snored softly on a cot in the corner of the office. Albavera considered him briefly, but Sack Suit said, "Let him sleep it off."

"Sure. He needs his beauty sleep."

244

Albavera took a pencil and paper, began scratching out the words, shaking his head, knowing the reaction he would soon get. Sure enough, after he handed the paper to Sack Suit, the man's gray eyes found Albavera.

"Just send the damned thing," he said.

"I'm not sending this," Sack Suit protested. "This is absurd. What kind of joke are you pulling?"

The drunk in the corner snorted, and rolled over.

"If I have to point that .32 in your face again, I'm pulling the trigger." Albavera walked to the window, and looked across the street. The telegraph keys clicked a moment, then again. He waited.

A response came.

Sack Suit began tapping out the rest of the message. He read the words aloud as he clicked out the message, signing it off with the name, "Signed. Dave Chance, Sergeant, E Company."

The drunk sat up. "Dave Chance?" He rubbed his eyes. "Dave Chance? Where's me Davy boy?"

His hands were like jugs, his fingers the size of railroad spikes. He didn't stand much taller than five-foot-three, and his breath stank of stale beer. The old man's eyes found Albavera, and saw the badge.

"You ain't Davy boy."

"Dave's a friend of mine," Albavera said. He stopped, thought about what he had just said. *A friend of mine.* And grinned.

The machine began clicking again. Sack Suit sighed. "They want to know what kind of joke is this?"

"Tell them it's no joke." Albavera didn't take his eyes off the man with the white beard. "Tell them Chance is alerting the soldiers at Fort Stockton."

More clicks.

"What's going on here?" White Beard asked.

Sack Suit said, "Captain Savage has gone stark-raving mad." He clicked out a final note, then waited. The clicking resumed, then stopped. Sack Suit bent over the machine, tapped out a message. Again. And again. He looked up at Albavera. "The line must be down. Had to have just happened."

Albavera stared back out the window. "A man came here today. Riding that gray Andalusian stallion, in front of that watering hole right over there. One of you see him?"

Sack Suit's negative response was cut off by White Beard's, "Yeah. Big fella. Mexican hat." He stroked his beard. "Kinda funny.

246

He's wearing one of them peso stars, too."

"He ride in alone?"

"Uh-huh."

"Is there a back door to this place?"

"No." Sack Suit shook his head. "But there's a window." He pointed.

"That'll do." Albavera kept away from the front window, turned down the lantern hanging from the ceiling, and went to the back wall. He pushed open the window, and started to step through it, pausing long enough to look over at the shadowy silhouettes of White Beard and Sack Suit.

"Oh, I'd stay inside if I were you. Away from the window. Probably on the floor. Maybe behind that desk — until the shooting stops."

CHAPTER NINETEEN

A half moon crept from behind a thin veil of clouds as Albavera slid against the back wall of the picket-walled depot. Gun in hand, he peered around the corner, saw nothing but shadows and boxes, and kept hugging the wall, easing toward the front of the depot. The banjo he heard was out of tune. Off to the west, a coyote cried out in accompaniment, answered by a cacophony of howls.

He had reached the edge of the building. Slowly, he stepped away, staying in the shadows, and looked around the corner.

Except for the saloons, most businesses across the street were closed, although a light drifted through the drapes hanging across the window in the adobe café. The aroma of strong coffee and baked bread reminded Albavera that he couldn't remember the last time he had eaten. He looked up and down the main road — hell, the only road — that ran through Sanderson, then focused on one saloon. He found his horse. Well, he was fairly certain that was his Andalusian, or rather the stallion he had stolen at Fort Stockton, tethered between a mule and what appeared to be a palomino.

The moon disappeared.

A shadow stood in the doorway to that saloon, the tip of a cigarette glowing red, then fading, glowing, fading. The figure kept his hands on the top of the batwing doors, staring out into the darkness, his head never turning. He was looking at the depot. Waiting. Wondering.

The hinges of the door squeaked, and the man stepped onto the dirt, the doors swinging behind him. In the darkness, Albavera couldn't make out the man's features, but he could determine the shape and size of the hat on the man's head. A sugarloaf sombrero. Albavera remembered him. One of those Rangers who had been outside the Iron Mountain Inn with Captain Savage. The bastard who had stolen Albavera's horse.

The cigarette glowed again, then darkened. Sparks flew and disappeared a few rods past the horses as the man began walking toward the depot. Apparently, he had flipped away the cigarette. As he drew closer, the light from the lanterns outside the depot office reflected off the badge pinned to the man's shirt.

Albavera nodded, satisfied. Indeed it was that horse-stealing Ranger. Good. He would have hated to have killed the wrong man.

Spurs jingled as the man made his way to the tracks, crossed them, and climbed up onto the platform. He stood in the shadows. Smart fellow. He was playing it safe. A revolver clicked. Albavera raised his .32.

The gunshot startled him, the muzzle flash blinding him for a moment. There was another gunshot, then a sudden darkness. Someone screamed. The banjo music ceased.

Albavera saw only red and orange dots at first. He smelled smoke, and heard the crackling of wood. Shadows began doing eery dances on the station platform.

He looked to his left. Flames crept up the picket walls, and he realized the man had shot the two lanterns, sending coal oil up and down the walls, the flames licking hungrily.

The door swung open. "Don't shoot! Don't shoot! It's —" Sack Suit leaped outside, ducking the flames. Another muzzle flash and deafening roar sent Sack Suit slamming against the wall, sliding down into a pool of blood, his coat smoldering from the flames.

The pistol roared again, shattering the window, but Albavera heard something else. Bracing his back against the wall, he turned, pointing the Smith & Wesson toward the rear. The moon reappeared, providing just enough light for Albavera to see the white beard, the hands raised high over his head. "Don't shoot," White Beard whispered.

The voice at the front of the depot was louder. "Come on out of there!" The Ranger stepped into the light, still looking at the door to the depot, not the west side of the building.

Albavera stepped around the corner. "I'm already out," he said, and shot the Ranger in the stomach.

The big man spun twice, but didn't fall. Albavera was surprised to see him still standing. And raising the long-barreled Colt in his right hand.

Albavera pulled the .32's trigger twice, feeling the little gun buck slightly in his hand, wishing he had Miss Vickie with him instead of that toy gun. The man took two steps to his side, his pistol booming, tearing a hole into the plank floor at his feet. His thumb worked the hammer, pulling the trigger again, then he was falling into the shadows. He rolled on his side, back into the light, spitting out a final curse, and soiling his britches.

Quickly, Albavera stepped toward the downed man. He looked across the street, saw shadows standing in front of the saloons, and that the light was out in the café. Shoving the empty Smith & Wesson in his coat pocket, he looked down at the dead Ranger, and pried the Colt out of his hand.

A board squeaked.

Turning, he saw White Beard, hands still held high over his head. Albavera looked over at the burning depot, and nodded at the dead man leaning against the wall in his sack suit. "Get him out of here. And best get a bucket brigade going if you want to save —"

A bullet carved a furrow across his left side. Cringing, biting back pain, Albavera rolled off the depot platform. He heard a gunshot, and the pounding of hooves. He came to his knees, raised the Colt, eased back the hammer, and squeezed the trigger.

The Colt clicked.

"Damn." He saw another muzzle flash from down the street, heard the hooves, and knew the man was riding toward him. Albavera flung the empty revolver into the dirt, and raced across the tracks, then across the street, sprinting desperately for the horses in front of that saloon. The spectators, seeing what was happening, quickly ran into the saloons, diving behind the walls, screaming and cursing.

A bullet tore off Albavera's hat. The mule brayed. The palomino pulled free, breaking its reins, and loping off toward Marathon. Albavera dived the final few yards. A bullet shattered a plate glass window. The Andalusian reared, but didn't run. The mule started kicking.

Albavera found the saddlebags on the Andalusian. A bullet buzzed past his right ear. The rider reined up, aimed a Winchester, and pulled the trigger. The hammer fell on an empty chamber.

"*¡Hijo de la puta!*" came a curse. The rider hurled the rifle to the ground, and reached for a holstered pistol.

Albavera shot him through the saddlebag, Miss Vickie blowing a hole through the leather, and a bigger one through the horseman. The man slammed hard onto the ground, his right foot hung up in the stirrup. The horse galloped west, dragging the dead man out of town.

Drawing a deep breath, Albavera pulled his hand out of the saddlebag, unfastened it, and withdrew the smoking sawed-off

253

Springfield rifle, Miss Vickie. He pressed his hand against his bloody side, glanced at a face in the shattered window, and said, "If you want to save that depot, you'd better get with it."

He brought up his left hand, sticky with warm blood, and walked wearily into the middle of the street.

"That's right." Speaking in a whisper to himself, but not caring who heard him. "Sergeant Dave Chance. Yeah. He knows Captain Savage well. 'He only has fourteen men. He can't afford to spare more than one.' Ha! Damned near got me killed. That's two men, Ranger Chance."

Men began spilling from the saloons, but in no hurry to put out the fire at the depot.

A bullet from behind him tore through the tail of his coat.

Albavera dropped, and spun.

Men dived back into the saloons, moving at breakneck speed.

A giant Mexican stepped into the light. He wore a thick beard, more salt than pepper, and a patch over his right eye. He pitched an old muzzle-loading rifle onto the dirt, and drew a machete from the scabbard.

Albavera hurled Miss Vickie at his head. The Mexican ducked. Just not low enough.

The sawed-off rifle, flipping stock over barrel, clipped the Mexican's left ear with the barrel, tearing a gash, knocking the big man to his knees.

He came up screaming, slashing into the night with the machete.

But Moses Albavera was no longer there. He was running. Cursing Dave Chance. "Three men. Not one. Not two. Three. Hell, Savage might have a whole damned army here."

He crossed the railroad tracks. White Beard had dragged Sack Suit's body off the platform, and stood to the side, hands raised again. Flames enveloped the picket building. Albavera looked at the platform, saw the dead Ranger, but not the man's pistol. He looked at the tracks. Turning, he saw the bloody-eared giant Mexican taking huge strides toward him.

"Old man." Albavera faced White Beard. "Where's my saddle? Saddlebags?"

White Beard studied him for a second, then looked at the Mexican. "I don't think you got time to saddle no horse, young fella, and get away from that hombre."

"I left them on that handcart. Where's the damned cart?"

"Hell, likely Paddy Keegan put 'em in that shed yonder." He pointed toward a side track that ran into a huge adobe warehouse.

Only a few yards ahead of the Mexican, Albavera stumbled across the sidetrack, leaped over a mound of thick wooden ties, and made it to the door. He jerked it open, and stepped inside.

He struck a match, looked right, then left, and saw the handcart in front of an old locomotive. Hearing the Mexican's heavy breathing, he blew out the match and fumbled through the darkness, feeling the leather of the bridle, the coolness of the metal bit, over a stirrup, then found the saddlebags. He reached inside.

Behind him, the Mexican stopped. A lucifer flamed to life, and the Mexican lit a lantern. *"¿Es esto mejor?"* The Mexican smiled.

"That's much better." Albavera drew a pair of socks from the saddlebag, and flung them to the dirt. He pulled out a knife from the sheath, and stood, crouching, waving the knife in his right hand, grinning. "Much, much better."

The big Mexican closed in, tossing the machete from right hand to left, left to right, his one eye glaring.

They danced around each other, stepping over iron rails, spikes, trash that littered the dirt floor. The machete sliced. Albavera sucked in his gut, and leaped backward. The Mexican laughed. Albavera's side throbbed.

Out of the corner of his eye, he saw White Beard step inside the building. He found a keg, turned it over, and sat down, pulling out a chaw of tobacco and a knife, settling down to watch the fight.

The machete blade flashed. Albavera spun, feeling the air whoosh by him, the momentum carrying the Mexican across the tracks. Albavera thrust his blade, but he, too was falling off balance, barely managing to keep his feet.

Both men's chests heaved. Albavera brought his left hand up, smelling the coppery odor. Seeing the blood in his hand, he wiped it on his trousers. His vest, which had cost him a fortune, was ruined. He ducked the machete's slash again.

Laughing, the Mexican said something, but Albavera didn't understand. His heart pounded against his ribs. He felt beads of sweat popping on his brow, rolling into his eyes. They burned as he blinked away the sweat.

The Mexican tossed the blade from one hand to another, cursing low in Spanish.

Albavera brought the blade upward in a deadly thrust, pulled back, and swung his left fist, slamming the Mexican's head. The man laughed. Albavera stepped back, shaking his hand, wondering if that behemoth's rock-hard head had broken all of his fingers.

The machete came at him again.

And missed.

Again, and again the man came at him, like a windmill, slicing the blade over and over, driving Albavera back. He blundered against a workbench, ducked, and sent a pack rat scurrying. The machete slammed into the bench between a screwdriver and a wrench. The Mexican tried to pull it free. Albavera thrust the blade at the Mexican's side, but the Mexican met him with a sledgehammer of a fist, sending Albavera onto his back. Shaking his head, he scrambled to his feet. The Mexican had freed the machete, and the blade tore fringe off the sleeves of Albavera's jacket.

He tasted blood. *That son of a bitch busted my lips.* One of his teeth felt loose.

Albavera avoided the machete once more, almost falling as he kicked over a box of iron spikes. He brought the knife up, but a vise gripped his wrist, pulling him close to the giant Mexican. He could smell the sweat, the blood, the cigarette smoke on the Mexican, as the giant drew him close. Albavera reached out with his left hand, and grabbed the wrist of the hand that held the machete. He squeezed. But the Mexican squeezed tighter. The knife fell from Albavera's hand to the dirt.

Bending his knees, he fell backward, and the Mexican went over him. Both men slammed against the engine's cattle catcher, and rolled off, ripping the Mexican's muslin shirtsleeve. Albavera's buckskin coat snagged on metal. He freed his arms, leaving the jacket on the metal catcher, and tried to scramble to his feet, looking for the knife he had dropped. The Mexican jumped on top of him, pinning him to the floor. Laughing, he brought the machete over his head. Albavera's right hand shot out, grasping for anything. He found something and slammed a railroad spike into the Mexican's side.

The man grunted. The machete slipped from his hands, and fell behind his back, landing between Albavera's legs. With an ugly roar, the Mexican leaned forward, his massive hands latching onto Albavera's throat.

He pulled the spike from the Mexican's side. Drove it in again. And again. The Mexican rolled off, releasing his grip on Albavera's throat, but grabbing his vest, pulling him on top of him. The left hand found the throat again, and pulled Albavera closer.

He began to crush Albavera's windpipe.

Albavera raised the spike again, and drilled it through the giant's eye-patch almost to the iron spike's bent head.

His eyes opened. He saw the white beard, his jaw furiously working on the tobacco in his left cheek. White Beard's head turned, and he sprayed the dead Mexican with tobacco juice. "You say you're a friend of Dave Chance?"

Albavera nodded. At least, he thought he had. He rubbed his throat, sucked in a ragged breath, spit out blood.

"So happens, I'm an old pard of his, too. Name's McGee. Mickey McGee."

Somehow, from the deep recesses of his mind, Albavera found that name. "Constantine gang," he said, his voice a worn-out whisper. "You killed one of them."

The man's brilliant eyes shined. "That's right. I reckon you wasn't lying about knowing me Davy boy."

White-bearded Mickey McGee, who looked nothing like Albavera had imagined, held out a meaty hand, and pulled him to a seated position.

Albavera looked at the Mexican he had killed. That was a mistake. He almost vomited. Then he looked up at the black engine. Rust covered the huge smokestack, the big engine smelled of grease and dust, and the catcher was bent, battered, and covered with blood from the Mexican and Albavera, not to mention his buckskin coat.

"What the hell is that?" he asked.

"That? Criminy, boy, that's a wood-burning 4-4-0 manufactured by Schenectady Locomotive Works of New York in eighteen and sixty-five. They don't build 'em like that no more."

"Will it run?"

CHAPTER TWENTY

Only two springs in Texas produced more water than Comanche Springs — which wasn't saying a whole lot. Yet out in West Texas, water meant life, even if it tasted like it had been flavored with rusty iron horseshoes and as bitter as gall.

The water brought freighters on the San Antonio-Chihuahua road, wayfarers on the Overland Mail route, and, before they had been pinned up on the reservation in Indian Territory, Comanches traveling the Great Comanche War Trail. All of which led to the establishment of Fort Stockton, first in the late 1850s, then in 1867 after the War Between the States. Outside the fort, a town sprang up, originally named St. Gaul, but about four years ago the residents had renamed it to match that of the Army post.

In the adobe headquarters building, Chance splashed water from the basin across his face, trying to wake himself up.

He patted himself dry with his bandana, and took the cup of steaming coffee the corporal offered him. He sipped it, surprised at its pleasant taste.

"Would you care to have a seat, sir?" The corporal, a thin man with a thick red mustache, motioned at a chair in front of a desk.

With a worn smile, Chance shook his head. He had been in a saddle for sixty miles. The last thing he wanted was to sit down.

The door opened, and in walked the major, a bald, bloated man wearing boots and a nightshirt, carrying the blue trousers with yellow stripes down the legs. Yawning, he made a beeline for his desk, and sat in the chair, barking an order for coffee to the corporal, before taking notice of Chance.

"All right, Ranger," the major said, as he kicked off his boots, and stood into the pants. "I'm Major J.R. Fields, commander of this post. What's so damned important that you haul me from a pleasant dream at" — he looked at the Regulator clock on the wall, and shook his head — "Christ Almighty, twelve-o-seven in the morning?"

Chance set the coffee on the desk, reached into his vest, and withdrew the note Hec Savage had written, handing it across the desk. "Major, I'm Dave Chance, sergeant,

Company E, Texas Rangers. I think you had better read this yourself, sir."

The officer opened a drawer, rooted around, and brought up a pair of spectacles, which he set on the bridge of his nose. He started to read, then stopped, looking up at Chance. "Chance, you say?"

"Yes, sir." He knew what was coming.

"I seem to recall —"

"Bad Water Saloon a few years back."

"That's right." He continued to look at Chance, sizing him up.

"Major, I really think you should read that letter. It's from Captain Hec Savage."

"Very well." His eyes dropped to the note. After a moment, his gray eyes looked up at Chance again as he turned to the second page. He frowned, finished the letter, and let the papers drop onto his desk.

"Are you serious?" the major asked. The corporal brought him his coffee. Major Fields opened another drawer, and brought out a bottle of rye, from which he poured two fingers, then added two more splashes, into the coffee. Looking back at Chance, he said, "Well?"

"Savage has killed, or had killed, three of his men," Chance replied. "I don't know what his plans are."

Major Fields picked up the note again.

264

"You rode up here from Presidio?"

"Marathon."

He looked up from the letter. "Nelson Bookbinder and I were at West Point together. He was a year behind me. A good man, Nelson, a good soldier, a fine friend. Do you think your captain is, as this letter claims, holding him hostage at Fort Leaton?"

Actually, Chance thought Captain Bookbinder and those other enlisted men were dead. Hec Savage had never been one for taking prisoners. Those he did capture alive were often executed shortly afterward by summary judgment. Yet Chance shrugged.

The major sipped his coffee. "Captain Savage can't be serious."

"If you know Captain Savage, sir, you know he's deadly serious."

"He's mad."

Chance nodded. "Fellow I know, should be in Sanderson right about now, agrees with you. He's sending a telegraph to Austin. Least, I hope he is."

As Chance filled in the story, Major Fields finished his coffee, pressed his fingers together, and rested his head against the tent his hands had formed. He drew in a deep breath, exhaled, and lowered his hands, looking into Chance's eyes.

"We can't wait for the governor to request help," Major Fields said. "There's not enough time."

"I understand that, sir."

"Besides, your captain is holding an officer and enlisted men of the United States Army hostage. I'll nail his hide to the barn door." He rose, barking out an order to the corporal. "Stone, send a galloper to Fort Davis. Right now." He folded Savage's letter, and handed it to Corporal Stone. "Have him deliver this note to Colonel McVicker, ask him to send as many troopers as he can spare to Fort Leaton. Have him request the sheriff of Presidio County assemble a posse to accompany his command." He began scribbling his orders on paper, talking as he wrote.

"We will follow Coyanosa Draw to Murphyville, and, with luck, meet the colonel and his men on the Alamito before they reach Presidio. Have the galloper tell Colonel McVicker that I cannot attest to the veracity of this letter, but we just cannot risk the lives of Captain Bookbinder and his men, nor those other hostages. Two women and a priest, by God."

"Not to mention a mayor and a barber," Chance added.

"Bugger the mayor," Major Fields roared.

"Bugger the barber. Worthless politicians." He signed and sealed the orders, handed them to Corporal Stone. "Awaken Captain Braden. Inform him that I will head the command, and the captain will be in charge of the post until my return. We will leave him with one company of infantry and anyone in the hospital or guardhouse. All others will go to Presidio. Two weeks' rations and thirty rounds of ammunition per man."

Stepping into his boots, Fields continued his orders. "When you have informed Captain Braden, have the trumpeter sound reveille. Then you will ride to town and inform Sheriff Vanwy that his presence is requested here immediately. We will organize a joint punitive action against Captain Savage and his gang of black-hearts."

Chance spoke up. "Fort Leaton is outside Vanwy's jurisdiction, Major. That's Presidio County."

"I don't give a damn. I don't think Sheriff Vanwy does, either."

"Yes, sir."

Corporal Stone saluted the major and hurried out the door.

"You want to come with us, Sergeant?" Major Fields stepped around the desk, pushing his trousers into his boot tops.

Chance finished his coffee. "With the major's permission, I'd like to try something else — just in case Captain Savage has other plans. But I could use a horse, sir. Preferably two." He thought about how hard he'd have to ride. "Better make it three. Mine is played out."

"Take your pick. And welcome. Just bring those horses back."

"You just take care of that sorrel. Cost me fifteen dollars."

"What're your plans, Sergeant?"

Chance grinned. "First, get some sleep."

The major gave him a look of skepticism.

Chance didn't feel like explaining anything. He needed the rest. He couldn't keep up that pace. If he rode out with the soldiers, he'd likely fall asleep in the saddle five miles south of the fort. It had been an exhausting, jarring ride from Marathon to Fort Stockton, and it wasn't like he had been taking it easy all week. He needed some shuteye. He'd sleep the rest of the night, get up early in the morning, and with three horses, head south back to Marathon. And then? Fort Leaton, to join Major Fields and those soldier boys? Sanderson, and wait on a reply to the telegraph Moses Albavera, maybe, had sent? Chance wasn't sure. Perhaps something would come to him before he reached Marathon tomorrow.

"Very well." The major was speaking. "You rest. I, however, must prepare for our expedition." Outside, the metallic blares of a trumpet sounded, and Major Fields went out the door. Left alone, Dave Chance picked up the bottle of rye the officer had left on the desk, and walked outside the headquarters building himself.

The trooper at the Fort Stockton stables let Chance take two bays and a liver chestnut. He threw his saddle on the bay with the blaze on its forehead, and led the other two horses out of the military compound buzzing with activity, and rode to the town, riding to the wagon yard at the southern edge of town. The Negro working there charged him two bits for the night. Chance let him have the last few swings from the bottle of rye.

Surprisingly, he slept well, but woke up stiff and sore. The sun was already rising, and he swore softly. He had wanted to be riding before the sun was up. After he pulled on his boots, he looked over the horses the Army had loaned him, getting a better view than he had gotten at the Army stables. He decided he liked the liver chestnut the best, so saddled it, and led the two bays, one with a blaze forehead, the other with three white feet, out of the wagon yard.

Stomach grumbling, he rode to the café just up the street from the wagon yard, tethered his horses to the hitching rail, and stepped inside to the smell of burned bacon and black coffee. He sat at the counter next to a couple of smelly wolfers, the only customers in the place. The waitress, a big woman with black hair pinned up in a bun, filled a mug with coffee without asking what he wanted to drink.

"Biscuits," he said, "and gravy." That should fill him up quickly.

"You got it, hon," she said in a Texas drawl, and walked to the kitchen to place the order, leaving the coffee on a potbelly stove.

He rubbed his eyes, flexed his wrists, and sipped the bitter brew. The two wolfers muttered something, and the bell above the door chimed as someone else entered the café. Chance looked at the mirror on the wall.

And ducked.

The bullet blew apart the coffeepot, sending it spinning, clattering, spraying the stove with liquid that sizzled against the cast iron. Cursing, the wolfers leaped across the counter, taking their plates and mugs with them, slamming hard against the floor.

"Not again," the waitress said from the kitchen. Her voice rose. "It's too early for gunplay!"

Chance left the stool, landing on his knees, and pushing himself to his right. He hit the floor with the Schofield extended in his right hand as a second bullet clipped his hat. He fired at the gent's waxed blond mustache, knowing he had missed, and rolled over.

Acrid white smoke clouded the small restaurant, burning Chance's eyes, fouling his nostrils. Glass shattered. The bell above the door rang out again as the man dived outside.

A noise came from behind him, and Chance rolled onto his back, bringing the .45 up. The waitress appeared, holding a pepperbox pistol.

Their eyes met. Chance lowered his pistol, and stood up, looking through the doorway, and out the window.

"Hell," the waitress was saying, "I figured it was them two wolfers shootin' at each other. But you? You're a Ranger."

Heading past the woman, Chance said, "So's the guy shooting at me." He walked through the kitchen, out the back door, and into an alley that smelled of trash and grease. He eased toward the street, keeping his finger on the trigger, the hammer cocked. A rooster crowed. Dogs yelped from all the gunshots. Chance hurried down the alley, crossed over to the other side, and hugged the adobe wall of a cobbler's shop. Across the road, he saw a figure running, leaping, landing on the far side of a water trough.

He had a clear view of the empty street. He made sure his three horses were safe, then focused on the water trough.

When Taw Cutter lifted his head, Chance fired.

The bullet tore off the Ranger's hat, and Cutter ducked. A moment later, he was up, running down the boardwalk, firing from his hip, but not coming close to hitting anything.

Chance sent one round after the fleeing Ranger, then ran in the opposite direction. Moving deliberately to the chestnut, he pulled the Winchester Centennial from the scabbard, and jacked a round into the chamber. Walking into the center of the street, he brought the big rifle to his shoulder.

The .45-70 roared. The bullet splintered a wooden column that held up the awning to the stagecoach station.

Cutter yelped, grabbed his right ear, stumbled, and ran across the street. Firing once, he performed a border shift, tossed his empty pistol from his right hand to his left, and drew another revolver from the holster on his right hip, all while running.

Impressive, Chance thought.

Cutter's second revolver thundered.

Not impressive. Chance stood far out of pistol range. He brought the rifle up, and drew a bead on the running figure of Taw Cutter.

He sensed . . . something. Perhaps he heard a noise. Maybe it was instinct, or just plain luck. But instead of pulling the trigger, he leaped to his side, as another bullet buzzed past him and dug into the sandy street.

Chance rolled onto his back, looking for a target, finding Eliot Thompson coming out of the wagon yard, working the lever of his Winchester.

He figured — knew it, actually, as well as he knew anything — that Hec Savage would send a rider to Sanderson. But Savage had sent two men to Fort Stockton. Chance worried if Moses Albavera had met more than one person in Sanderson, wondered if that big black man had been killed.

He couldn't fret over that. He had more

pressing matters.

Such as that Winchester repeater Eliot Thompson was about to fire.

CHAPTER TWENTY-ONE

Chance was a dead man. He knew that as he tried to find the Ranger down the street in his gun sights. Next to Doc Shaw, Eliot Thompson was probably the best rifle shot in Company E, and Chance lay in the center of the street, with no place to hide. Thompson appeared to be grinning as his finger tightened on the trigger.

A gun roared, but Chance didn't see any smoke from Thompson's Winchester. Instead, Thompson was catapulted to his side, sending the rifle cartwheeling across the road. A gray stallion, lathered with sweat, loped around the corner of an adobe jacal across from the wagon yard, and Chance recognized the dark figure in the saddle. The Andalusian shifted into a weary gallop. Chance rolled over, came to his knees, and aimed the Centennial at Taw Cutter. Seeing Thompson down, and another rider thundering into town, Cutter loosened one quick, fruitless shot at Chance, and kicked open the closed door to a saloon. He disappeared inside.

Chance looked at the sign above the doors. BAD WATER SALOON. "Great," he sighed, and looked back.

Thompson had crawled to the Winchester, and was using the rifle as a crutch. He pushed himself up to his knees, the left side of his shirt soaked with blood. Moses Albavera reined in the Andalusian, and slid from the saddle, shoving Miss Vickie in the holster, and reaching into the pocket of his buckskin coat. Thompson let the rifle fall, and reached for a .45 holstered, butt forward, on his left hip.

A small pistol bucked in Albavera's right hand, the bullet driving into Thompson's gut.

" 'No . . .' "

Another shot.

" 'Niggers . . .' "

Another shot.

" 'Allowed . . .' "

Boom!

" 'In . . .' "

Boom!

" 'Savage.' "

The hammer clicked empty. "Isn't that what you said, Ranger?" Albavera swung around, crouched, and ran toward Chance, leaving the Andalusian in the street, leaving the bullet-riddled body of Eliot Thompson in the dust.

Chance was on his feet, waved his hand at the Bad Water Saloon, and sprinted across the street. A bullet kicked up dust in front of him. Chance answered, firing from the hip. He reached the adobe wall of the saloon a few rods from the door. Albavera leaped over the hitching rail, and flattened himself against the wall next to Chance. He reloaded the sawed-off Springfield, then broke open the Smith & Wesson .32, ejecting the five spent casings. Reaching inside his coat pocket, he brought out a handful of bullets, and thumbed them into the cylinder.

"What the hell are you doing here?" Chance said tightly, keeping his eyes on the front door and window to the saloon.

"You're welcome." Albavera snapped the .32 shut. "Hell, man, I just saved your life."

"I wanted him alive." Chance spit, and wiped his mouth. "And I told you to go to Sanderson."

"I did. Sent your damned telegraph. Killed that Ranger with the Mexican hat."

"Bucky Bragg?"

"I didn't ask his name. He didn't give it."

"How'd you get here so fast?"

"It's a long damned story. Maybe I can tell it to you over a morning bracer." He pointed the .32's small barrel at the door.

"I could use a drink," Chance said.

"Hey." Albavera raised his head. "Isn't this the Bad Springs Saloon?"

"Bad Water," Chance corrected.

"Who's inside?"

"Taw Cutter. He's got one six-shooter. And there's no back door to this place."

"He might have found the scattergun the beer-jerker keeps behind the bar," Albavera said.

"Maybe." Chance looked down the street. The two wolfers, the cook, and the waitress were standing in front of the café, keeping a respectful distance from any potentially stray bullet. A couple dogs on the porch in front of the Comanche Springs Bank were barking, growling. Nobody else dared show his face.

Albavera shook his head. "I don't care much for shotguns. If memory serves, that's a sawed-off Greener behind that bar. Twelve gauge."

"It's not your concern. I figured you'd be in Mexico by now."

"Where's the sheriff?" Albavera asked.

"Rode off with the Army boys to Fort Leaton."

"Not all of them, I'm sure. We could ask the soldiers for some help."

"There's only one man in there."

"Uh-huh." Albavera slid the Smith & Wesson into his coat pocket, pulled the Springfield from the holster, and thumbed back the hammer. "And Savage could only afford to send one man to Sanderson. Hell, Chance, there were three."

Chance turned, unbelieving. "Three?"

"That's right. Three. The bastard who stole my Andalusian and two Mexicans."

"Mexicans?"

"Yeah. I know Mexicans when I see them, especially when one's about to tear my head off with a machete."

Chance looked back at the doorway. "Well, I'm not leaving Taw Cutter here. Besides, this is a civilian matter. Army's got no jurisdiction here."

"Suit yourself. How you want to handle it?"

Staring again at the big Moor, Chance started to say something, but couldn't find the right words. He shook his head, and turned again to the doorway. Suddenly, he swung back around, reached out with his left hand, and fingered the badge Albavera had pinned on his vest. Their eyes met.

Albavera grinned. "I deputized myself.

The Rangers also owe Corbett's Hardware Store in Sanderson for a box of .32s, since you didn't give me any extra ammunition."

"Didn't occur to me." Chance eased his way toward the door, his back braced against the adobe. "This isn't your fight."

Albavera followed him. "The hell it isn't. I don't tolerate horse thieves."

"You got your horse back."

"And I'm damned sure not letting a bunch of ignorant, murdering racists run me out of this country. 'No niggers allowed in Savage.' We'll see about that. I'm with you, Ranger Chance."

Chance yelled at the doorway. "Cutter! There's no way out. Throw your gun out, and come out with your hands high."

"Come and get me!" a panicked voice cried from inside the dark saloon.

Still staring at the door, Chance whispered, "Where do you make him?"

"Behind the bar." Albavera shook his head, sighing, and added, "Likely with that Greener in his hands." With his left hand, he drew the .32 from his coat pocket, and thumbed back the hammer.

"I want him alive. I'll go through the window. You come through the door. I'll come up on the left. You cover the right."

"Who's got the center?" Albavera asked,

but Chance was already moving.

Pulling the trigger to the Winchester as he leaped, Chance watched the glass window shatter as he dived through the opening. He landed on a poker table, which collapsed under the force of his impact. Rolling onto the floor, shards of glass tore into his hands as he worked the Centennial's lever.

Albavera ducked through the doorway, keeping low, snapping a shot from the .32 in his left hand that shattered a jug of mescal on the bar. Moving to his right, the sawed-off Springfield in his right hand, he dived to the floor, overturning a table. He crouched behind it, using it for shelter.

Chance came to his knees, swinging the rifle barrel from one side to the other, letting his eyes grow accustomed to the darkness.

Both men had expected to be greeted with gunfire. Instead, they heard only the barking of dogs outside. Gunsmoke drifted toward the ceiling, catching rays of sunlight that streamed through the broken window and doorway.

The place smelled of gunsmoke, sawdust, and spilled whiskey.

Albavera peered around the corner of the table, focused on the bar, scanned the top, the sides, then looked over at Chance, who motioned him to one side of the bar. The black man nodded in acknowledgment, and began creeping across the saloon's hard-packed earthen floor. Chance moved to the opposite end.

He leaned against the side of the bar, sucked in a deep breath, slowly exhaled, and dived to the floor, the Winchester ready. Eighteen feet down the bar, he saw Moses Albavera do the same.

They raised the barrels of their weapons, and quickly slid behind the bar.

"Where the hell is he?" Albavera mouthed.

Carefully, Chance stood. He peered at the shadows, the corners. Nothing. Albavera looked at the low ceiling, but there was no place for anyone to hide up there. Barely enough room for a rat. Chance stepped back, aiming the barrel underneath the bar, but found only bottles, bung starters, and trash. Albavera ran his tongue over his cracked lips. The two men looked at each other.

"Trap door?" Albavera asked, audible now.

"Hell, I don't know." Chance placed the cocked Centennial on the bar, and reached for a bottle of tequila.

Albavera took a couple steps behind the bar, holstering Miss Vickie and moving the Smith & Wesson to his right hand. He pointed, and looked up as Chance splashed clear liquid into a dirty glass. "The Greener's gone."

Chance glanced under the bar, again scanned the room, and slid the glass across the bar toward Albavera.

Outside, the dogs had stopped barking. Muffled voices could be heard.

Chance filled another dirty glass and killed the tequila in two swallows. His eyes scanned the ceiling again, then he began kicking the baseboard on the bar. He refilled his glass, and picked it up with his left hand.

Albavera lifted his glass, and stepped in front of stacked barrels marked WHISKEY. One of the barrels toppled and caught his arm, knocking the .32 and the glass of whiskey to the floor. Taw Cutter leaped from behind the high stacked barrels, slamming the giant muzzles of the Greener shotgun into Albavera's throat. "Leave the Winchester on the bar, Chance, or I blow this nigger's head clear off."

Chance's right hand froze on the Centennial. "Let him go."

"No way. I'm backing out of here. You move, and I kill him."

Chance shook his head. "Then I kill you."

"I don't think so, Chance." Cutter's smile was crooked. "You always were too damned soft." He tugged on Albavera's shoulder. "Start backing."

Albavera obeyed.

Chance kept his hand on the Winchester, but didn't make any attempt to lift it. His left hand brought the glass of tequila to his lips. He sipped, and stood there. Watching.

Albavera slid around an overturned table, tipped over a chair, and felt the barrels of the Greener bite deeper into the flesh under his chin.

The two men stopped. "Don't try nothing smart, darky," Cutter said, his voice tight. The man stank of sweat, horseflesh, and leather.

"Man, I can't see where I'm going," Albavera said. "You try backing up with a shotgun under your chin. Don't shoot me just because I stumble. I'm trying to keep my feet."

"Just move," Cutter said.

At the bar, Chance sipped his drink.

"All I'm doing," Cutter said, his voice tense, "is taking the darky out of here. You stay put, Chance. I get on my horse. I ride away. All three of us get to go on living."

Chance swallowed the tequila. Took another swig. *Cutter won't do that. As soon as he is out the door, he'll blow Albavera's head off.*

Cutter would have the upper hand then. He'd have Chance pinned inside that bucket of blood. He swallowed, took another sip. Looking away from Cutter, Chance locked eyes with Albavera.

He stopped as he reached the door.

Cutter's fingers squeezed hard. "Keep moving, nigger."

Albavera stumbled again, but jerked back his head, slamming it into Cutter's nose, and dived to his left, saying, "Go to hell."

The Centennial was aimed waist high at the doorway. Chance's finger had never left the trigger, and the .45-70 had been cocked. As Albavera dived to his left, the rifle roared. Both barrels of the shotgun discharged, shrouding Cutter's face in white smoke, but only briefly. The .45-70 caught him in his midsection, sending him sailing through the doorway and onto the street.

Chance finished the tequila, set the empty glass down, and came over the bar, jacking another round into the Winchester. Moving toward the door, he watched Albavera pick himself off the floor, and Taw Cutter writhing on the ground.

Albavera slapped his ringing ears, and shook his head. His eyes met Chance's, and the two men stepped through the door, stopped underneath the awning, and looked down at Taw Cutter.

"God," the Ranger said, choking on blood that poured out of his mouth, and seeped from his busted nose. "God . . . God . . ." He trembled, coughed, and, staring at the blue skies until his eyes lost focus, died.

Said Albavera, "Thought you wanted to take him alive."

Replied Chance, "Changed my mind."

"Good."

"Not so good." Chance lowered the hammer on the Centennial. "Now we don't know a damned thing about what the hell Captain Savage is really planning."

"Yeah, we do." Albavera drew the yellow page of a telegraph from his pocket, held it out for Chance. "Read this."

CHAPTER TWENTY-TWO

Elbows on his desk, head bent, Captain Miles Braden smoothed his mustache as he read the telegraph again. He cast his eyes at a crudely drawn map, then, releasing his mustache while shaking his head, he stared up at Dave Chance and Moses Albavera. His elbows remained on his desk as he held out his palms and said, "I don't see what this proves."

Seething, Chance jabbed his finger at the telegraph. "That's from Colonel Thomas. Ordering Captain Savage and Company E to Murphyville to make sure there's no trouble when the eastbound S.P. arrives."

"So?"

Tapping harder, Chance said, "There's a quarter of a million dollars on that train. In gold bullion."

"I read that."

"Then don't you see?"

"See what?"

"Jesus. Savage is going to rob that train. That's why he sent your soldier boys south to Fort Leaton. To get you and the law, everybody out of the way." He moved his finger to the map. "There. Moses took that off a Mexican bandit he killed in Sanderson. It marks that." He tapped. "Cathedral Mountain. That's south of Murphyville. Calamity Creek. That's where Don Melitón Benton's sheep operation is headquartered. Savage didn't go to Fort Leaton. He went there. Major Fields and Colonel McVicker are going to Fort Leaton for nothing. That's what Savage wanted. To get the Army out of the way."

Braden shook his head. "Orders from Austin and a map taken off a dead Mex. Those don't prove anything. And you said yourself Savage has only fourteen men."

"Eleven." Albavera spoke softly, carefully examining his fingernails. "Three have gotten themselves killed."

Ignoring Albavera, the captain continued, "That money will be well guarded. Savage doesn't have enough men to pull off such a bold move."

"He's got help," Chance said. "Juan Lo Grande."

Captain Braden sniggered. "Really, Sergeant Chance, do you think your Ranger captain would form an alliance with any Mexican, especially Juan Lo Grande?"

"For a quarter of a million bucks," Chance said, "he'd join Lucifer himself."

Added Albavera, "I'm fairly tempted myself."

Chance stiffened. That Moorish gambler didn't know when to shut the hell up. Chance told Braden, "Lo Grande sent those two Mexicans to Sanderson. Plus, Moses and I killed a couple more in the hills between Fort Davis and Marathon. Lo Grande's in this, sure as hell."

"You don't know that for certain."

"The hell I don't." Actually, Chance was guessing, but it had to be. It all made sense.

The captain waved his finger at Chance. "You brought in a note from Captain Savage that says he is holding an officer and enlisted men of the Third United States Cavalry — my outfit, mind you — and will kill them, and other hostages unless payment is received on Sunday afternoon." Braden lowered his arms. "Major Fields left me here. Didn't want to share the glory —"

"Then get some glory for yourself," Chance said, frustrated, feeling like he was wasting time trying to pry the Army officer off his ass. "Send your troops to Murphyville. We can attack Don Melitón's camp."

"Those are not my orders, Sergeant."

"Captain Savage always told us that orders were open for interpretation. Actually, he said there never was an order written that wasn't made to be broken."

Braden shook his head contemptuously. "That's just like you undisciplined Texas Rangers. West Point teaches us otherwise."

"Captain, don't be so obtuse."

Braden's muscles tightened, and he slowly rose, speaking in a harsh voice. "Get out. Both of you. Get out. Before I have you thrown off this post, or into the guardhouse."

Outside, Chance angrily pulled his hat on his head, turned back to the door and started to open it, then changed his mind.

"Too bad the Ninth Cavalry isn't stationed here anymore," Albavera said, fingering a bullet hole in his hat. "Black soldiers. White officers, mostly, but smart fellows. They aren't obtuse."

"You're right." Chance let out a sigh of exasperation, and looked across the parade grounds. The American flag popped in the wind. A few soldiers marched from the north end to the south. A horse whinnied in the stables.

Asked Albavera, "What exactly does obtuse mean?"

"I'm not sure." Chance stepped off the stone porch, and gathered the reins to the chestnut. "Just something Grace Profit called me once." He took the lead rope and pulled the two bays behind him, heading toward the corral.

Leading the Andalusian, Albavera followed. "Where we going?" the black man asked.

"That stallion of yours is half dead. We'll get you some horses."

A lanky trooper in a stable frock met Chance and Albavera at the stables. Chance waved a greeting, and smiled. Luckily it was the same soldier who had helped him pick out his horses the night before. He hooked a thumb toward the headquarters building. "Captain Braden sent us to get three more horses for my pard."

"Morning," Albavera greeted, and pushed back his jacket to reveal the badge on his vest, before he handed the stallion's reins to the soldier. "You take fine care of this Andalusian. He's special."

"I'll say." The soldier spit a mouthful of tobacco juice into the dirt. "Man who owns him has posted a fifty dollar reward for his return."

Albavera frowned.

Chance grinned. "Guess you just made fifty bucks, trooper. Pick out three of your fastest horses, if you will. And hurry. We're burning daylight."

As the soldier led the stallion into the stables, Albavera approached Chance, tilting his head toward the headquarters building. "You figure that pasty white captain'll come after us for stealing government mounts?"

"It'd be nice. Give us some more men after they realize we're right and their captain is a damned fool. But I don't think Captain Braden has the guts to leave this post."

It was well past midnight when they reached Marathon, their horses — Chance on the bay with the three white feet, Albavera on a buckskin — hanging their heads, panting, about played out. Their mounts weren't the only things half dead. They had been in the saddle for fourteen hours, leaving the four other horses they had ridden in the desert north of town. Over the past thirty-six hours, Chance had ridden about one hundred and twenty miles. Albavera had ridden that distance and sixty miles more, plus fed wood into the firebox on a Schenectady 4-4-0 locomotive on another sixty-mile leg.

Both men eased from the saddles in front of the depot. Chance stared at the big black locomotive, creaking, hissing, smelling of wood smoke and grease, while Albavera stamped his legs to get the blood circulating again.

A yawning, white-bearded face appeared in the window of the cab, and Mickey McGee let out a wild yelp, then bounded out of the cabin. He gripped Chance's arms, said something, and wrapped his arms around the exhausted Ranger. "Damn, Davy me boy, it's grand to see you. Just grand." He released his bear-hug, stepped back, and began scratching his beard. "Where's the soldiers?"

Chance shook his head.

"Sheriff?"

Another shake.

"Who you got?"

Chance hooked a thumb at Albavera, walked to the saddle, and jerked the Winchester from the scabbard, saying, "And you."

Shuffling his feet, McGee said, "I see."

"You sober?" Chance asked. He leaned the Centennial against a drive wheel, and began unsaddling the bay.

"Sure, Davy. Moses neglected to tell me that Captain Savage burned down the only saloon in Marathon. Had I knowed that, I probably wouldn't have volunteered."

"Since when did you become an engineer?" Chance tossed the saddle into the open door of the cattle car.

"Since Moses and me got this little baby huffin' and puffin' about as hard as Sean O'Rourke was when we told him what we was plannin' to do. But I've ridden in enough locomotives, shared enough jugs with enough engineers, it's not too hard to figure out how to make one of these things go and stop. Hell of a lot easier than layin' track, that's for sure."

Moonlight shined on the locomotive, and the engine's headlamp sprayed the tracks with light. Lights were also burning at the depot, and a few windows glowed at the Iron Mountain Inn, but the rest of Marathon was dark, asleep. Chance stepped back. Behind the tender were two cattle cars. Too much. "Best uncouple that last car, Mickey," Chance said. He threw the bridle behind the saddle, and patted the bay's neck. The bay barely acknowledged any affection.

"Grace has a black mare in the livery," Chance told Albavera. "We'll bring her. And borrow Mr. Kipperman's Appaloosa."

They drank coffee in the cab while waiting for the pressure to build up in the boiler. All three men were sweating. Albavera leaned on a shovel, and Chance picked a wood splinter from the palm of his hand. McGee shook his head. "How the hell do you plan on stoppin' Captain Savage and that Mexican badman?"

Chance folded the blade to the knife, flipped it to McGee, and rubbed his right hand on his trousers, picking up the coffee cup with his left. He didn't answer.

"One of you could go see the sheriff at Fort Davis," McGee said. "Or the soldiers there."

"They're likely halfway to Presidio by now," Chance said. "We don't have much time."

McGee shook his head again. "Well, how about we take this train all the way through Murphyville. Meet up with the eastbound S.P. Warn them what's goin' on."

"They wouldn't believe us," Albavera said.

"They might."

Chance shook his head. He had considered that option on the ride from Fort Stockton, but had dismissed it. "No, Mickey, the captain's sure to have some men, his or Lo Grande's, probably both, in Murphyville. They see a train come barreling through heading west, they'd get word to Savage. He'd figure out something was wrong. And wouldn't have any use for Grace or that prostitute from Terlingua."

"Isn't he holdin' some others captive, too?" McGee asked.

"Could be. Those soldiers might be at Fort Leaton. Along with that barber and the mayor. The captain maybe left one or two men behind, to keep the Army and the law at bay, keep them talking, trying to get those prisoners released, keep them away from the S.P. tracks and that load of money."

Savage, however, couldn't have sent Grace Profit and Linda Kincaid all the way to Presidio. He couldn't afford to spare any more men. They had to be at La Oveja. Or . . .

Albavera cleared his throat, and finished Chance's thought. "Those women . . . Savage could have killed them."

Chance nodded. "Yeah. I've thought about that. But Captain Savage has always been decent, as far as women are concerned. Part of his code. You treat a woman good. Doesn't matter if she's a whore or a saloon owner. You treat her like you would your mother or sister."

"I hated my sister," Albavera said. "And she hated me."

Chance finished the coffee, ignoring Albavera's comment. "I think Savage took those women to La Oveja. You get this train moving, Mickey. Take us to about five miles east of Murphyville. Moses and I'll ride into the mountains. Maybe we can get those women out of there."

"Then what do I do?"

"You wait."

"Never was much good at waitin'. How 'bout if I borrow one of those horses in that livery, ride down to that goat farm with you?"

"Sheep ranch," Chance corrected.

"Sheep, goats, they all stink like hell."

Chance shook his head. "I don't want you getting hurt, Mickey."

"What about me?" Albavera asked.

"I don't care," Chance said.

"Boy," McGee said, putting his hands on his hips. "You seem to be forgettin' that I saved your arse a few years back. It was me that stoved in Robert Constantine's head. Don't you worry none about Mickey Mc-Gee, Davy boy. I can take care of meself just fine."

Chance nodded. "All right, Mickey. Fetch a horse and saddle. But make it quick."

As soon as McGee had left the cab, Albavera tossed the dregs from his cup out the window, and checked the gauge on the boiler. "That makes it three against . . . how many men you think Lo Grande has with him?"

"Twenty. Thirty."

Albavera chuckled. "You think they can handle us?"

"I told you to head across the border after you sent that telegraph to Austin. You didn't have to come back."

"But I like you, Ranger Chance."

Chance started to say, *I like you, too,* but stopped himself. He opened the furnace, grabbed another piece of wood, tossed it into the flames, and looked across the street.

In the moonlight, he could see Mickey McGee leading a horse on a halter, lugging a saddle in his other hand. The horse turned its head, whinnied. Down the road, came another horse's answer. Mickey stopped, stared down the dark street, then began to run.

Muttering an oath, Chance closed the iron door to the furnace, and reached for the Winchester Centennial. Slowly, Albavera drew the sawed-off Springfield.

"Stay here." Chance slipped off the engine.

In the darkness came the pounding of horses.

"How fast can you get this thing moving?" Chance asked as Mickey ran past to the cattle car.

"Not that fast," McGee said.

Chance worked the lever of the Winchester and stepped onto the street. Albavera climbed down from the cab, and helped McGee load a piebald gelding up the ramp and into the cattle car. McGee ran to the engine, Albavera started to close the door to the cattle car, but stopped, and walked to Chance's side.

"Told you to stay put," Chance said.

"Orders are open for interpretation. Besides, there never was an order written that wasn't made to be broken." He put his hand on the stock of the Springfield.

A dozen riders loped into view, and quickly formed a semicircle around them. Lights began glowing in the windows of the homes across the street, and down at the hotel, as eleven vaqueros on horseback aimed Spencer repeating rifles at Chance and Albavera. The twelfth rider nudged his horse closer, and Chance figured, maybe, just maybe, he had found some help. Better help than the Army. Of that he was certain.

Providing, of course, those vaqueros

didn't kill him, Albavera, and McGee in the next few minutes.

"Evening, Don Melitón," Chance said, and lowered the hammer on the Centennial.

CHAPTER TWENTY-THREE

With a blend of grace, dignity and gringo trader, Don Melitón swung from the saddle, handing the reins to the vaquero closest to him. He said nothing, just stroked his white goatee, the moonlight giving his features a pale glow, staring first at Moses Albavera, then at Dave Chance. The man's eyes revealed nothing. He was still dressed in the *calzoneras* and suede jacket, and slowly removed the black hat, holding its stiff-edged brim in his hands. Then, his face never betraying any emotion, he lashed out, sending the coarse, horsehair braided stampede string slashing like a whip across Chance's face.

Chance flinched, brought his hand to his cheek and looked at the blood on his fingertips. He let his arms fall to his side, as his eyes met Don Melitón's.

"That," the old man said, "is for Fort Davis. I am not one to be left bound like some common criminal."

Blood dripped down Chance's face. He stood still, staring at Don Melitón as the nobleman reached with his left hand, and fingered the peso badge pinned to Chance's vest. Suddenly, he ripped it off, tossed it in the dirt, and ground it with the sole of his boot. "You have been busy, *el rinche.*" His voice was chilling.

"I had nothing to do with your two vaqueros getting killed," Chance said.

"*¡Silencio!*" His accent sounded more Missouri than Mexico.

Chance kept talking. "The hell I will. Captain Savage killed your two men." Bracing himself for another burning lash as Don Melitón swung back his hat, prepared to strike Chance again, he blurted out, "I warrant he's killed more, if you have anyone at La Oveja."

Hand and hat froze behind the old man's head. His eyes showed curiosity. "What? What do you mean?"

Catching his breath, Chance wiped the blood off his cheek, while explaining. "Savage has hooked up with Juan Lo Grande. They plan to rob the eastbound Southern Pacific when it hits Murphyville."

A laugh escaped the old man's throat. He shook his head, and returned the hat to his head. "You take me for a fool?" Shoving Chance aside, he stood face-to-face with Moses Albavera.

"It's true," Chance said to the don's back. "They've teamed up to rob the eastbound Southern Pacific when it hits Murphyville. I'm pretty sure he's holed up at La Oveja. Waiting for the train."

The don fingered the badge on Albavera's vest, looked into the man's dark eyes. "You killed my son," he said in a tight whisper.

Albavera nodded. "Seemed like the thing to do."

Don Melitón backhanded him, stepped away, and put his hand on the Allen & Wheelock in his sash, his thumb on the side hammer.

They hadn't noticed Mickey McGee in the cab of the locomotive. Probably wouldn't have ever seen him if he hadn't released the steam, and blown the whistle at the moment Don Melitón drew his single-shot pistol, the same time the moon disappeared behind a cloud.

Steam belched from the Schenectady engine, and the whistle screamed, panicking the horses, and the don's riders. Gunfire erupted. Horses reared, bucked, and spun. The engine lurched forward, and McGee yelled, "All aboard!" He fired a shot from a

Remington revolver into the darkness.

A bullet tore through Chance's left hand, as he dived, extending the Winchester. Another round clipped his boot heel. Swinging the barrel, he caught Don Melitón Benton's ankles, dropping him into the dirt. A rider thudded nearby, the breath whooshing from his lungs, the horse he had been on loping east through town.

Spanish curses and shouts rang out as the engine groaned. Warnings for the vaqueros to hold their fire, that they might hit *el patrón*.

The train moved.

So did Albavera. The sawed-off Springfield cut loose like a cannon, and another horse fell into the darkness, kicking, thrashing in its death throes. The moon reappeared. Dogs barked. A rooster crowed. Coyotes wailed in the desert that surrounded the town.

Chance scrambled to his feet, as Albavera jerked the old man up, grabbing his single-shot .22, pressing the barrel into Don Melitón's temple.

"Come on," Chance said, aiming the Centennial from his waist, taking in what he could make out in the moonlight.

Three riders were down, one holding his shoulder, writhing on the ground. One

304

horse lay dead. Two other horses were bucking, their riders pulling leather, desperately hanging on. Another horse spun, stamped its hooves, swung its head left to right, fighting the bit. Yet a bunch of rifles remained pointed at Chance and Albavera.

They couldn't shoot, though. Not with Albavera holding their patrón close, not with that pistol cocked and glued to the old man's head.

"You slip, old man," Albavera said, "and you join your son in hell." He picked up the pace.

Chance led as they ran across the empty lot, then behind the Iron Mountain Inn. He tossed his rifle through the open door, grabbed the handle, and swung himself into the cattle car. The train was picking up speed. The vaqueros, those still mounted, rode down the street. Chance gripped the wood with his right hand, leaned down, and reached out with his bloody left hand.

"Take his hand!" Albavera commanded.

The old man did, but his hand slipped off because of the blood. He tried again, made it. Grunting, Chance squeezed as hard as he could, surprised to find his muscles cooperating, and pulled Don Melitón into the car. He sat up, grabbed for Albavera, and missed.

A bullet splintered the door. Another whined off the iron wheel. The vaqueros cursed. Another shot lost itself in the distance, then Mickey McGee fired a quick succession from the Remington. A horse stumbled, threw its rider into the dust.

The train passed the path that led to the church and cemetery, chugging, grinding, picking up speed.

Moses Albavera dropped the .22, leaped, and landed in the cattle car.

Another bullet ricocheted off the tender. Inside the cattle car, the three horses borrowed from the Marathon livery stamped their hooves, snorting. The whistle screeched again. No. That was no train whistle. That was Mickey McGee cutting loose with a rebel yell as the 4-4-0 engine began pulling away from the don's riders, heading west into the blackness as another cloud swallowed the moon.

A match flamed to life, and the cattle car brightened as Albavera lit the wick to a lantern, and turned it up. He peered out the open door, the wind cooling him as he stared into the blackness. Leaning against the rough, ventilated wooden wall, Chance bit back pain as he wrapped a bandana around his bloody hand.

"You want me to burn that hand, stop that

bleeding?" Albavera asked.

"No!" Chance snapped. "I don't want you touching me."

"Testy." He turned away from the door, and stared at Don Melitón Benton. The man sat there, wooden, in the middle of the car. Stiff, unblinking, mad, he wiped Chance's blood off his own hand on his pants leg.

"That is twice I have let you surprise me," Don Melitón said. "There won't be a third time."

"Damn right." Chance tied the bandana tight, grimacing, reaching up with his right hand, and pulling himself to his feet. The car wobbled. "Next time I'll just kill you."

"Like I said," Albavera whispered. "Testy."

"Shut up, Moses." Chance wobbled over until he stood in front of the old man. Stood there, weaving to the car's motion, beads of sweat popping on his forehead. "You think I'm a fool, old man?"

The don looked up.

"I had my prisoner." He thumbed at Albavera. "I could be in Sanderson. Could have taken him to Fort Stockton. I could be riding to Galveston. Why do you think I'm still here" — he pointed again behind him — "with that son of a bitch?"

Don Melitón said nothing.

"Captain Savage killed three Rangers. He killed two of your men. He has taken Grace Profit hostage. Maybe some others. Or maybe they're all dead. He's planning to rob the Southern Pacific of a quarter of a million dollars. He's working with Juan Lo Grande. That's why I'm here. And he's holed up, for now, at your sheepherding camp."

No change of expression on the don's rugged face.

"The Army, the Presidio County and Pecos County law are all down at Fort Leaton. Thinking that's where Savage is. They've given him plenty of rein. There's nobody to stop him or Lo Grande. Except me" — he pointed again — "and him" — he nodded at Don Melitón — "and you."

The don blinked.

"How many men do you have at La Oveja?" Chance asked.

No answer.

"Christ." Chance kicked out, almost lost his footing, and had to regain his balance. He looked over at Albavera. "Moses, throw this arrogant bastard out of this damned car."

When Albavera started to stand, the don caught his breath, and said, "Miguel Aquiles and his grandson."

"That's all?" Chance asked.

"There is not much to do until the ewes begin lambing in the spring."

Chance knelt, rubbed his left hand, the bandana already soaked through with blood. He looked into Don Melitón's eyes. "Will you help us?"

Smiling without humor, the old man shook his head. "Help you?" He jutted his chin toward Albavera. "Help the man who killed my only son?"

"Your only son was a creep," Chance said. The man stiffened, his eyes narrowing, but Chance didn't let up. "And you know it. Tell him what happened, Moses."

Albavera cleared his throat. "I told him at Fort Davis. Remember?"

"Tell him again."

"Well, we were playing poker in Shafter. A Mexican lady came in, selling tamales. Prince took one, tasted it, told her it was terrible, shoved it in her face, so hard he knocked her to the floor. I came to her defense. Prince and me exchanged —"

"I've heard your story," Don Melitón interrupted.

His eyes drilling through the old man, Chance said softly, "And you know Moses is telling the truth."

"I owe my son," Don Melitón said stiffly.

"That much, I owe him."

"How much do you owe Miguel Aquiles and his grandson?" Chance asked. "Or their next of kin?"

The train groaned to a stop in the gap between the Glass and Del Norte ranges, the skies beginning to lighten into a dull gray in the east. Albavera and Chance lowered the chute, and let their horses out, Don Melitón following with the third horse. All the mounts were saddled.

Lantern swinging in his hands, Mickey McGee ran down the side of the tracks, and slid to a stop when Don Melitón mounted the horse he had taken from Marathon.

"Hey . . ." McGee began.

"Change of plans, Mickey," Chance said, swinging into the saddle. During the night, he had taken off his boots — a vaquero's bullet had knocked off one boot heel — and pulled on a pair of calf-high moccasins, Apache style, from his saddlebags. "Don Melitón's coming with us."

"But —"

"He knows La Oveja. Better than anyone. And we only have three horses."

The lantern lowered as McGee's shoulders sagged. He pouted. "What am I supposed to do? Sit here and wait?"

"Exactly." The horse spun around, ready to run. Chance had to pull hard on the reins. "Don Melitón'll need that revolver of yours."

Slowly, Mickey pulled the revolver from his waistband.

"Loaded?"

"Six beans in the wheel." He spun the revolver on his finger, and offered the walnut butt to the old man, who took it, flipped open the loading gate, and rotated the cylinder. Chance watched the don, half expecting him to thumb back the hammer and kill him and Albavera, but the man snapped the gate shut, and slipped the revolver inside his sash.

"Have you any extra shells?" the don asked.

Grumbling, McGee reached inside the mule-ear pocket of his trousers, and pulled out a handful of brass cartridges, dropping them in Don Melitón's palm, watching him slip the bullets in his jacket pocket.

McGee was talking. "You don't leave a man much, Davy boy."

"The don's vaqueros should be here in a couple hours," Chance said. "It'll be dawn by then. You send them after us. We'll need all the help we can get."

"It'll take you a couple hours to get there

yourself."

Chance nodded. "More if I keep talking to you." The horse spun again. "Mickey, if we're not back by three o'clock, you take that engine, and you go barreling down those tracks. Through Murphyville. You don't stop until you see that eastbound coming. You tell them what's happening, what we're doing. You got enough wood to get you that far?"

His head bobbed, but he said, "Thought you said Savage would have the town watched, that if some unscheduled train rolled through, he'd know his plan ain't gonna work."

"He'll know that in a couple hours anyway," Chance said, and heeled the side of the black mare. The horse exploded in a fast lope, kicking up dust, hooves pounding the desert floor. Don Melitón Benton followed on the piebald McGee had picked out for himself, and Moses Albavera fell in behind Benton on a sure-footed Appaloosa. McGee watched them in the predawn light until they disappeared over a ridge, then, grumbling like a child who had been rebuked by his parents, kicking stones with the toes of his boots, he walked back to the cab of the hissing locomotive.

CHAPTER TWENTY-FOUR

Flickering light from the candelabra on the adobe wall reflected in the glass Hec Savage raised to the candles. He held it there for a moment studying the liquid, then brought the drink to his lips, satisfied. "Old man Benton makes mighty fine peach brandy, don't you think, Grace?"

Across the cherry-wood table, Grace Profit shrugged. Her glass remained in front of her, untouched.

Smiling, Savage finished his drink, and fetched a gold watch from his vest pocket. He rose, walked to the keg, and refilled his glass, draining it before he walked back to the table, and stood behind her. He reached over her shoulder, and laid his empty glass beside her full one, then brought his hand back, and rested it on her right shoulder. His left hand fell on her other shoulder, and he began squeezing. Grace stiffened.

"You should relax," he told her.

"You should get your damned hands off me."

Savage chuckled. "Would you prefer that greaser Lo Grande's?" He released her shoulders, and slid on the table so that he faced her. She looked quite lovely. Of course, the room at La Oveja wasn't well lit, and the shadows hid her blemishes. Not that she wasn't a handsome woman. More than handsome, actually, and a woman who could take care of herself.

He picked up her glass. "I think this tastes better than that bust-head you serve, Grace."

"The men I serve aren't interested in taste. My whiskey gets them drunk. That's what they want."

"But you should want more."

She stared ahead at the wall. Savage reached down, lifted and turned her head with two fingers underneath her chin. "Remember," he said, "our little conversation on the ride over here? I could buy you a new saloon. A fancy one, with fine drinks."

He left his hand on her face, but Grace reached over and removed it. Savage could see the candlelight flickering in her pupils, like a rattlesnake's tongue. Like a serpent's diamond eyes.

He dropped his hand back to his side.

"What would you say if I told you I was about to come into the sum of a quarter of a million dollars?"

"You plan on selling your kingdom of Savage to Germany?"

"No."

"England?"

He shook his head. "The Southern Pacific is bringing it."

"I thought you only wanted a hundred thousand from the railroad."

He laughed again.

"The U.S. Mint needs gold to make its coins. Gold's often shipped to New York, you know. They take the bullion, sell it on the gold market for greenbacks. There's two hundred and fifty thousand dollars in bullion due to stop in Murphyville for water and a new crew on its way east."

Her lips parted, closed. She shook her head. "You'll never get away with that," she said after digesting what he'd told her.

"Who's to stop me?" He began rolling a cigarette. "By now the Army's loping down to Fort Leaton. They'll get there, surround the fort, and prepare for a siege. Only there's no one to talk to. Nobody's left inside that fort, but it'll take those stupid damnyankees a day or two before they figure that out."

"What about those hostages?" Grace asked, though she knew the answer.

"You know me, Grace. I'm no good with prisoners. When the Army finally storms through the gates, they'll find the late Mayor Childress and Congressman Hendry in the stockade."

She swallowed. "And Father de la Vega?"

He shook his head. "And if they look hard enough, they might find Captain Bookbinder and what's left of his bluebellies at La Mota Mountain."

"You're sick."

"No, I'm Savage." He laughed, and lit his cigarette. "Meanwhile, Austin's scrambling. I bet Colonel Thomas doesn't know what the hell's going on. He thinks he has a Ranger captain gone loco, but he can't communicate with anyone west of Sanderson. He'll try to organize a force, but he won't be able to get anyone to Presidio County until Tuesday or Wednesday. They'll be heading west, and we'll pass each other, like ships sailing across the dark seas, because I'll be riding east. By the time he figures it out, I'll be in Mexico."

She laughed. "For that much money, the Army won't be stopped by any border."

"They'll go through channels, though. First, they'll contact the Rurales at Ojinaga.

Then the Rurales at San Pedro." He took a long pull on the cigarette, and blew out smoke through his nostrils. "Alas, the Rurales in both villages are now under the command of Juan Lo Grande."

Grace reached for the glass of brandy, before remembering that Savage had polished it off. She leaned back, considering Savage again.

"Impressed, eh?"

"Repulsed."

He blew smoke in her face, but she didn't react.

"You'll never get away with it, Hec."

"Who's to stop me? By now, your friend Dave Chance is dead."

It was Grace Profit who laughed, a warm, musical sound, that caused Savage to straighten. "Dave? Dead?" Her head shook. "I don't think so, Hec."

Savage flicked the cigarette across the room, showering the adobe wall with sparks. Apparently, she had touched a nerve. She kept at it. "Besides, how do you plan to transport that much gold to Mexico? It's eighty, ninety miles to the border, and, like you said, those bluebellies won't be fooled at Fort Leaton forever. You'll never be able to cross the border at Presidio."

He smiled again. "Who said anything

about Presidio? I said east, remember. We're just gonna ride those rails all the way to Sanderson."

A pretty good plan, Savage had always thought. They'd take over the train at Murphyville, and keep that bullion on the S.P. — all the way to Sanderson. They'd leave the train there, in that big warehouse on the sidetrack. Out of view when that westbound came barreling through to reach Murphyville or Marathon. They'd load the bullion onto wagons, and head south to the Rio Grande. The border was a hell of a lot closer from Sanderson than it was from Murphyville, and they wouldn't have to worry about running into any Army patrols in case those yankees he'd sent to Fort Leaton got smarter. They wouldn't have to worry about running into Juan Lo Grande's bandits, either.

Savage grabbed the two glasses off the table and returned to the keg.

Lo Grande had ruined that, of course. He and his men were supposed to stay put in Ojinaga, get to the sheep farm after Savage and his men had robbed the train. By the time Lo Grande had figured out he had been double-crossed, Savage and his men would be headed down the Rio Grande, on the Mexican side, of course, to Matamoros, where they'd board a ship in that port city and sail to Argentina. A quarter of a million dollars would go a long way in Buenos Aires. For that much money, he could tolerate living with a bunch of ignorant greasers.

But Savage would have to figure out another plan. Lo Grande had brought twenty-six men with him. Savage had only eleven, fourteen when Taw Cutter, Eliot Thompson, and Bucky Bragg returned. Still, he wasn't worried. Lo Grande's men were nothing but a bunch of dirty bean-eaters, and he'd yet to meet ten damned Mexicans equal to one of Savage's Rangers.

He filled both glasses with brandy, and walked back to the table, offering Grace a drink, which, this time, she accepted. He slid onto the chair across from her.

Her eyes were mesmerizing. He started to say something, when he heard a noise. His right hand darted to one of the revolvers on his hips, and he sat up, staring at the doorway. Juan Lo Grande, smoking a cigar, one arm wrapped around the neck of the disheveled whore from Terlingua, another on the butt of one of his fancy Colts, grinned. He brought his hand up over Linda Kincaid's face, and removed his cigar, blowing a plume of smoke at the ceiling. His right had remained on the revolver.

"Amigo, is it not about time for us to leave for Murphyville?"

How long has he been standing outside that door? Savage wondered, but his face showed no alarm. Besides, what had he told Grace that Lo Grande, or that damned whore, could have overheard? Nothing important, and it didn't really matter. Lo Grande's presence had forced him to start thinking of a new plan anyway. He'd have to get rid of Lo Grande somehow.

Permanently.

Savage brought out his watch again, released the cover, read the time, snapped it shut, and dropped it back into his pocket. "We got some time yet."

Waving the cigar at Savage, Lo Grande said, "But not as long as you would have Juan Lo Grande think. Is that not right, mi amigo?" He returned the cigar to his mouth, catching Linda Kincaid's throat in the crook of his arm. She looked too battered to know anything.

When Savage's lips flattened, Lo Grande's grin widened, and kept stretching. He almost doubled over, laughing so hard, pulling Linda Kincaid down with him. He straightened, shoved the prostitute away, and pointed the cigar at Grace Profit.

"*Señorita,* el capitán, he tries to fool Juan

Lo Grande, no? He tells Juan Lo Grande that the train is coming to Murphyville on Sunday. That is what everybody is saying. Those politicians, those law dogs, those Army officers, they are *muy* smart." He paused long enough to return the cigar to his mouth, and sucked on it, but it had gone out. He tossed it to the floor, and walked to the keg of brandy.

"But the train, all that gold, it is due to come to Murphyville on Saturday." There were no glasses, so he knelt under the keg, turned the spigot, and let brandy splash into his mouth, his Adam's apple bobbing. His thirst slaked, he turned off the spigot, and pulled himself up, wiping the excess brandy off his face.

"El capitán, he must think Juan Lo Grande is a fool. He must have forgotten that it was me" — he tapped his chest — "Juan Lo Grande, who let him know about the gold being shipped. It was my idea. My plan." The smile began to fade. "If not for Juan Lo Grande, Capitán Savage would be sitting on his hindquarters in that presidio on the Rio Bravo dreaming about one day catching Juan Lo Grande."

"Juan Lo Grande," Savage said, "seems to have forgotten that I received orders from Austin about that trainload of gold. I knew about it."

Clucking his tongue, wagging his finger, Juan Lo Grande shook his head. "No, no, señor. You may have known about the shipment, but not how much gold was on board. And you never would have dreamed about stealing it." He sighed. "And now, he tries to fool Juan Lo Grande. Tries to take all that gold — too much for one man to spend, too much for even fourteen *rinches* — for himself, and leave old Juan Lo Grande and his *muchachos* to remain poor, humble *bandidos*."

He hooked his thumbs in his sash. " *'E tu, Brute.'* "

A noise startled both Lo Grande and Savage, and they turned toward the doorway, had their revolvers halfway out, before stopping the draws.

"Easy there, boys," Doc Shaw drawled as he stepped into the light, the High Wall rifle nestled under the crook of his left arm. "You both are mighty touchy."

Something was different about Shaw. Grace realized that his hat was gone, replaced by a railroader's cap. He brought his right hand up and tugged on an imaginary cord, then let out a loud, "Whooooooooo. Whooo. Whoo. Whoooooooooo!" He broke out laughing, and said, "All aboard."

Grace Profit killed the brandy, and set the empty glass on the chair. Linda Kincaid stood in the corner, absently twirling her bangs on one finger, her eyes vacant.

"It's about that time, gents," Shaw said.

"We got some time," Savage said again.

"What if the train's early?" Shaw asked.

Savage frowned. Lo Grande clapped his hands. "You have a good man there, *rinche*. I like the way he thinks." He tapped his temple. "*Muy* intelligent. Takes no chances. He might ride for me someday."

"All right." Savage eased his .44 into the holster. "Let's go."

"*Bueno*. I will cut this *puta*'s throat and we shall ride."

"No." Savage's command came out like a bullet.

Lo Grande turned. Grace's fingers balled into fists.

"Amigo," Lo Grande said. "It is —"

"Don't quote your Shakespeare, Lo Grande. It ain't right."

"What? That I quote Shakespeare? He was a brilliant writer, my friend."

"That's not what I mean." Though, Savage thought, it wasn't right for Juan Lo Grande, a damned Mexican, to be quoting an English writer, a white man. He pointed at the Terlingua whore. "You leave her be. You're not harming a woman."

"We cannot leave her here."

"Where's she going? She'll stay here."

"But —"

"No buts. She stays here. She stays alive." Hell, she was half dead already, thanks to Lo Grande and his men.

"But she can tell the law —"

"The law'll know who we are and what all we've done whether that whore's alive or not. She stays. She lives." His hand rested on the butt of the Merwin Hulbert. "You want to argue that point?"

Slowly, Lo Grande shook his head. "No. It will be as you say, el capitán."

Savage figured that son of a bitch would send some of his riders back there after they'd left, to ravage and kill Linda Kincaid. He didn't like that, but didn't know how he could stop it from happening. Then he realized that would be two less bandits he'd have to worry about.

The Mexican tilted his chin at Grace. "But what of her?"

Savage helped her out of the chair. "She comes with us."

Grace looked up at him, curious.

He'd be damned if he'd let Lo Grande's men get their hands on her. Besides, she might come in handy. "Just in case," Savage said, smiling with his lips if not his eyes. "I promised I'd buy you a new saloon, Grace. Remember?"

CHAPTER TWENTY-FIVE

For thirty minutes, they stood among the Mexican walnut trees, Dave Chance and Don Melitón Benton, watching, waiting. Behind them Moses Albavera held the reins to the horses, making sure the animals kept quiet. The morning sun warmed them, shining through the massive branches. The only noise came from the bleating of the sheep, and the trickle of water flowing over rocks in Calamity Creek.

Finally, Don Melitón spoke, his voice bitter. "I should have known better than to believe anything you told me, *rinche.*"

Chance's stomach knotted. He tried flexing his fingers in his throbbing left hand, let out a sigh, and stepped into the clearing. Slowly, he turned, looked back at Albavera, as if seeking reassurance. The black man's face was blank. Running his hand across the beard stubble on his face, shaking his head, Chance turned back and studied the compound of La Oveja.

Deserted.

How could he have guessed wrong? He took off his hat, and ran his fingers through his hair. He would have sworn he had been right. Savage and Lo Grande had to be there. It had all seemed so palpable. He studied the compound again. Something wasn't right.

"Where are your Rangers, señor? Where is Juan Lo Grande?" With contempt, Don Melitón spat in the dust, and strode toward the horses.

It hit Chance suddenly. He finally figured out what was wrong. "Where's your sheepherder?" Chance called out defiantly. "Where's his grandson?"

That stopped the old man. Sheep were scattered everywhere.

"Ground's been chewed up by horses," Albavera said. "And, unless my eyes are failing me, there's a lot of horse dung in those corrals."

The old man turned, his face solemn, the anger gone.

A moment later, a horse whinnied.

The sound of hooves echoed down the canyon, and Don Melitón and Chance rushed to the horses, putting their hands over the animals' muzzles. Chance drew his

Schofield, easing back the hammer. The three men looked down the trail. A few minutes later, two horses splashed across Calamity Creek and came into view.

In a mighty big hurry, two Mexicans loped down the path, scattering ewes, and rode through the open gate at the stone fence. The taller one said something, prompting a chuckle from the fat, gray-bearded one, as they reined in their mounts, and swung down from the saddles, wrapping the reins around the top post of one of the corrals. The tall man ran into one of the buildings. The fat one took the other.

Inside the closest building, a woman screamed.

Chance took off running.

He was through the stone fence, gun in hand, heading toward the corrals when the heavy graybeard stormed through the open door, hurrying to the other building. He spotted Chance charging toward him out of the corner of his eye. The fat man slid to a stop, shouting, "Eladio! Eladio!" He jerked an old cap-and-ball pistol from his waistband.

Chance fired. Dust flew off the adobe wall next to the big man's head. Still running, Chance snapped off another shot.

The Mexican jumped to his right, rushing

his shot. The bullet sailed far to Chance's left. He didn't even break stride, and pulled the trigger again. The big man dropped to a knee.

At that moment, the tall one, Eladio, appeared in the doorway, his laugh dying in his throat. He shoved a figure behind him, reaching for a silver-plated pistol in a concho-studded holster on his left hip. *"Esta es mía,"* he said, thumbing back the hammer on his Remington.

Chance fired again, still running. The fat man's head exploded in a fountain of crimson, and Chance dived to his left. Another gun roared. The tall Mexican stopped laughing and started screaming as he fell, his left arm shattered by the chunk of lead fired from Moses Albavera's sawed-off Springfield.

Chance loosed a shot that splintered the doorjamb. The Mexican pulled himself to his knees, tried to slam the door, but it stopped about halfway open. By then, Chance was on the portal, catching his breath. His eyes found the fat Mexican, dead. Breaking open the Schofield, he ejected the spent shells, and filled every cylinder with a live round.

Moses Albavera flung himself on the other side of the door. He, too, quickly reloaded his rifle.

The two men's eyes met.

Before Chance could speak, a shout came from inside. The language was Spanish, the voice pained, rapid, as if he spoke while grimacing. Albavera shot Chance another look.

"He's talking too fast for me," Chance said. "You catch any of that?"

Albavera shook his head.

Don Melitón spoke, his voice calm as he walked across the yard. "He says if you come inside, he will kill the girl."

"What girl?" Albavera asked.

The old man shrugged. He reached down and pried the old revolver from the dead Mexican's hand.

They heard another panicked shout in Spanish.

"He says for you to drop your pistols. To back away toward the corral."

More shouts.

"He says to do this now. He does not want to harm the girl."

Chance seethed.

The Spanish continued.

"He says he will not hurt you, either. All he wishes to do is to mount his caballo and return to Juan Lo Grande."

The Mexican yelled a final demand.

"Do so, now, he says, or the girl will begin her stay in Purgatory."

Don Melitón examined the revolver in his hand, then let it fall atop the dead man's back, and walked toward the corral. Swearing an oath underneath his breath, Chance laid the Schofield on the flagstone portal, and began backing his way toward the corral, slipping one hand behind his back, near the Smith & Wesson .32. Albavera shook his head, but finally leaned the sawed-off Springfield against a cottonwood column, and joined the old man and Ranger at the corral. The don called out in Missouri Spanish, and, a short while later, the tall Mexican, his face soaked with sweat, his left arm dripping blood, appeared behind the ashen face of Linda Kincaid.

The tall man stopped when he saw the body of his comrade, and slowly brought up the Colt, using it to make the sign of the cross over Linda's chest. He whispered something to her, and she stepped forward, slowly easing toward the two horses tethered to the corral, the barrel of the pistol pressed against her ear. The bandit's eyes shot from Chance to Albavera to the don, and back again.

Stopping, the Mexican waved the pistol at the three men, who carefully moved away from the horses until they stood beside the well.

He spoke to Linda in Spanish, but she didn't understand. He swore, backed to the posts, and tried to use his left arm to grab the reins to a lathered bay gelding. His arm wouldn't work. He spoke again, a hoarse shout, and grabbed the reins with his gun hand, releasing Linda, using the horse as a shield.

Chance's hand tightened on the butt of the .32.

The horse, frightened by the smell of blood, snorted and began backing away. Twisting its head, it started to rear, and then the Mexican was on the ground, facedown. Linda ran toward Don Melitón, and the horse galloped out of La Oveja.

Water splashed against the man's paling face, and his eyes fluttered open as he groaned. Reaching for his left arm, he found it wrapped tightly with a dirty rag torn from his shirt. The three men standing above him slowly came into focus. Beyond them stood the *puta* from Terlingua.

Don Melitón dropped the gourd ladle, and knelt beside the bandit. He spoke softly in Spanish. The Mexican, growing defiant, snapped a response.

The don cuffed him with his backhand. He asked the same question in the same tone.

The Mexican swallowed. He asked for water.

Don Melitón's head shook. He repeated the question.

That time, the Mexican answered.

"They left last night," the don translated.

The Mexican spoke again, rapidly, fervently, until he was out of breath. His face became a mask of pain. Groaning, he reached over and tugged on his left shoulder, pulling up his knees, biting his bottom lip. He gasped out something else.

"He asks if I will carry his confession to his priest in San Pedro," Don Melitón said.

"We don't have that much time," Albavera said.

The don spoke again. The Mexican stared at him, lips trembling, tears streaming down his face, and he answered. Then began crossing himself, muttering a prayer, a confession. Whatever it was he was saying, he never finished, for Don Melitón drew the revolver he had retrieved from the dead bandit's back, thumbed back the hammer, and while Chance was reaching for the pistol, shouting, "No, damn it, no!" the gun roared, so close it burned the Mexican's face. The bullet tore through the man's nose and blew out the back of his skull.

"Damn it!" Chance swore, kicking a loose stone across the grounds. "Damn you all to hell, Don Melitón."

Albavera hooked a thumb at Chance stomping back and forth. "In case you were wondering, old man, he wanted him alive."

"This *pendejo,*" the don said tightly, "killed Miguel Aquiles and Romolo, the grandson of my sheepherder." He shoved the revolver into his sash, his hands trembling, his eyes welling with tears. "Romolo was only thirteen years old. This *hijo de la puta* did not deserve to draw another breath for one second longer. He and his *amigo*" — Don spat in the direction of the dead fat man, still on the portal in a lake of drying blood — "came back here to ravage this woman" — he pointed at Linda — "and then kill her."

"Why did they leave her alive?" Albavera asked.

"Captain Savage."

The woman's voice startled the three men. They seemed to have remembered her presence only when she spoke.

"Lo Grande was going to kill me. Captain Savage said no. He wouldn't let him." She sank to her knees, and began sobbing.

Chance slipped between the don and Albavera, knelt beside the crying prostitute, and put his arm around her shoulder. "That's all right, ma'am. Go ahead and cry. Let those tears run their course."

She buried her head into his shoulder. He put his other arm around her back, pulled her close, and squeezed her tightly.

They had ignored her. Well, not ignored. They'd left her alone. It hadn't occurred to them, as frightened as she had appeared, so wrecked, so brutalized, to ask her anything. Until she had spoken.

"Was Grace here?" he asked.

"Yes," was her choked reply.

"Where . . . ?" Chance couldn't finish.

"The captain took her." She straightened, twisted her head, bit her lip, and sucked in a deep breath. When she exhaled, she said, "Captain Savage said he might need her. In case something went wrong."

"They're going to rob the Southern Pacific?" Chance asked.

She nodded.

"Murphyville?"

"I'm not sure."

Albavera cleared his throat. "Train's not due in Murphyville till Sunday. That —"

"That's not true." She shook her head. "I heard them talking. Savage was talking to

335

Grace. Lo Grande had me. We listened outside the door. Then we went inside."

"The train's due Sunday, ma'am," Chance said.

She shook her head again. "That's just what they wanted everybody to think. The train's due" — she swallowed — "Saturday."

Today!

Chance fell back against the corral post. He brought his pointer finger to his mouth, considering what Linda Kincaid had just told him. He looked up at Albavera, then over to the don.

"No, now I remember." Linda's head bobbed. "Captain Savage said he'd ride those rails all the way to Sanderson. He said that when we were listening, Lo Grande and me. They are going to Murphyville. I guess they'll take the eastbound to Sanderson."

Chance reached over his head, gripped a pole, and pulled himself to his feet. "The schedule at Marathon said Sunday." He looked at Albavera for confirmation.

The Moor nodded. "But a couple S.P. workers from Sanderson told me they were ordered to get that telegraph wire repaired by Saturday. Said it twice." He tilted his head at Linda Kincaid. "I think she's right. Railroad brass, the law, they wanted everyone to think the train would be coming in a day later than it really is."

"Or this is a special run."

"Regular train comes through Sunday. Sure. That makes sense."

"Savage will leave the train in Sanderson."

Albavera was nodding. "I saw a bunch of freight wagons in town. Empty. Right by the railroad tracks."

"But there is no town to speak of south of Sanderson," Don Melitón spoke. "That is Coahuila. Lo Grande never goes that far east. He is a Chihuahua man."

Chance wet his lips. "Maybe that wasn't part of Lo Grande's plan."

"It wasn't." Linda Kincaid told them of the conversation she had heard in the dining room of La Oveja just hours earlier.

They grained and watered their horses. Chance tightened the cinch on the saddle of the buckskin the fat Mexican had ridden in on, and took Linda Kincaid's hand, helped her into the saddle, then swung up on the black mare.

"We'll never make it to Murphyville in time," Albavera said as he mounted his horse.

"I don't intend to try."

Albavera's eyes brightened. "The train. Mickey McGee."

Chance nodded.

The don mounted his horse.

Turning to Linda, Chance said, "Miss Kincaid, we're going to have to ride mighty hard, over some rough country. You sure you don't want to stay here?"

Her eyes told him she never wanted to see La Oveja again.

Chance bit his lip. He didn't like it. But he had no choice.

He tugged on the rein, started to urge the black out of the compound, when a bullet tore off the horn on his saddle. The bay mare pitched, but Chance was already flying out of the saddle, the Schofield practically leaping into his right hand.

He hit hard in a cloud of dust. Horses screamed. Bullets whined. Albavera cursed, came past him, jerked Linda Kincaid from the saddle, and fell on top of her.

Chance rolled over. Dust stung his eyes. He blinked, making his eyes hurt worse. A bullet clipped the snubbing post in the corral. Chance crawled to the side of the well, came up in a seated position, filled his lungs, and tried to find a target.

As the wind took the dust away, he saw Don Melitón dropping the reins to his horse, calling out something in Spanish, standing in the open, unafraid. The Colt revolver remained in the old man's sash. He continued to speak in Spanish, walking toward the open gate, holding his hands over his head, palms outward. Not offering to surrender, but telling those shooters in the walnuts and cottonwoods to hold their fire.

Suddenly, it hit Chance. Those bullets hadn't come from Juan Lo Grande's men, or Hec Savage's. They were the don's vaqueros, who had made damned good time.

"It's all right," Chance called over to Albavera.

He started to holster the .45, started to stand, then thought better of it. He shot Albavera a worried glance.

He mouthed the words, *Or is it?*

CHAPTER TWENTY-SIX

Thick clouds of smoke belched out of the 4-4-0 American Standard locomotive as it slowed, hissing steam. It groaned to a stop in front of the Murphyville depot, which was nothing more than an old piece of rolling stock that had been set up alongside the iron rails. Hec Savage gripped a lamppost and leaned over, checking out the rest of the train.

A tender. Three cars. A caboose.

Good. No passengers. Except for the guards behind those bolted doors of the boxcars.

He swung back, nodding a good morning at the smut-faced engineer and fireman as they climbed out of the engine and onto the platform. Two of Savage's men were already bringing down the arm to the water tank over the tender, jerking the chain, letting water replenish the tank. The fireman went over to help, but one of the Rangers, Tom O'Brien, told him, "That's all right, pal. Me and Joe's got it. Go get yourself some break-fast."

"Thanks," the fireman said. "Reckon we'll do just that."

From the caboose came a fat man, panting, as he hurried alongside the tracks.

So far, so good. Letting out a sigh of relief, Savage looked across the street at Murphyville.

The town rested in a valley in the Davis Mountains foothills, most of it along a creek that ran along the foot of a small mountain. Tents and dugouts were slowly being replaced by adobe structures, log cabins, even a few frame buildings with their white-washed false fronts. Typically, the streets and saloons would be full on a Saturday, with railroaders, cowhands, and the wives and daughters of ranchers coming in to do their shopping. That morning, however, the streets were empty. Every shade of every building along Front Street was pulled shut. Even the bakery hadn't opened, although the fireman and engineer crossing the street hadn't noticed yet.

The good residents of Murphyville knew their place, and their place that day was inside. They'd seen or heard Savage and Lo Grande and their men ride into town before dawn.

"Are you Capt'n Savage?" The conductor whipped a handkerchief, already sopping wet, from the pocket of his corduroy jacket, and mopped his face.

Savage tapped his badge. "I am."

The man started talking, but Savage hardly listened. He was looking over the fat man's shoulder, staring at those cars, wondering if one of the doors would open. They didn't.

"Who are those men?" the fat man blurted out.

When he turned, Savage saw Doc Shaw and Oliver Drago climbing into the 4-4-0's cab.

"Relief for your crew," Savage told him.

"I don't know 'em."

"You know every engineer and boiler-man on the Southern Pacific?"

The man returned the wet handkerchief to his pocket. "I know Dickie Gleason. He's supposed to be replacin' Aaron West here. Hey! Hey, you there!"

He charged forward like a bull, pointing a stout finger at Doc Shaw, who hung out of the cab's opening, staring, uncertain.

"Where the hell's Dickie Gleason?" the man boomed.

"Dead." Savage's answer stopped him. He spun around, and his mouth opened in protest when he spotted the Merwin Hulbert in Savage's right hand. "Join him."

The .44 cut short the fat man's cry. Savage waved the barrel of the smoking gun at Shaw, motioning him to hurry, and started off the platform. He never bothered looking at the man he'd just shot, nor the engineer and fireman as they stopped in the middle of Front Street, halfway to the bakery. A cannonade erupted from the alley between the hotel and butcher's shop, and the two railroaders crumpled into the dirt.

Rangers P.G. Foner, Harry Jones, and Munge McSween quickly joined Savage in mid-stride as the other Rangers poured out of the boxcar-turned-depot. From behind the barn and livery, Mexican bandits rode up and down Front Street. Others leaped from their hiding places in the alleys, or on rooftops.

Savage and his three men reached the first car. He looked across the street, nodded, and saw Juan Lo Grande fire a round that sang off the coupling. Savage banged the butt of his .44 against the door.

"Open up, Lieutenant. It's me. Hec Savage. Texas Rangers."

No answer. Another bullet thudded in the car above Savage's head.

"Damn it, open up!" He nodded an unspoken order at Foner, Jones, and Mc-Sween, and the Rangers jerked out their revolvers. They fired at the Mexican raiders — the bullets flying harmlessly well over their heads.

"Open up!" Savage thundered.

Above the din of gunfire, the pounding of hooves, and the whistling from the engine, Savage thought he heard a reply. "I have my orders."

Savage rammed the Merwin Hulbert harder. "The hell with your orders. We're under attack."

"I'm sorry."

Savage swore under his breath. He looked at Harry Jones, and shot him in the groin.

Jones fell, gripping his crotch, screaming in agony. The faces of Foner and McSween turned pale. They stopped shooting and stared at Savage, wondering if they'd catch the next bullet.

"Damn it, Lieutenant!" Savage yelled. "My men are getting cut to pieces out here." Another bullet punctuated his statement. So did Jones's pitiful wails.

"The game's up," Savage said. "Let us in. Else we're all dead."

On the ground at Savage's feet, Jones began pulling a Colt from his holster. Savage shot him in the head.

"For the love of God, man!" Savage banged on the door again.

The door opened, and a young man in a blue blouse and trousers reached down, offering Savage his gloved right hand. Another man knelt beside the lieutenant, jacked a round in his Winchester, and fired, knocking one of Lo Grande's men out of the saddle.

Savage let the lieutenant pull him inside. He hit the floor, rolled over, and filled his lungs with the musty air from the cramped, dark boxcar. P.G. Foner and Munge McSween went in right behind him, and the door slammed shirt. The lieutenant rammed the bolt shut, but not before the man with the Winchester fired another shot.

"This all the men you got?" Savage asked. He counted four, not including the lieutenant.

"Six each in the other two cars." The lieutenant had broad shoulders, a hawkbeak nose, pockmarked face, and a cleft in his chin.

The train lurched forward, slamming the lieutenant against the wall. He caught himself, did a little dance, and regained his balance.

"Where's the Gatling gun?" Savage asked.

"Right here, Capt'n," an Irishman answered. He was feeding a magazine into the top of the gun.

"We're moving," the lieutenant said.

Just like that, the train stopped, and the lieutenant stumbled forward. Savage managed to catch him, keeping him upright. The man stank of sweat, his breath smelling like a week's worth of cigarettes.

"Thanks," the lieutenant began, but the word caught in his throat as he felt the Merwin Hulbert's muzzle pressed against his stomach. The gun roared, igniting the blue blouse, and the lieutenant fell on his back, choking on the blood that filled his throat, and poured from the corners of his mouth.

Munge McSween shot the Irishman by the Gatling gun. P.G. Foner rammed a Bowie knife to the hilt underneath the ribs of the guard closest to him, ripped the blade loose, and slashed the throat of another man, who was fumbling with the flap on his holster. Savage and McSween shot the last man at the same time, Savage's bullet tearing into the redhead's heart, McSween's piercing his back.

Smoke filled the car, stinging the eyes of each Ranger. Savage grabbed a hat off the floor, and beat out the flames on the dead lieutenant's chest. He made a beeline for the door, coughing, then telling McSween,

"Get that Gatling ready. Move it to the door. Cover the street."

Light shown through as the door swung open, and Savage leaped down from the car, holstering his revolver, and moving down the tracks toward the next boxcar. Lo Grande's men stayed in the streets, or on the roofs, peppering the final car with gunshots. Savage tried to still his heart, found himself sweating like that conductor he'd left dead on the platform. He looked down at the depot, saw Demitrio Ahern hurrying Grace Profit out of the building, off the platform.

"Take her to the caboose," Savage ordered. "Be damned quick."

Ahern rushed past Savage, half dragging Grace behind him, and shoved her onto the platform at the back of the caboose, then turned, thumbed back the hammer of his Sharps, and stood there waiting.

Joe Newton and Tom O'Brien, who had been filling the tank with water, scrambled into the tender, and lay atop the pile of wood, aiming Winchesters at Lo Grande's men.

From the livery stable ran Steve Coffman, Bill Barr, and J.K. Scheidner, hauling buckets in each hand, liquid sloshing on the streets, splashing their chaps as they ran.

Coffman and Barr doused the side of the second car. Scheidner ran to the third car, threw the contents from his two buckets onto the bullet-riddled frame of that car.

Savage shot another glance at Lo Grande, then used the butt of his .44 as a knocker.

The gunfire fell silent.

"All right, gents," he said. "We've just given this box car a bath of coal oil. I don't have much time. You step out, and live. Or you stay in, and fry." With his left hand, he pulled out his pocket watch, opened the case, and said, "You have ten seconds to make up your minds, or burn alive."

He wet his lips.

"One. Two."

Those guards had their orders, just like the guards who worked for the express companies. Stay in the express car (fortified special boxcars, in this case). Keep the door locked. Open it for no one. If someone breaches the door, kill him. Defend that payroll with your life.

Hell of a price to pay for fifty dollars a month.

"Three. Four."

The door opened. A revolver flew out. Then a handful of Springfield rifles and other pistols. Six men eased through the door, and jumped down, hands held high.

They stood there, panting, praying, and sweating.

"If I were you," Savage said, "I'd go that way." He pointed at the opening between the two cars. "You head to that street, Juan Lo Grande will kill you."

The guards did as he said, footing it toward the Davis Mountains foothills. From the streets, he heard Spanish curses. Lo Grande bellowed something, but Savage kept walking down the side of the tracks to the third car, turning just long enough to see Coffman and Barr climb into the second car.

From the hotel's roof, a rifle popped. Savage looked up, saw one of Lo Grande's butchers firing at the guards fleeing toward the hills. He couldn't tell if those bullets were finding their targets, and he really didn't care. He knocked on the door of the car in front of the caboose, and yelled at its occupants. The wood, reeking of coal oil, would burn like a tinderbox. They could live, he said, or roast. Their fellow guards were running for their lives. He'd give them ten seconds.

Those men had a lot more mettle. Savage reached ten, and struck a match across his gunbelt. The lucifer flamed to life. "Match is lit, boys. Once this fire starts, nobody leaves that car alive."

"Hold it!" came a quick shout, and the door slid open.

The guns came out first, then the men, and again, Savage directed the guards to start hoofing it toward the hills. They ran, but Lo Grande's men didn't try to gun them down. Savage had figured they wouldn't. Now, they'd want to save their ammunition.

To use on the Rangers.

"Amigo!" Lo Grande reined in his horse.

"Get in the car," Savage told Scheidner. Ignoring Lo Grande, Savage started walking toward Ahern and the caboose.

"Amigo, mi capitán, wait. We have done it." Lo Grande eased his horse closer to the tracks, but the animal danced nervously, and he gave up a few yards from the tracks. Still grinning, he said, "We are rich, amigo. Rich beyond your wildest dreams."

Now, Savage thought, as he reached the caboose, gripped the wrought iron railing with his left hand, put his right hand on the butt of one of his revolvers. *Now comes something from William Shakespeare.*

" 'But be not afraid of greatness; some are born great, some achieve greatness and some have greatness thrust upon 'em.' "

"Which are you?" Savage called out. He

climbed onto the platform. He didn't care what Lo Grande said, just wanted to keep that son of a bitch talking. He put his hand on the doorknob.

"Amigo. *Por favor,* I cannot let you go inside that caboose."

Smiling, Savage released the handle, and turned to face Lo Grande. The Mexican's smile vanished. He looked up and down the train, noticing for the first time, that Savage's men were well hidden. That train made a hell of a fort, and most of Lo Grande's men were in the street. Sitting ducks.

Just like Lo Grande himself.

"I'm afraid," Savage said, "that this train has a schedule to keep."

He drew as he ducked, heard Demitrio Ahern's Sharps boom from the far side of the caboose, and saw a Mexican spill out of his saddle. Smoke and flame belched out of the first car, then the two other Gatling guns joined in, spraying Front Street with lead. Horses reared, screamed, fell, and died. Riders were cut to ribbons. Dust flew off the ground like grasshoppers.

Lead ripped into the facade at the top of the hotel. The bandit stood, twisting in a macabre dance, and somersaulted off the roof, crashing through the awning and landing on the boardwalk. The Gatling swept across the other rooftops, ripping through wood, adobe, and the bodies of the sharpshooters Lo Grande had placed there.

Savage snapped a shot, but Juan Lo Grande, lucky bastard, had slipped over the saddle of his horse. The horse went down, and Lo Grande took cover behind the dead animal.

The train jerked, almost spilling Savage. A bullet whined off the iron railing. Another shattered the window to the door. He recovered, aimed, and pulled the trigger. The wheels to the engine spun, caught, and the train moved, slowly at first. Gunfire roared again from two of the boxcars. Ahern's rifle barked. The air smelled of brimstone and death. A horse galloped past. Savage fell back, and fired again. Reaching up, he grabbed the doorknob, fell inside, and kicked the door shut. The far door opened, and Demitrio Ahern slipped into the caboose, working the breech to ram in another big shell.

Lying on the floor, face pale, hands covering her ears, was Grace Profit. She looked up.

Hec Savage smiled.

The train began picking up speed. Doc Shaw had said he reckoned that the engine would top out at maybe fifty miles a hour. They'd leave Lo Grande's men — what was left of them, anyway — far, far behind. Should have enough time to unload their fortune in Sanderson, and light a shuck for Mexico.

A final burst from one of the Gatling guns rang out as the 4-4-0 locomotive pulled Hec Savage, his surviving Rangers, Grace Profit, and two hundred and fifty thousand dollars worth of gold bullion east, out of Murphyville, toward Marathon and Sanderson.

CHAPTER TWENTY-SEVEN

Smoke hung about the ceiling of the boxcar, which reeked of the acrid stench of gunpowder and stale sweat, but to Hec Savage the place smelled of wealth. Sunlight beaming through the open side door reflected off the gold bar he held in his hands, and he couldn't help himself. A tear or two almost welled in his eyes, and he practically giggled like a schoolgirl. The bar had to weigh close to twenty-five pounds. He tried to figure that out: Twenty-one dollars an ounce at twenty-five pounds? It was too damned complicated for him.

He looked up, beaming, and saw a grinning J.K. Scheidner with a doctor's stethoscope hanging around his neck. He heard Demitrio Ahern mumble something. He stood, weaving as the boxcar rocked, and brought the bullion bar closer to his chest. Grace Profit was looking at him, the wind rushing through her hair, her eyes on the safe Scheidner had just opened.

"Maybe," Savage said, "you're thinking, 'By God's grace, Captain Savage was right. He can afford to buy me that fancy saloon in Argentina.' Maybe you're thinking, 'Lord, Hec Savage isn't so repulsive after all.' Is that it, Grace?"

She turned, looked out the open side door, and watched the desert fly past her.

"You want me to open up those other safes, Capt'n?" Scheidner asked. "In the other boxcars?"

Savage staggered back against the wall, amazed again by the weight of the bar. He knew when he'd hired J.K. Scheidner that having a safecracker on the payroll might come in handy, but he had been thinking if they happened to find some old strongbox some outlaws had taken from a bank, or if they managed to raid Juan Lo Grande's fortress south of the border. He'd never expected to have this.

He moved back, and looked into the safe. Nine other bars sat there, so damned beautiful. Ten bars were likely in the other safes in the other boxcars.

"Capt'n?" Scheidner asked again.

"No," Savage said. "And keep that door there locked." He pointed to the regular door at the front of the car. Those weren't ordinary boxcars. They were built like a fort, with heavy, reinforced doors in the front and back, and the regular sliding door on the side, all equipped with bolts thick and heavy as railroad spikes. The walls of the cars were so thick none of the bullets fired by Lo Grande's men had come close to penetrating them. "Don't want to tempt the boys. You'll open the other safes when we reach Sanderson."

It had taken Scheidner only twenty minutes to open that one. He could be cracking those safes while they hitched up teams to the wagons once they were in Sanderson.

"Let's go," Savage said. Clutching the bar tight against his heart, he headed back for the caboose.

Horses stomped around the compound of La Oveja, slaking their thirst from the troughs by the corrals.

Don Melitón spoke sharply in Spanish to two of his vaqueros. They answered, *"Sí, patrón,"* and one of them helped Linda Kincaid into the saddle before the two men mounted their own horses, and led the Terlingua whore through the stone fence and toward Calamity Creek.

"They will take her west to the town of Marfa," Don Melitón told Chance. "That seems to be the safest place. For now."

Chance nodded. He looked at his left hand. He should change that dirty bandana he had used for a dressing, and clean up the wound, but had no time.

"They will stay with her until they hear otherwise from me. If Captain Savage or Juan Lo Grande want her, they will have to go through Benito and Tomás."

That, Chance figured, would take a lot of doing. Linda was safe. Now all he had to worry about was Grace Profit.

After he gathered the reins to the black mare, Chance swung into the saddle. Beside him, Moses Albavera was already mounted. The don climbed with dignity onto the back of his horse, adjusted the stampede string to his hat, and stared hard at Chance, but did not pay any attention to the black man beside him.

"I hope to God you are right," the old man said. Chance took that as a warning. If he were wrong . . .

Well, he wasn't wrong. He knew that. Hoped he did, at least.

Across the flats, the mountains rising in the background, the train barreled down the tracks, the smell of smoke and cinders obscuring the aroma of coffee brewing on the stove in the caboose. Like a ship in gale seas, the car rocked violently, so much that Hec Savage had trouble maintaining his balance as he tried to grab a cup.

"How fast do you think we are traveling?" Demitrio Ahern asked.

"As fast as she'll go." Savage fell against the north wall, knocking a map to the floor, and, shaking his head, continued to weave his way toward the coffeepot.

"I hope Doc Shaw does not blow a boiler." Ahern looked seasick.

Savage had reached the stove. He loosened his bandana, using it to grip the handle of the pot, and filled his cup, splashing some of the liquid on the stove. He looked across the caboose, found Grace Profit rocking in her chair to the rhythm of the car's violent dance. "Coffee, Grace?"

She shook her head.

He turned toward Ahern, was about to ask him the same question, but Ahern had jerked the rear door open, stumbled outside, and was heaving over the back of the caboose. The door banked open and shut as Ahern vomited. Savage laughed, and tested the coffee, gripping the wall with his right hand. He looked at the desk beside the front door, saw that bar of gold sitting there, shining so brightly, so beautifully, and sipped more coffee.

While Albavera hurriedly threw wood into the furnace, Chance started to load their horses into the boxcar.

"No, you ain't!" Mickey McGee roared.

"Why the hell not?" Chance asked. He looked down the tracks. No smoke. No train. Not yet.

"Because I ain't killin' no horses," McGee said. "Rangers and colored boys . . . don't mind killin' them, but I ain't killin' no horses."

With that, McGee simply stuck his head back inside the cab, and helped Albavera stoke that fire.

Muttering an oath, Chance pulled the black mare away from the box, patted her side, and pulled off the headstall, tossing it into the cattle car on top of the saddle. He did the same with Albavera's horse, and both animals wandered off in search of something to graze. Chance walked toward the locomotive, having second thoughts about their plan.

He had suggested that they try to derail the train that would be coming from the west, maybe loosen the rails, maybe pile up rocks and debris on the tracks.

"We don't have the tools for that, or the

time," McGee had said.

"Well," Chance had suggested, "let's just stay here, and leave this train to block their way."

McGee was adamant — "Obtuse," Albavera had called him. "That would give them boys the advantage," McGee had replied. "I ain't givin' them vermin no chance at all. I'm takin' the fight to 'em."

Surprisingly, Don Melitón had agreed with the railroader. So had Albavera, and they had come up with another plan. As Chance gripped the railing on the old 4-4-0, Don Melitón rode up, his men right behind him.

"We might be able to slow that train, but we won't be able to stop it," Don Melitón said. "A horse cannot outrun a train, especially not as tired as our mounts will be."

"I know," Chance said. "I appreciate this."

Don Melitón and his vaqueros would be decoys, drawing fire from the outlaws on that train, while Chance, Albavera, and McGee . . . Chance shook his head.

Don Melitón pointed a long finger at Albavera. "As I told you at La Oveja, this changes nothing, pendejo. You and me'll settle our accounts after this is over." Just like that, he faced the Ranger again, tipped his hat at Chance. *"Vaya con Díos."*

Chance nodded a silent reply.

"*¡Hijo de la chinga!*" Ahern roared from the rear platform.

At first, Savage thought the half-breed Mexican was referring to his stomach woes, but suddenly Ahern was stumbling through the door, reaching for his Sharps.

About that time, one of the Gatling guns opened fire.

"Get down," Savage told Grace. He dropped his cup, drew a .44, and followed Ahern onto the platform. Another Gatling spoke up, kicking up dust a dozen or more yards in front of a bunch of hard-charging horsemen. Ahern knelt, pulled back the hammer, and squeezed the trigger. The carbine's bullet sailed harmlessly over one of the rider's heads.

"Hold your fire, damn it." Savage had to grip the iron railing to keep from being tossed off the caboose.

The front door swung open. Savage turned and aimed the Merwin Hulbert through the open rear door. He held his fire, as Scheidner threw his hands up, yelling, "Don't shoot, Capt'n. It's me!"

"Get back to that Gatling gun, man!" Savage snapped.

"I'm out of ammunition for it, Capt'n.

361

And those gents are out of range for my revolver."

One of the other Gatlings ceased firing.

Hell, it wasn't like anybody on that train could hit a moving target, not as bad as those coaches were rocking, as fast as that train was hauling. On the other hand, it wasn't like one of those riders could hit anybody on board.

Those thoughts had just crossed Savage's mind when Ahern sang out, *"Madre mía."*

Savage looked down. The Sharps carbine clattered on the platform, and bounced over the side, smashing in the dirt. Demitrio Ahern sank back against the caboose, both hands gripping his stomach. Blood poured between his fingers. He looked up at Savage, his eyes revealing shock, his face paling. He started to lift his right hand to begin the sign of the cross, but the caboose lurched, and Demitrio Ahern slumped against the iron rails. Another bullet thudded in the wooden wall of the caboose.

Savage dived back inside, and slammed the door shut.

Those riders were damned good shots.

"Where's Demitrio?" Scheidner asked.

"Dead." Savage danced across the floor to the other door. Crouching, he stepped onto the platform between the two cars, looked north, then south. The guns had fallen silent aboard the train, but the horsemen would loosen an occasional shot. Savage counted about a dozen riders on the southern side of the tracks. A bullet whined off a piece of iron. He looked to the north. Another dozen men on that side.

"Lo Grande's men?" Scheidner asked, as Savage returned to the caboose, and slammed the door shut.

"No." He holstered his gun. "I don't think so."

"Then who?"

"Don Melitón Benton's."

"That old man? What the hell would he be doing attacking a train? You think he knew about the gold? Think he's trying to rob this train for himself?"

Savage answered the Ranger with a withering stare.

Scheidner wet his lips, then ducked as another bullet thudded into the outside wall of the caboose. He gave his commander a hopeful look. "What are we gonna do?"

"Nothing," Savage said. He looked at the gold bullion. "We'll outrun those idiots. We'll —"

He never finished. The whistle screeched from the engine. Almost immediately, the brakes on the train squealed, showering the desert flats with sparks. The engine groaned. Savage slammed against the door, Scheidner slid across the floor and Grace was tossed out of her chair.

Cursing above the metallic noise of the brakes, Savage reached up, grabbed the doorknob, and started to pull himself up, then felt himself hurled backward, hearing a deafening roar, before his world turned black.

A gloved hand pulled the iron door open, blasting Dave Chance with heat, and he shoved in two more pieces of wood before the furnace door slammed shut. Moses Albavera helped pull him to his feet, and Chance, wiping the soot off his face, leaned against the back of the cab, caught his breath, and turned to fetch a couple pieces of wood from the tender. Albavera looked at the gauge on the boiler, and shot Mickey McGee an *I hope you know what the hell you're doing* look.

McGee leaned his head out the window, came back in, pushed the throttle, and held his breath.

"You hear something?" Albavera leaned out the locomotive.

Chance could barely hear the words over the roar of the engine. Albavera pulled himself back inside, rubbed his eyes. Both men heard the noise then, and McGee peered out the window. Chance set the pieces of wood on the floor, put his hand on the butt of the Schofield. McGee's hand pulled back on the throttle, and the train began to slow. He looked at his two helpers, and said, "Iffen I was you two, I'd disembark this locomotive right about now."

"You haven't stopped it yet," Albavera protested.

"This train don't stop. In fact, it's about to speed up."

McGee's eyes convinced Chance. As the train slowed, he leaned out the cabin, and launched himself into the air.

He landed on his moccasined feet, tumbling violently, uncontrollably over cactus, stones, and through one creosote bush. He heard the roar of the passing boxcar, and prayed his momentum wouldn't carry him back up the embankment, onto the rails, and under the wheels. Then the train was gone, and all Dave Chance could hear was the pounding in his head, and several yards away, the curses of Moses Albavera.

Spitting out sand and blood, Chance pulled himself to his feet. His left arm was broken between his wrist and elbow. He grabbed his hat, snagged on that creosote bush, and slammed it on his head. Blood seeped from his split lips, from his busted nose, down both arms. He pulled the Schofield from its holster, blew the dust off it, making sure it would still cock. He dropped it back into the holster, and reached for the Smith & Wesson .32, but it was gone. He looked down along the rails, but couldn't find it. By then he was standing over Albavera, who was sitting up, shaking his head, testing the sawed-off Springfield.

Chance extended his hand. Albavera took it, letting the Ranger pull him to his feet.

"You look like crap," Albavera said, wiping blood off his forehead.

"You're no Mona Lisa." Chance grimaced as pain shot up his left arm, which dangled uselessly at his side.

"What's the matter with your arm?"

"Broken."

"Wonder we didn't both break our necks." He shoved the Springfield into the holster. They took three steps, and stopped.

Black smoke belched out of the Schenectady locomotive as it sped down the tracks. Beyond that, another black 4-4-0 engine began screaming, whistle blaring, brakes sounding. About fifty yards from the tracks, Don Melitón's vaqueros reined in their horses.

The engine driven by Mickey McGee picked up more speed as he opened the throttle. As the other train tried to stop, men leaped from the top of the tender, out of the cab, and from one of the boxcars. At the last moment, Mickey McGee hurled himself out of the Schenectady engine.

"Christ Jesus Almighty," Dave Chance said, and closed his eyes. Doubt seized his mind. *What if I'm wrong? What if Savage and Lo Grande didn't rob that train? What . . . then?*

Chapter Twenty-Eight

The American Standard had slowed to a crawl when the Schenectady, going wide open, slammed into it with a crushing, earsplitting impact that lifted the Standard's rear wheels off the track, and sent the cattle car pulled by the Schenectady flipping over violently on the northern side of the tracks, the tender toppling over to the side. The Standard's drive wheels landed, and the engine fell on its side on the southern side of the track.

Tom O'Brien, the Ranger who had dived off the top of the tender before the trains collided, was trying to drag himself away. He turned, raising both hands as the 4-4-0 toppled on him, silencing his screams.

The first boxcar rammed into the tender, slamming it off the tracks on the northern side. Smashed and splintered, it fell on top of the tender. The second car also lurched to the northern side, rolling over on its top, side, top, before landing near the cattle car from the westbound train. The final boxcar cartwheeled over the wreckage of the Schenectady, collapsing the roof on impact. The caboose spun off to the southern side, flipped twice, coming to a rest on its wheels, which sank deep into the sand. Almost immediately, smoke poured from the open back door, then flames consumed the rear of the caboose. Flames also shot out from the wreckage of the second boxcar. Dust and smoke quickly obscured the scene.

It had happened in only seconds.

Then the boiler of the Schenectady exploded.

The eruption rocked the desert valley, sending chunks of metal and wood through the air like grapeshot. Two Rangers stumbling from the wreckage were cut down, a spray of pink mist marking their demise. On the southern side of the tracks, Don Melitón's vaqueros tried to control their horses. One mount fell dead, killed by a piece of metal that had penetrated its brain, pinning its rider under its dead weight. Another horse sent its rider sailing over his head, and took off in a gallop south, away from the carnage.

The explosion from the boiler knocked Chance off his feet. He staggered upright, holding his left arm, biting back pain. Ahead of him ran Moses Albavera, the Springfield in his hands. Chance cried out, and took a few steps, not knowing how much more he could endure, how much farther he could go. He pushed himself, then tripped. His legs refused to run. He careened along the sides of the tracks, chest heaving, arm throbbing, head pounding, ears ringing. Again he spit out blood, caught the scent of smoke, of death, and stopped beside a body lying a few rods from the rails.

Kneeling, Chance rested his right arm on Mickey McGee's shoulder. The Irishman's eyes fluttered open. "Hey, Davy. We stop 'em?"

"Yeah." He looked at McGee's legs, tucked underneath him at an ungodly angle.

"Them was the Constantine boys, wasn't they?" Blood seeped from the corners of the railroader's mouth, out of his nose, and ears.

The Constantines? That was a long time ago. "Yeah." Chance squeezed the shoulder. McGee didn't respond. Probably couldn't feel anything.

"I got Robert good, didn't I? Was Robert I got, wasn't it?"

"It was." Chance smiled weakly. "You stoved in his head with that sledgehammer."

"Better than drivin' spikes." McGee tried to grin, but coughed up a bloody froth. "Saved your life, didn't I?"

Chance nodded, pushed himself to his feet, and looked down the track at the bedlam.

"I bet the T&P'll give us all medals. I got Robert. You gunned down Will. Hell, I didn't even know you was packin' iron, Davy. Never seen you shoot a revolver before."

"Mickey," he said, not daring to look back at his friend's wrecked body. "I've got to go."

"I know, pard. You go on. You get Greg Constantine. Get him for me. I'll just rest . . . shut my eyes . . . for a wee bit."

Chance moved away, drawing the Schofield, coming to the hissing, creaking, steaming overturned American Standard engine. He looked across the tracks. Flames had enveloped the Southern Pacific car, had spread to the ruins of the nearby cattle car that the Schenectady had been pulling. Above the smell of grease, of oil, came the stench of burning flesh from inside that boxcar. Again, Chance closed his eyes.

The report of a pistol snapped him back to his senses.

Pushing himself away from the wrecked

engine, he saw the surviving Rangers running toward Don Melitón's men, firing, charging. Up ahead, Moses Albavera had dropped into a prone position, fired the sawed-off Springfield, and rolled onto his back, trying to feed another shell into the breech.

Chance shook his head. He staggered on, fell to his knees, and looked at the other cars. "Damn you, Mickey. You didn't tell me you planned on ramming that train. Derailing it might have injured some people, but not like this.

"Grace!" he called out.

Down the way a horseman stopped, slashed out with a large Bowie knife at a Ranger, but the horse stepped in a hole, and down went horse and rider. The Ranger, wearing a cap, not a hat, leaped over. They disappeared in the dust. When the horse stood up, and the dust had settled, it was Doc Shaw leaning low in the saddle, furiously whipping the horse with his Sharps, galloping south.

Shaw was getting away, but where was Hec Savage? In which car?

Chance looked back at the mass of metal that had been a 4-4-0. He had seen two men leap from the engine before the collision. Captain Savage wouldn't have been there.

That was too far from the gold. He looked at the smoke rising from one of the cars. Remembered the smell of burning flesh. Choked down bile.

The first car? The one lying on the other side of the tracks, by the tender? Maybe. He looked at the final car, crushed into kindling. Saw the smoke from the caboose. Saw the door shudder two times, three, then kick open.

Maybe Savage is dead? No, not that son of a bitch.

Vaqueros thundered across the rails from the northern side of the tracks. The last one reined in beside the caboose, and fired a round from the Spencer. Smoke and flame belched from the doorway, and the rider slid from the saddle. The horse turned, started to run, but stayed, held by the reins wrapped around the dead vaquero's wrists.

Suddenly, Chance's vision blurred. He closed his eyes, shook his head, and let his eyes open again. The flaming caboose was spinning, faster, faster, faster.

Chance looked at the pistol he held. He saw three Schofields, three hands, and then they, too, went blurry, and started spinning. He tried another tentative step, felt the Schofield slipping from his fingers, and crashed, falling hard, the warm sand rushing up to meet him.

Some woman was screaming. Grace wanted to tell whoever it was to shut the hell up. She opened her eyes, coughed from the thick smoke that stung her eyes, burned her lungs, her throat, and realized that those screams were coming from herself.

Determinedly, she made her mouth close, and the screaming stopped. She heard the crackling of wood, then a terrific explosion. The earth moved beneath her and she fell backwards. She pulled herself up, and fell immediately back onto the floor, her ankles burning with intense pain. Something trickled down her cheek, and she smelled, then tasted, blood.

Lifting her head, she tried to remember where she was. *The caboose. The train.*

She remembered.

Feeling the pain in her ankles again, she began swatting the smoldering hem of her skirt. At first, she thought they were on fire, but no. She reached up, found something to grip — the edge of the desk — and pulled herself up to her knees. Heat began to sear the side of her face, and she could smell the sickening stench of burning hair. She crawled across the floor, strewn with debris, away from the fire.

Suddenly, she realized something else, and desperation gripped her. If she didn't get out of that damned car, she'd be burned alive. She tried to stand, but the pain in her ankles shot up her legs, and she almost fainted. She dragged herself farther away from the thick smoke, the intense flames. Something stopped her. Turning, she saw the smashed face of the Ranger, Scheidner, his eyes open, only no longer seeing. She wouldn't have recognized him if not for the stethoscope hanging from his neck.

She choked back a cry, made herself crawl over his dead body, and touched something else, cold and hard.

The heavy bar of gold, the reflection of the flames shimmering.

Above her, fire swept across the ceiling. She made herself move faster, until she had backed into the wall. Turning, she saw the door, and she slid toward it. Reaching up, she gripped the knob, hot from the heat of the fire. The knob turned, and she pushed with her back against the door. It didn't budge. She bit her lip, sucked in fiery air that burned her lungs and made her cough. Squeezing her eyes shut, she pushed on the door again, harder, feeling the searing heat from the flames, choking on the smoke.

That woman started screaming again.

Something smashed her hand, and she let go of the knob, hearing a man curse. She opened her eyes, but could see little from the smoke. A hand grabbed her shoulder and pulled her up. The door flew open. Something popped. A gun. A revolver detonated close to her ear, leaving her momentarily deaf. The grip on her shoulder was released, and she fell onto the platform, sucking in cool, fresh air as she tried to pull her legs out of the burning caboose.

She thought she heard spurs singing out, heading back into the coach, then returning. Rough hands lifted her, and shoved her down the steps. She fell onto the dirt, and let out a loud yelp. Rolling over, clawing, pulling herself away from the burning caboose, she saw the hooves of a horse. A Mexican lying nearby was facedown, the reins wrapped around his wrist.

Boots thudded beside her. She heard another shot, smelled gunpowder. A horse raced by her, and she saw a rider, his boot caught in one stirrup, dragged through the creosote and prickly pear.

Suddenly, Grace felt herself being lifted.

"Come on!" a voice rang out, but she could barely make out the words. She looked, blinked, and realized she was being held by Captain Hec Savage. His nose was a bloody pulp, and a wicked gash creased his forehead.

Her head shook.

"Move!" She heard clearly him that time.

"I . . . can't." Biting back tears, she cried, "My . . . legs!"

"Damn." He grabbed her, and half dragged her to the horse.

"Hold it!" That wasn't Savage. Somebody else's voice sounded like it was coming from the deepest well.

A gun roared underneath Grace's arm. A groan followed, then a gasp, and a horse's whinny. The sound of something crashing to the ground was followed by the pounding of hooves.

She smelled the stink of leather and sweat.

"Get on!" Savage commanded.

"I can't," Grace wailed.

Savage cursed again. Holding her upright, he swung into the saddle. He reached down, pulled Grace up, throwing her arms and head over to the side, her stomach pressed between the saddle horn and the horse's neck. A rough hand slammed into her back, and stayed there. The gun roared again, then she felt herself bouncing around like a sack of grain, her head smashing against the horse. She smelled dust, vomited.

That woman wasn't screaming anymore.

She was cussing like a railroader.

Moses Albavera ran, holding the Springfield with both hands. He watched a Ranger ahead of him drop to his knee, bring up a Colt, saw the flash from the muzzle, and felt a bullet zip past his ear. Barely aiming, Albavera pointed the sawed-off rifle, and fired. The Ranger jerked, and fell hard on his back. As Albavera ran past him, he glanced at the dead man, recognizing him from Marathon. He had been one of those guys with Savage. What was the name? Newton. That's right. Newton.

Worthless bastard.

Not even slowing his pace, Albavera pushed out a bullet from the shell belt, and worked open the breech.

Riders came barreling across the flats from the west, from Murphyville.

Albavera slid to a stop. He wet his lips. "Who in the hell . . . ?"

He realized the answer before he had finished asking the question. Quickly, he came to his feet, signaling at Don Melitón's vaqueros, waving the Springfield in the direction of the approaching riders. "Lo Grande! Lo Grande!" he yelled, pointing at the men.

A vaquero looked at him, then toward the

riders, and shouted something in Spanish.

Several horses wheeled. One rider slipped from the saddle, then jacked a fresh round into the Spencer. The vaqueros opened up, spilling two — no, three — of Lo Grande's men from their saddles.

Albavera's rifle had been reloaded, and he didn't even remember doing it. He pulled back the hammer, dropped to his knee, aimed — but stopped himself. They were still out of range for a sawed-off rifle.

A horse whinnied, and Albavera turned, falling on his back, raising the Springfield. About a dozen riders came loping in from the east. More of Lo Grande's men?

Then we're finished.

Albavera sat up, and let out a cheer. They were white men. Railroaders from Sanderson. That merchant, Kipperman, and some other gents from Marathon — including the burly Mexican who'd damn near gutted Chance with a pitchfork when they had first arrived in Marathon.

They galloped past, firing, charging the Mexicans of Lo Grande.

Albavera stood. Letting the dust pass, he looked left, right. "Where the hell is Dave?" He realized he had asked the question verbally, though nobody could hear him. He turned, running behind the dust, hearing the gunfire, then a shout, *"¡Ándale! ¡Ándale!"* Through the dissipating dust, he saw, just like that, the Mexican bandits turning their horses, galloping south.

A bullet whined off a rock. Another Ranger screamed. Dropping his gun, he ran, stopped, and lifted his hands over his head.

The roof of the caboose collapsed as Albavera drew near. Turning his head, he shielded his face from the sparks and smoke that flew into the sky. When he lowered his arms, he saw the body of a vaquero lying near the ruins of the caboose. Then he saw another man, lying faceup in the sun, a gun in his hand, a bullet in his chest.

Albavera lowered his Springfield, tried to shove it in the holster, but missed, and let the weapon fall into the dirt. He swallowed, as best he could with a throat so dry, and kneeling, put his hand on the shoulder.

The eyes opened.

"¡Paren a ese hombre!" came a cry, and Albavera looked up. Vaqueros galloped or sprinted in his direction, every damned Spencer among them aimed at him. Keeping his right hand on the shoulder of the man lying in front of him, he raised his left hand into the air, and looked back down at Don Melitón Benton.

The old man moved his lips, spit out a

little trickle of blood, and said, "Don't worry."

Albavera eyes returned to those vaqueros coming at him. He quickly studied the area, hoping to find Dave Chance, or maybe Mickey McGee. He saw neither. He figured they were both dead . . . and that he'd likely soon join them.

"If it's just the same to you, Don Melitón," he said in a dull whisper, "I reckon I'll worry some. I reckon I'll worry a hell of a lot."

CHAPTER TWENTY-NINE

"You're a real ugly son of a bitch to wake up to."

Dave Chance ground his teeth against the pain shooting through his left arm, and let Moses Albavera gently pull his right arm until he was sitting in the sand by the railroad tracks. His vision blurred for a moment, and the air stank of death, of burning wood and oil. Smoke from the wreckage drifted across the sky like clouds. Horses snorted, stamped their hooves, and whinnied nervously. A few men cried piteously, *"Agua . . . agua . . . por favor . . ."* Men walked among the bodies and debris was strewn across the desert flats.

Chance screamed his bloody head off.

He practically doubled over when Albavera set the broken arm, spitting out tears and curses, pushing himself back up, slowly realizing that his left arm didn't hurt quite as bad as it had. After he caught his breath, he gave Albavera the coldest stare he could muster.

Albavera grinned. "Next time, you might watch who you're calling a real ugly son of a bitch. Especially considering how much your face has been worked over. Here. Let me brace that arm. I'll fashion a sling out of a bandana."

"I didn't know you were a doctor."

"I'm not. But I got plenty of experience in accidents."

"Where's Grace?" Chance asked after Albavera had braced the arm with a dead cactus limb and eased it through a bandana he had looped and tied around Chance's neck.

"Savage took her with him." Albavera jutted his jaw south.

Chance wet his lips. He let out a long sigh, one of relief. The answer he had expected was *She's dead.*

"I figure we'll be going after him." Albavera pulled Chance to his feet.

"I'm going after her."

"I'm riding with you."

Their eyes locked. Albavera pointed south. "Juan Lo Grande and about ten or twelve of his men rode after them."

"Damn."

"Uh-huh. And we don't have any horses."

"Sure we do." Chance pointed at several riderless mounts. "Already saddled."

"Well, before we light out of here, you'd better come with me. It's Don Melitón."

The old man's eyes slowly opened, saw Rodney Kipperman kneeling over him, his hands bloody. He searched the faces of the vaqueros who stood, shading him with their sombreros, solemn. At last, his eyes landed on Dave Chance.

"I am dying," he spoke quietly.

Chance's eyes dropped briefly. "I am sorry, Don Melitón."

Don Melitón answered with a curse more in line with a Missouri bushwhacker than a Spanish nobleman. "I want no pity." He swallowed, let out a little cough, and braced himself against the pain. For a long time, he squeezed his eyes tightly shut, his lips pressed together, sweat peppering his forehead. Rodney Kipperman, the Marathon merchant, wrapped strips of linen across the old man's bare chest.

"How is he?" asked someone in the crowd.

"I ain't no doctor," Kipperman snapped. "But you heard him."

The don's eyes opened again. "I want you, Sergeant Chance, to find the man who has killed me."

"That I plan on doing, Don Melitón."

The old man's head shook with surprising strength. "It was not Lo Grande. It was your *capitán,* Hec Savage."

"I figured that. I'll find him."

"Find him. Kill him."

"You got my word."

"Our word," Albavera added.

"This I want . . . more than I want to avenge the death of my son." His eyes moved to Moses Albavera. "You were right. Both of you. My son was worthless." He coughed.

"My vaqueros will attend to matters here. They will take me home" — the old man's voice began to fade — "to die. With dignity."

"*Sí, patrón,*" one of the vaqueros said.

"They will not molest you," Don Melitón said, and weakly lifted a finger toward Albavera. "You . . . are . . . free. . . ." He closed his eyes again, and his muscles relaxed.

Kipperman bent his head to the old man's chest. When he straightened, he said, "He ain't dead. Not yet anyhow."

A bearded vaquero knelt. "We will attend *el patrón.*"

Kipperman and all the Anglos in the crowd were dismissed. Slowly, Kipperman stood, wiping his bloody hands on a cloth rag. "You want us to come with you,

385

Ranger?"

"No." Chance shook his head.

"Are you out of your damned mind?" Albavera whispered in his ear. "Savage isn't alone. One of his Rangers rode out after him. Tall man with a big rifle."

"Doc Shaw," Chance said, guessing.

"That evens the odds, but we need to think about Lo Grande. He has a dozen men. Maybe more." Albavera put his hand on Chance's right shoulder. "We could use all the help we can get, pard."

Stubbornly, Chance pulled away from the big Moor. "Mickey McGee's lying over yonder, dead with a broken back. Don Melitón's lying here, about to be called to Glory. I'm not getting any other volunteers, any other amateurs, killed, Moses. Hec Savage is a professional. I'll do this alone."

"Not alone," Albavera said. "I'm a pro, too."

Chance faced the merchant. "I appreciate the offer, Mr. Kipperman, but I think it would be best if you and these men handled things here. Take Mickey McGee's body. Take real good care of Mickey." His voice started to crack. He stopped.

What was that he had told Moses Albavera? About the graveyard in Marathon? *It will get even more crowded before I'm all done.* Something like that. Only he had never expected one of those graves to be for a friend of his. He certainly hadn't planned on seeing Don Melitón Benton dead.

Without waiting for an answer from Kipperman, without another word, Chance spun on his heel, and started walking to a horse. Moses Albavera quickly caught up with him. "You can't even saddle your own horse. Not with that arm of yours."

"Like I said, the horse is already saddled."

He stopped by a dead man, pried a lever-action rifle from the man's hands. He worked the lever, blew dust off the rifle, and eased down the hammer. It was an 1881 Marlin, .40-60 caliber. Held ten shots. The dead man had a bandolier across his chest. And a Ranger badge. He looked at the dead man a little more closely.

"Munge McSween," he said, and jerked off the badge, pinning it to his own vest, replacing the one Don Melitón had ripped off back in Marathon. He fumbled with the buckle to the bandolier before Albavera mumbled something, and dropped beside him. "Here. Let me do that."

Chance didn't protest. Ten minutes later, they were riding south.

It felt like someone was slicing the bones in

her feet and legs with razors. Tears of pain blinded her as she bit down tightly on the stick Hec Savage had put in her mouth. The fire in her legs burned harder, and she broke the stick with her teeth, spit it out, cursed. Her fingers clawed into the hot sand. She prayed she would pass out, but her prayers went unanswered.

There was a final moment of agony, and suddenly the pain lessened — but didn't stop. Grace Profit figured she'd always be hurting, but those razors had quit cutting into her bones. Her fingers relaxed. She felt her head being lifted, felt a cool rag brushing the tears off her cheeks.

When Grace opened her eyes, she saw Hec Savage's battered, bruised face.

"I don't reckon you'll be trying to run away from me," he said with a smile. "Not with both of your ankles busted."

The rag vanished. A moment later, Savage brought a pewter flask to her lips, and she drank. That seemed to dull the throbbing in her ankles. She drank some more.

"Easy." Savage pulled the flask away from her, letting rye whiskey roll down her cheeks. "Save some for me, Grace." He took a swig, and dropped the flask into his pocket. "How do you feel?"

She didn't answer.

"Not much I can do." He looked around at the desert. Grace followed his gaze. They were shaded by a mountain to the west. She heard water trickling over rocks, and guessed they were on Calamity Creek. The mountain looked like Elephant Mountain, but that would mean they'd traveled a far piece since . . .

Since . . . what?

She tried to remember. Since the train had . . . derailed.

No . . . there had been a collision. The face of the dead Ranger in the caboose popped into her mind. It was a miracle she had survived. She remembered the heat, the smoke, the caboose on fire. Pictured Savage carrying her out. Pictured the man Savage had shot off his horse, Don Melitón Benton.

Savage's voice sounded tired. "I laced your boots up as tight as I could. That's about all I can do. For now. Till I get you to some old sawbones."

"In Argentina?" She realized those were the first words she had spoken. Her voice sounded strained.

Savage stared at her. The flask returned, but to Savage's lips, not hers. After swallowing, he shook his head. "I don't think one bar of gold bullion will get us all the way to Buenos Aires, honey."

"We could go to Terlingua." She swallowed. "Or, better yet, Fort Davis."

He smiled. "They might hang me in Terlingua. Besides, that's getting too close to Juan Lo Grande's country. And they'd definitely do me grave harm were I to show my face in Fort Davis. No, I'm still thinking if we can make it to the Río Grande, cross it, we can follow that river east. You up for that, Grace?"

There was no time to answer. Hoofbeats sounded, and Savage lowered her gently to the ground, gave her his hat as a pillow. He stood, drawing one of his Merwin Hulbert revolvers. She watched him step to the horse, using it as a shield, then heard the hammer click as he lowered it, and pushed the .44 into the holster.

The Ranger, Doc Shaw, rode into view, that big rifle cradled across his lap.

He eased the weary mount past the captain and Grace, and she heard the mount drinking water from the stream. Shaw grunted as he dropped from the saddle.

"Well?" Savage asked.

"Lo Grande's got his men spread out. Cutting for sign."

"How many men does he have?"

"I couldn't tell. Eight at the least. Fifteen, sixteen at the most." He drank water from a canteen. "But he could have some men south of here."

"Anybody else?"

"Not that I saw."

"All right."

Shaw spit. "No, Captain, it ain't all right. Our horses are worn out, and we can't keep riding in Calamity Creek to hide our trail forever. Look at that water, Captain. This creek'll be dry in two or three more miles. Besides, even if Lo Grande's men can't find our trail, it'll be obvious what we're doing. It's not like we can follow this creek north."

Silence. Grace tried to turn her head, but that made her legs hurt, so she gave up. Letting her head sink into Savage's hat, she stared at her feet, let out a sigh, and listened.

"We get to the Big Bend, closer to the river, we can hide out," Savage said. "Rest our horses."

"For how long?"

"I don't know, Doc," Savage thundered. "However the hell long it takes. Then we can sneak across the border, head east."

The silence returned, shorter this time.

"It's sixty," Shaw said, "maybe eighty miles to the river."

"I know that."

"Weather's warming up."

"Weather's not the only thing warming

up," Savage said. "I can feel Hell — so can you — if Lo Grande or the law catches us."

Shaw let out a sigh. "More than two hundred thousand dollars in gold . . . just . . . pissed away."

"Have a drink, Doc."

"Is this what I traded my badge, maybe my life, for, Captain? Two fingers of tequila."

"It's Manhattan rye."

"Oh, well, that makes it all worthwhile, don't it?" She heard him drink, heard the empty flask drop into the creek. "How's the strumpet?"

"She's no strumpet, Doc. She's a good woman."

"How is she?"

"Both ankles busted. I got her boots on tight."

"She can't walk."

No reply.

Shaw cleared his throat. "We've got Lo Grande's men behind us, trailing us. Only a matter of time before they find us. By now, Colonel Thomas must have every Ranger, every sheriff, every marshal, every man in Texas who can handle a gun on a train bound for Marathon or Murphyville. And Don Melitón —"

Savage's snort cut off Doc Shaw. The captain sounded jovial when he said, "We don't have to worry about that old fool."

Grace closed her eyes. She thought she might cry, not for her predicament, but for Don Melitón. He had always been a good man. To her, at least.

After that statement sunk in, Shaw continued. "Well, the Army will soon find out you didn't leave anyone in Fort Leaton — anyone alive, that is — and they'll be on your ass like a roadrunner on a rattlesnake. When I lit out after that wreck, there was a posse raising dust from Marathon-way, and I bet Murphyville has raised a posse by now. And that big ass nigger, the one Dave Chance had with him, I spied him running alongside those rails, too."

"The Moor?" Savage sounded skeptical. He recalled the name. "Moses Albavera?"

Opening her eyes, putting the memory of Don Melitón behind her, Grace laughed. "I told you Dave wasn't dead."

"Shut up."

"She's likely right, Captain," Doc Shaw said. "I'm betting Bucky, Taw, and Eliot are either dead, or in jail. My guess is dead. They won't be joining us, Captain. It's just the two of us. To split . . . what, one bar of bullion? Eighty-four hundred dollars?"

"That's still a hell of a lot of money. More than you'd make in five years."

"Forty-two hundred, if we split it, Captain. Split it evenly. Either way, it won't buy us nothing out here."

Leather squeaked. She could imagine Savage resting his hands on the butts of his holstered revolvers. "You got something on your mind, Doc. A suggestion, I guess. Spit it out."

"We've got two horses, and both are on their last legs. We've got a hard ride to the border. She'll just slow us down. Get us caught. Get us killed. Now I know how much you appreciate a good woman, and I was raised that way, too. But it would be best for us to leave her behind."

"Let Lo Grande's men find her?" Bitterness accented Savage's statement, and the thought left Grace trembling.

"We could shoot her. Or slit her throat."

"No. I won't harm the fairer sex, especially a fine figure of a woman like Grace Profit."

"We could leave her here in the shade. Or hidden in the rocks up on Elephant Mountain. Maybe Lo Grande's men won't find her. Hell, we can leave her a pistol. She can defend herself better than a lot of men I know. Or, God willing, when Lo Grande's men are gone, someone will be sure to come by, looking for us. She could fire a shot, bring some men, white men, to her. Get those busted legs of hers tended to."

More silence. The captain was considering it.

"The point is, Captain, we're three people with only two horses that are half dead. We'll never make it to Mexico that way."

The wind blew. The water flowed.

Captain Savage let out a weary sigh. "You're right, Doc."

CHAPTER THIRTY

The body lay facedown in the creek, the head partially buried in the sand, naked, the ears cut off. When Moses Albavera turned the corpse over, he discovered another indignity.

"God," he said, dropping the dead man. "His pecker's been cut off and stuck in his mouth."

"I got eyes." Chance swung off the dun, wrapping the reins around a large rock. He felt relief. When Albavera had first spotted the circling buzzards that morning, he had feared they would find Grace Profit underneath Elephant Mountain. He waded into the stream, letting the trickling water soak his moccasins, and knelt, massaging his left shoulder as he looked at what once had been Doc Shaw.

He put his hand on the corpse's head, turned it slightly. "Skull's smashed. That's probably what killed him. But Savage slit his throat just to be sure."

"Why'd he do the . . . rest?"

Chance rose. "He didn't. That's the handiwork of some of Lo Grande's boys. Help me get him out of this creek."

He vocalized his theory while Albavera dragged Shaw's body to an arroyo that ran alongside the mountain into the creek. "Savage, Grace, and Shaw stopped here, probably to rest and water their horses. Two horses. Three riders. Something had to give, and that turned out to be Doc Shaw's head." Savage had brained him, but Chance had to give the captain some credit. Doc Shaw was looking at him when his skull got caved in. That meant Savage knew Lo Grande's men were close by, on his trail. He used stone and knife, rather that one of those .44s. A shot would carry a long way out there, and bring Lo Grande right to them.

"They found him anyway." Albavera let Shaw's feet fall onto the water-smoothed rocks.

"Yeah." Shaw climbed out of the arroyo, and made a beeline to a mound of horse apples. "Cut off his ears as trophies. Robbed him of his clothes, everything, including his dignity. That's why they cut off his dick." He knelt, picked up a turd, and broke it open, testing the moisture with his fingers, then dropped the crap, and wiped his hands on his chaps. "They're four hours ahead of us, or thereabouts."

"And Savage?"

Chance shrugged. "I don't know. But I doubt if he has much of a head start." He walked to the dun, gathered the reins, and pulled himself into the saddle.

"What about him?" Albavera gestured at the dead man in the arroyo. "Should we bury him?"

"Doc didn't bother burying Ray Wickes." Chance kicked the dun into a walk.

Albavera took a final glance at the body before walking to the blood bay mare.

About a hundred yards downstream, Chance pointed toward some tracks in the sand that pointed northeast. One of Lo Grande's riders — he guessed there were four others who had butchered Doc Shaw's corpse — had taken off to find Lo Grande and the others, and let them know they had found Savage's trail.

"So" — Albavera pulled the sawed-off Springfield from his holster — "this party'll be even bigger."

Nodding, Chance drew his Schofield.

The Marlin shot high, but Chance still managed to kill a scrawny mule deer late the next afternoon. They made an early camp, resting the horses while Chance butchered the deer and roasted steaks.

"You think that fire's a good idea?" Albavera asked.

"My stomach thinks so."

"Well, at least the weather's decent."

Two days later, a blue norther hit, dropping the temperature forty degrees in less than an hour, turning the Big Bend region into a sheet of ice. The wind blew furiously, lashing out as Hec Savage helped Grace Profit into the saddle. Sleet stung like rock salt. Frigid air burned their lungs with each breath.

"Keep your head bent low," Savage called to her. "We'll be inside a warm building, sipping hot coffee, eating warm tortillas in an hour."

She looked at him. Her lips moved, but he couldn't hear her over the roaring wind. Somewhere, the limb of a juniper cracked, broken by the weight of ice. Savage raised a gloved hand to his ear.

"I can't feel my legs."

That was probably a good thing, he figured. He'd seen her legs earlier that day. The bruises, deep purple, even black in places, had reached halfway up her calves.

After transferring the contents of his coat pocket to the empty pockets of his vest, Savage pulled off his coat, and draped it over her back. "Just hold onto the horn," he told her, and mounted his own horse. He grabbed the reins of her mount, and pulled horse and rider behind him.

The wind was at their back, pounding them with sleet and a harsh wind. They kept to a deep arroyo, the sides full of junipers, which protected them a little from the weather, but not much. For the past couple days, Savage and Grace had hidden in a cave in the Big Bend, resting their horses, resting themselves. It wasn't bad, having Grace Profit crippled with two busted ankles. He could leave her in the cave, while he went out to scout, or find some grub. It wasn't like she was going anywhere. Hell, she couldn't even mount a horse, and she knew better than to scream if she heard someone outside the cave. She understood what would happen to her if Lo Grande's men caught her.

Lo Grande. That troubled Savage. He had seen nothing of those bandits since he had killed Doc Shaw. It was like those damned Mexicans had given up, or been swallowed up by the rugged, mountainous high desert country.

Maybe the Army or a posse of Rangers had caught up with Lo Grande. No . . . no, he would have heard the gunshots. Sounds carried a long distance out there, and if Lo Grande and his men were dead, the men who had killed them would still be combing the countryside for Hec Savage.

Maybe Lo Grande had given up, crossed the border, returned to Ojinaga or San Pedro. Savage had to snort at that thought. Give up? Lo Grande? After being double-crossed? After being robbed of a fortune?

Savage couldn't risk staying any longer, though. The horses were refreshed, ready. He knew he needed to get across the border, and start heading east. Eighty-four hundred dollars was a long way from two hundred and fifty thousand, but it could buy him a lot. It could keep him from getting hanged.

He had hoped the storm would blow itself out. Instead, its intensity picked up. His fingers were numb, and he was wearing gloves. His lips were chapped, his face felt raw. He cursed his luck. His horse stepped in a hole, stumbled. Cursing again, he lurched forward and back as the horse regained its balance, then plodded along.

"How about a glass of tequila, Grace?" he

yelled back. "Beefsteak and beans? Maybe even some coffee? That sound all right to you? Maybe even a nice straw bed?"

He didn't expect her to answer. He kept riding, head bent, lungs aching.

They reached the end of the arroyo. "All right, honey, you need to hang on tight to that horn. We gotta climb out of this. The river's only another mile or so. We'll be in Mexico in no time."

Twisting in the saddle, he looked back at the horse he was leading.

"Ah, hell."

The saddle was empty.

It was the damnedest thing. She didn't feel cold at all.

She couldn't remember slipping out of the saddle. One minute she had been riding, head low, body aching, bitterly cold, and the next thing she knew she was lying on a bed of rocks, nose seeping blood, hands scratched all to hell, ankles burning like a son of a bitch.

But she wasn't cold.

She had lost Savage's coat. Didn't recall when. She looked southwest, down the arroyo, but saw only falling sleet. She looked in the other direction, but sleet blasted her face. Rolling over, cursing from the pain in her legs, she stretched her right arm ahead, grabbed a rock, and pulled herself forward. Reaching with her left hand, she grabbed a root from a juniper, and dragged herself a little more.

Grab . . . drag . . . grab . . . drag . . . grab . . . drag . . .

She stopped, desperately trying to catch her breath. A tear rolled down her cheek. Her legs burned terribly, but at least they weren't numb, as they were when they'd first left the cave. She rolled over, tried to guess at the time, but saw only white and gray.

Rolling back onto her stomach, she pressed her face on the ice-covered ground. That cooled her off. It would be so easy to just close her eyes, go to sleep, let the sleet cover her. So easy to just give up.

So easy to lie there and die.

"Like hell I will."

Her eyes shot open. She bit her lower lip. Reaching out, she found a rock slippery with ice, and dragged herself a few inches more. Then reached with her left hand.

Grab . . . drag . . . grab . . . drag . . . grab . . . drag . . .

She reached the edge of the arroyo, shielded partly by an uprooted juniper and mounds of sand and rocks. The wind and sleet moaned over her head. Grace pulled herself up until her back rested against the wall. Leaning forward, she put her hands on her knees.

Pain rocked her. She fell back.

Another tear stung her cheeks, and she could no longer hold the river. Tears flooded, and she choked out sobs. Snot and blood froze underneath her nostrils. She sucked in bitterly cold air through her mouth. Her teeth hurt.

She leaned her head back, and tried to figure out just what she could do.

She couldn't walk. Could barely crawl.

Looking up at the arroyo wall, three feet above her head, she knew she'd never be able to climb out there. Not with both of her ankles broken. Maybe somewhere else, but to leave the protection of the downed juniper . . . she'd never make it. It had to be twenty degrees. The wind made it feel even colder.

This is desert, she told God. *It isn't supposed to be like this.*

This is hell. It's supposed to be hot.

She wrapped her arms around her ribs, began rocking back and forth, back and forth, shaking her head, trying to figure out how she was supposed to pray.

Rough hands grabbed her shoulder, lifted

her back. Her eyes fluttered open.

"Dave?" she cried out, wanting to reach for him — wanting to kiss him. "Dave!"

"Grace." The voice sounded so distant.

Suddenly, she shivered. "No," she said.

"Grace," Hec Savage said again, shattering the vision of Dave Chance. Taking off one of his gloves, Savage put the back of his hand against her cheek, against her forehead.

"Christ, Grace, you're burning up." He stood, looked on the other side of the juniper, then turned, looking back down the arroyo. "Where's my coat? The coat I gave you?"

She shrugged.

He lifted her to her feet. She moaned, and fell back against the arroyo wall.

"Did you jump out of the saddle? Or fall?"

"I . . . don't . . . know." She was still sobbing. Couldn't stop crying. Couldn't stop shaking. Her stomach rumbled. She thought she might throw up.

"We gotta get you to a doctor," Savage said. "Even a bean doctor. To shelter. Something. Come on. Lean on me, honey. I've got your horse. Our horses. Right over yonder."

He lifted her over his shoulder, and like a sack of wheat, got her into the saddle. She leaned over, and sprayed vomit over the horse's withers. Savage pulled a handkerchief, and wiped her mouth. He cleaned the mess off the horn and the horsehair, and tossed the piece of cloth onto the ground.

"Here." He cut off a string behind the saddle, wrapped it around her wrists, and secured her to the horn. "Now you won't fall off. Come on. Don't you fret none, Grace, my dear. I'll have you to some Mexican pill-roller and you'll be dancing before you know it. Maybe we'll make it down to Buenos Aires after all. Maybe I can still buy you a nice little saloon. Got to be cheap down that way. 'Course, you'll still have to be making your own whiskey. Don't think we'll be able to afford any Manhattan rye."

He talked as he mounted his horse, kept talking as he pulled Grace behind him, back down the arroyo, then up and out. He kept talking about Buenos Aires, about his old ranch in Bexar County, about growing up in Texas, about those damned Mexicans, about his years as a Ranger, about the first time he had laid eyes on Grace Profit, about her whiskey, about Juan Lo Grande, about how he had hated to have killed Doc Shaw, even about Dave Chance.

It didn't matter that Grace couldn't hear
what he said.

407

Chapter Thirty-One

There wasn't much to the village of Boquillas del Carmen, which lay just over the Mexican border where the Rio Grande flowed into Boquillas Canyon. Silver and lead mining had begun there a few years ago. The Consolidated Kansas City Smelting and Refining Company had built a processing plant on the American side of the river, and a cable tramway to bring ore across the border. After processing, it was shipped to the railroad in Marathon.

Sometimes, when the miners got paid, the cantina bustled with activity, and, sometimes, when the gringos working at the processing plant got paid, they crossed the river to partake of cheaper beer, tequila, and Mexican women. But on a night like that one, Boquillas was dead.

The only light Hec Savage saw came from the little adobe church at the edge of town, which consisted of a few scattered homes and businesses, and a ramshackle corral and livery. He eased his horse down the sleet-crusted street, and pulled the one carrying Grace Profit toward the Catholic church.

A door opened, then shut. Savage reined up and aimed the Merwin Hulbert at the peon woman who had stepped out of her jacal. Giving his shadowy figure a moment's glance, she pulled her cloak tightly, and hurried across the street toward the church. Savage followed her, studying the shadows, the buildings, watching the woman as she entered the church, closing the door behind her.

He rode past the well in the center of the street. Stopping in front of the church, he climbed down from the saddle, pulled the heavy bags off the back of his horse, and slung them over his left shoulder. Next, he drew Grace's mount over to the hitching post, wrapped the reins around it, and sliced through the rawhide that held her pale hands to the horn. She was half dead, her breathing ragged, her body cold to the touch, but she was still alive. He draped her over his right shoulder, and moved to the door.

Inside the adobe building, he immediately felt warm — God's blanket of love, he thought mockingly, or some such nonsense

— and carried Grace and the saddlebags past the peon woman lighting a candle to the pew nearest the potbelly stove at the front of the church. Two priests in their scratchy brown woolen robes, bound at the waist by plain cords, hoods over their heads, watched from the altar.

"Get down here, damn you," Savage roared at the priests. "This woman's hurt. Sick. Needs some help. *Socorro. Socorro.*" Not pleading for help. Demanding it.

Stepping away, he holstered his revolver, and patted the saddlebags as the priests moved off the altar and crossed the flagstone floor. The woman lit her candle and hurried to the pew, kneeling, whispering something in Spanish, brushing Grace's wet bangs off her forehead.

"Her ankles are busted," Savage said. "Both of them."

The woman removed her cloak and wrapped it around Grace's body.

Savage wet his lips. He wanted a drink and wondered if he might be able to find some communion wine in that miserable excuse of a church. When he turned back toward the priests, his right hand dashed for the Merwin Hulbert on his right hip.

"No," the priest said — only he wasn't a priest. Or if he were one, he was the first man of God Savage had seen pointing a cocked Starr revolver at his belly. Savage's hand gripped the butt of the .44, but he slowly let go, and raised his hands.

The priest pulled down his hood with his left hand, and said something in Spanish. The other Mexican went to Savage and took both pistols from their holsters, dropping them by Grace Profit's boots on the pew, then shoved Savage toward the altar. The priest with the Starr spoke again in Spanish, and the second man hurried out of the church and into the darkness.

Savage turned. "You *sabe* English?"

The man just stared at him with hard eyes.

"English. You *sabe* English?"

"Silencio," the man said.

"Ah, hell's fire," Savage said, and he knew. He knew it before the second padre returned, followed by six other Mexicans, including one holding a bottle of tequila.

" 'All's well that ends well.' No?" Juan Lo Grande took a slug of tequila, tossed the bottle to another bean-eater, and strode up the aisle to the altar.

"Allow me, amigo." He pulled the saddle-bags off Savage's shoulder. "Ah, this is heavy. Very heavy."

He laid the bags on the pulpit, and opened one, stared inside, and raised his dark, smiling eyes at Savage. *"Muy bien."* He opened the other bag, and frowned. "One bar. That is all?"

"You saw what happened. Damned law dogs rammed our train. I was lucky to make off with that."

Lo Grande wiped his mouth with the back of his hand. He stood, gave Grace Profit and the woman tending her a brief glance, then positioned himself in front of Hec Savage. "How much is one bar worth?"

"If Doc Shaw was right, about eighty-four hundred dollars American."

He nodded. "That is better than a coffin and a cross, no?"

"How'd you know I'd come to this miserable excuse for a burg?"

Lo Grande shrugged. "When you were in the Big Bend, Juan Lo Grande thought" — he tapped his temple — "where would Hec Savage go? The only suitable crossing is at Boquillas Del Carmen. It was also the nearest place with grog. With tequila. So here I came with some of my men. Other men are at Ojinaga and San Pedro. Though I doubted you would be foolish enough to go there. More are riding along the river between the Cibolo and the Maravillas. In such weather, too. What brave men Juan Lo Grande has. We would find you if you dared enter Mexico."

He stepped closer. "But to be honest, I did not think you would come to Mexico. I thought you would ride west, maybe to El Paso. Or north. Everyone would think you would race to the border, and Hector Savage is too smart a man to do what everyone would think."

He laughed, shaking his head. "But, no, Capitán Savage is not so smart. He is as dumb as every other *bandido* who is too lazy to work for an honest living. This is what I thought. Or maybe I thought, *los rinches* would kill you in Texas. In which case, poor Juan Lo Grande could never collect his share of the bullion we steal together. We steal together . . ." The words trailed off. " 'Men at some time were masters of their fates. . . .' " Lo Grande's smile vanished. "The streets of Murphyville run red with the blood of many of my men, capitán."

He cuffed Savage across the cheek with his backhand.

Savage spit in Lo Grande's face.

That was the last thing Savage remembered for a while.

The sleet had stopped by the time Dave Chance and Moses Albavera came out of the Sierra del Caballo Muerto — Dead

413

Horse Mountains — on the Texas side of the Rio Grande, but the wind had not relented.

At least it was blowing at their backs as they rode alongside the banks a while, then entered the frigid but shallow water.

"You sure you know what you're doing?" Albavera had to shout over the wind and splashing water to be heard.

Actually, Chance wasn't sure of anything anymore, but it seemed as good a guess as any he had. "Only place Savage could cross is here," he said with more confidence than he felt.

"Yeah, but there's a town here," Albavera argued. "Seems to me that your captain would want to avoid any towns."

Chance snorted. "Boquillas del Carmen isn't much of a town."

At which point, they were in Mexico.

He ducked underneath an ice-covered tree limb, and let the horse pick its path up the bank, then followed a small trail through rocks and brush until they hit the main road. Side-by-side they reached the outskirts of Boquillas. Long before they saw the faint outlines of the town in the dark, laughter reached them.

"Hey," Albavera said easily. "Looks like the miners have gotten paid. I'll be in that cantina, dealing stud, relieving those poor souls of their pay while you search this dot on a map for Savage."

Chance didn't reply. He swung off his horse, and wrapped the reins around the top rail of a corral next to a crumbling adobe building. Light glowed from the windows of the cantina. A barrel-chested Mexican staggered out, yelling something over his shoulder, and carrying what appeared to be a rope in one hand, and a jug in the other. He headed for the church at the west end of town.

There wasn't much to Boquillas. The cantina. A church. A few sod, stone, and adobe structures. The mine headquarters, and the office of the village alcalde. Yet the corral was full of horses, and lying alongside the adobe wall were saddles and tack far too fancy to belong to any miner, especially some hard-rock miner in a dumpy little village like Boquillas.

The wind had stopped, the storm blowing itself southeast. Chance heard the creaking of leather as Albavera dismounted, heard him draw his sawed-off Springfield. Apparently, something about the scene struck the gambler as false, too.

One of their horses whinnied. A stallion in the corral answered, snorting, and stamping its hooves. Chance's horse kicked out, its hooves striking a pile of adobe blocks.

The man with the rope and the jug stopped underneath the awning of the church. He rubbed his beard, and started walking toward the corral.

Crouching, Albavera took off, leaving his horse behind, and rounded the corner of the adobe wall.

"*¿Qué es lo que pasa?*" the Mexican called.

Chance knelt, pushed his hat off, fell onto his good hand, and called out weakly, "*Amigo . . . me siento enfermo.*" *Hell, I sound as Mexican as Don Melitón or Captain Savage.* Yet the Mexican rounding the corral must have been too drunk to have noticed. After an exaggerated groan, Chance pretended to gag. "*Necesito un médico.*"

He heard the Mexican's footsteps, saw his soiled boots.

"*¿Bueno, qué le pasa?*" The Mexican reached down, and Chance lifted his face. The Mexican jumped back, dropping his jug, yelling, "*¿Cómo? !Dios mío!*"

Chance saw the shadow behind the Mexican about the time the Mexican felt the presence. He was turning, reaching for an old cap-and-ball relic in his waistband when the barrel of Albavera's sawed-off rifle clobbered his skull, and he sank into the melting ice and mud with a small groan.

Albavera slid beside the unconscious Mexican, and looked at his jacket. "Rurale."

"Bandit," Chance corrected, drawing the Marlin from the scabbard, "in a Rurale uniform."

"One of Lo Grande's men?"

"That would be my guess."

A roar of laughter exploded out of the cantina.

Albavera found the bandit's pistol, and heaved it behind the adobe blocks. "Well, if Lo Grande's here, and those boys are celebrating . . ."

Chance tilted his jaw at the church. "I don't think this old boy was going to confession."

He looked across the town. Light shown from the church's windows. The door opened, and a figure emerged, "Celso!" he yelled. "Celso!" Muttering something, he waved his hand toward the cantina, and returned inside the church.

Chance rubbed the beard stubble on his chin. "I'm going."

"But —"

"I don't care what you do." Chance crouched, and took off in a low sprint down the street. Albavera stifled a curse, and ran after Chance, keeping his eyes and the barrel of the Springfield trained on the door to the cantina. Once past it, they ducked beside the well in the center of the street, and caught their breath, before continuing until both men were standing flat against the adobe wall, on either side of the door.

Chance's left arm throbbed in the sling.

"We don't know how many men are inside," Albavera said.

Chance figured most of those men were in the cantina, and pretty well roostered on tequila by now. "Let's find out." He thumbed back the hammer of the Marlin.

"I've never shot up a Catholic church before," Albavera said.

"I was raised Baptist. You?"

Albavera shrugged. "Pagan."

Chance grabbed the pull, pressed the lock, and pushed the door open. Stepping into the church, he moved to his right. Albavera went in, Springfield ready, and dived behind a pew to his left.

The door banged against the corner and slammed shut behind them.

CHAPTER THIRTY-TWO

When Chance was in the church, when he saw Hec Savage standing, on a wobbly chair on the altar, a rope around his neck, the other end secured to a viga, hands tied in front of him, Chance's mind flashed back to Fort Stockton and the Bad Water Saloon.

He had just slapped the handcuffs on an unconscious Dawg Goolsby after buffaloing the murdering son of a bitch with his .45. Later, he figured his mistake in thinking the patrons of a bucket of blood like the Bad Water Saloon would respect the badge on his vest, that they wouldn't come to the aid of a wanted felon. And that he should never holster his revolver or turn his back on armed men in a saloon. But he was a greenhorn lawman back then, and had barely lived to learn a valuable lesson.

He heard the footsteps, but remained focused on getting those bracelets on Dawg Goolsby.

As he turned, unsuspecting, a whiskey bottle — empty, naturally — smashed across his forehead.

They dumped a spittoon on his face, the tobacco juice burning the cuts on his forehead and over his eye. The juice and water burned his eyes, blurred his vision. He blinked, tried to speak, but something was tightening around his throat, burning, cutting. When his vision cleared at last, he realized he was standing on a rickety chair in the center of the Bad Water Saloon, wearing those iron cuffs he had been putting on Dawg Goolsby. A rope was tight across his neck, looped over a beam in the saloon's ceiling, and secured to a whiskey barrel behind the bar.

"Well, well, well." Dawg Goolsby threw down a shot of scamper juice, and thumbed back the hammer of a Schofield — Chance's revolver — and laughed. "A new Texas Ranger. Come to Stockton to protect the innocents. Thought he'd deliver June Goolsby to the gallows."

"June?" One of the patrons laughed.

Goolsby shot his hat off.

The laughter died.

"Well," he said, blowing smoke from the barrel, and turning back to face Chance, "let's see how you like dancing with a rope 'round your neck as a partner." Cocking the hammer,

Goolsby took a couple steps closer to the chair, extended his arm, aimed, and pulled the trigger.

The bullet splintered one leg, and Chance almost slipped. The rope bit deeper into his neck. His lungs and brain screamed for oxygen.

"Nice shot, Dawg!" one of the patrons cheered.

"Gun pulls a mite to the right," Goolsby said, earring back the hammer again.

The hell it does, Chance thought. *You're just too damned drunk to shoot better.*

But he knew Goolsby's aim wasn't that far off. The next shot broke the leg, and the chair tilted forward. Chance gagged, almost slipped, somehow maintaining his balance, but it was hopeless. He was about to black out, slip off, and fall into eternity.

The doors to the saloon crashed open, and a shotgun roared as Chance twisted, turned, and felt the chair overturn. The rope pulled on his neck. The world went black.

When he came to, Dawg Goolsby was lying dead, his chest torn apart by buckshot fired by Hec Savage's Parker shotgun. One barrel had caught Goolsby as he turned. The other had cut through the rope above Chance's head and sent him crashing to the floor.

"One Ranger ought to have been enough to

take care of Goolsby, young fella," Savage said. "I don't cotton to Rangers who need someone to back their play. Remember that."

Chance had.

Chance braced the rifle's stock against his hip. Holding it with his good hand, he swept it across the church, pulling the trigger. A man in the coarse woolen robe of a priest slammed against the wall, dropping a double-action revolver, groaning, sliding down, leaving a trail of blood on the white-wash behind him.

Another man jerked the chair from underneath Savage's feet, and dived behind the pulpit. A second man in a priest's robe staggered from a rear room, dropping basket-wrapped bottles of wine on the floor, reaching for a revolver. A woman kneeling in front of the first pew lifted her head, screamed, ducked, and repeated a rosary.

Chance tried to work the Marlin's lever with one hand, but gave up and drew his Schofield. He aimed it at a man in the back of the church. The bandit's pistol bucked first, the bullet sending splinters from the back of the pew into Chance's cheek. He ducked as another bullet whined off the back wall.

Albavera came up, aimed the Springfield

422

at the "priest" grabbing for his gun.

"Not him!" Chance yelled. "The rope!"

Albavera shot him a quick glance, then turned the Springfield. Hec Savage was swinging, twisting, his legs kicking. Albavera's gun sang out, and the hangman's rope severed. Savage crashed to the floor, rolled, and quickly disappeared.

Laying the Schofield on the floor, Chance grabbed the Marlin, and looked across the aisle at Albavera as he reloaded the Springfield. "Here. Catch." He flung the rifle across the aisle. The butt landed on the flagstone, and flipped the rifle across the Moor's legs.

From outside came curses, shots, and the pounding of feet. Two more bullets lodged into the door before it was opened.

Chance and Albavera raised their weapons. A figure in a brown robe ran inside, slamming the door behind him. He turned, his face paling. A pewter cross hung around his neck. He was Mexican, but something about his face told them he was truly a man of God. Even the two *bandidos* at the front of the church held their fire.

"If I were you, padre," Chance said, "I'd bolt that door."

"And duck," Albavera added.

Chance wasn't sure if the priest understood English, but he quickly began drawing a long oak bar through the iron brackets, securing the door.

"No, padre, no!" someone yelled from the front of the church.

Albavera moved down the back row toward the wall. Chance picked up the Schofield, and did the same on the other side. When they reached the end of the pews, they turned and looked at each other. Chance held up three fingers. Counting, he mouthed the words.

One . . .

Two . . .

Then he stood. So did Albavera. He fired first, at the bandit in the robe, off to the side, near the pulpit. The Marlin's slug tore through the Mexican's shoulder, and he crumpled to the floor. Chance took off down the side aisle. Above the ringing in his ears, he heard the priest shout something.

Another figure appeared, and snapped a shot at Chance, blasting a *santero* on a shelf. Chance turned, tried to steady the Schofield, then heard another shot, and saw smoke belch from behind the first pew. The Mexican in the center aisle cried out. He fired, putting a round into the ceiling as another shot tore through his chest, but the man was dead before he fell across the back of a pew. He dropped his pistol, and toppled to the floor

The sounds of gunshots died. The smoke slowly dissipated. The woman in the front of the church prayed in Spanish. Men pounded at the front door, but the oak bar refused to give. Chance and Albavera trained their guns on that first pew. Hec Savage was behind it, and he had a gun. Unconcerned, the priest walked down the center aisle, crossing himself, shooting angry glances at Albavera and Chance. "Have you no decency? Have you no shame? How dare you stain this hallowed place with blood, with violence!"

His English was pretty good.

"Is there a back door to this place?" Chance yelled.

The priest glared.

"Answer me!"

"No." The priest gestured at the front door, which was shuddering, but not breaking. "This is the only entrance."

Chance nodded, walking toward the first pew, his gun cocked.

A voice stopped him. Stopped the priest. And Albavera, too.

"Is that you, Sergeant Chance?"

Instinctively, Chance ducked behind a pew, and brought his gun up level, bracing his arm against the back of the wooden seat. "It's me, Captain," he said at last.

"I thought so. Reckon we're even now. For Fort Stockton."

Chance tried to think of some reply. Couldn't.

"Grace is up here with me, Dave. So is some greaser woman praying to be delivered."

Chance tried to swallow, but couldn't work up enough spit. "Thought you didn't hold with harming womenfolk."

"Times have changed."

The doors strained. The Mexicans outside shouted. A gun was fired, but the bullet couldn't penetrate the thick door.

"You and him drop your weapons. Or I blow Grace's head off."

The pounding on the door continued.

"You might need our guns, Captain."

"I don't think so, Dave. I'll ask that padre for sanctuary. Till Lo Grande's boys decide it ain't worth it. Not with old Juan Lo Grande lying dead."

So that was Lo Grande in the center aisle.

"You are not worthy of sanctuary." The priest resumed his walk. "You come into this house of the Lord with guns. You kill." He stopped by the dead man, Lo Grande, and began blessing the corpse.

"Guns on the floor, boys." Savage's voice had an edge to it.

Cursing, Chance let the Schofield drop. Across the church, Albavera tossed the Marlin on the seat of a pew, and unbuckled his gunbelt. He laid it and the Springfield on the next pew.

"It's done, Captain," Chance said.

"How do I know?"

"You've my word on it, Captain. Just let Grace alone."

His tied hands, holding a Merwin Hulbert revolver, appeared first. Then grunting, Savage pushed himself to his feet, the rope still wrapped around his neck. He tried to smile, staggered back, and sat on the pulpit. He motioned Chance and Albavera to come on up.

The priest finished with Lo Grande, then moved to another corpse.

The pounding on the door continued.

"It's over, Captain," Chance tried.

Savage grinned. "For you. Not me. Hey, you, woman. Come here. I want you to cut this rope off my hands. Take this rope off my neck. I can't do it. Not without tempting Sergeant Chance" — his eyes shot across the room — "or his Moor."

The woman lifted her head. Rising, the priest repeated Savage's instructions in

Spanish.

"Come on," Savage ordered. "Take the knife off that dead one there. *Muy pronto, por favor.*"

The woman moved forward, leaned over the dead man, and slipped a knife from its sheath. Seconds later, Savage was standing, flexing his muscles, and the woman was sitting on the front pew, her head bowed, her lips moving in a silent prayer.

The pounding on the door continued.

Chance eased to the front row, and saw Grace Profit lying there, so pale, so haggard. His face tightened. He knelt beside her, and took her hand in his own.

"I could have left her in the Big Bend, Dave," Savage said. "Could have left her to die. But I'm no monster. I brought her here. To save her life. Damned near cost me mine."

Eyes still on Grace, Chance whispered. "It still might."

Savage snorted. "Padre, you go to that door. You tell them boys that their leader is dead. You tell them that I've asked for sanctuary, and you've given it to me. You tell them to ride out of Boquillas for San Pedro, or to hell for all I care, and you tell them to get gone and get gone now. They'll trust you. They believe in God. Believe in a man like you. I seen it with my own eyes in San Pedro. They ride for the devil." He looked at Lo Grande's body and chuckled. "Rode for the devil, I mean. But they got the faith. Do it."

The priest stared. Savage cocked the pistol. The priest turned, and walked up the aisle toward the door.

Savage let out a long breath. Reaching into his vest pocket with his left hand, he pulled out a little gold cross, and held it up in the candlelight. "Here, Dave. You might want to kiss this. Make your peace. You and your Moor." He sent the cross sailing across the altar, and reached again in his pocket — for the makings of a smoke.

At that moment, the Mexican woman looked up. Screaming something in Spanish, she yelled a pitiful cry of anguish so piercing it caused Chance's skin to crawl. Caused Savage to drop his tobacco pouch. He started to ask . . .

Then saw the other Merwin Hulbert, the one he had left on the pew, in the woman's hand. He saw the muzzle flash, and felt the bullet slam into his chest. Heard another explosion, and felt another bullet strike his side — like he'd been struck twice by a sledgehammer. His gun slipped from his hand.

Dave Chance turned, yelling. Moses Al-bavera dashed across the room. The woman was screaming, crying. Putting the muzzle of the .44 under her chin, she turned toward the priest, begging. She pulled the trigger as Chance launched himself, futilely, toward her, yelling, "Don't!"

The priest knelt by the dead woman, cover-ing her face. He crossed himself, crossed her, his head bowed.

"I hate . . ." Hec Savage, still standing, though he was leaning on the lectern for support, spit out a glob of blood. "Hate to see a woman hurt . . . even one that . . . has . . . killed me." Blood trickled from his lips. He looked at the priest.

"What was it . . . she . . . was saying?"

The priest finished his prayer, and stared up at Savage with merciless eyes. "The crucifix belonged to her son. Jaime Bautista Moreno, a lieutenant with the Rurales in San Pedro. He was murdered on the river west of here. She said that you must have killed him, so she was sending you to hell before joining her beloved son in heaven."

"I'll be . . . damned." Hec Savage laughed. Coughed. "That's . . . hell . . . justice . . . ain't it?"

He let go of his hold on the lectern, and fell dead.

CHAPTER THIRTY-THREE

"And then?" Grace Profit cringed at the pain in her ankles. "How'd we get out of that church in Boquillas?"

Chance shook his head. "Don Melitón and his vaqueros rode up about ten minutes later. God-fearing men or not, Lo Grande's men were ready to set fire to the church. The don . . ."

Grace sat up in her bunk. "I thought Don Melitón was dead. Captain Savage shot him."

"Oh, the don was lying in an ambulance. His segundo did most of the talking."

"I can imagine how."

Chance smiled. "Well, Lo Grande's men took off. The don said he was going to Meoqui. Said he trusted the doctors down there better than —" He cut himself off, tried to swallow down what he had said.

Grace laughed. "Well, these sawbones here haven't cut off my legs yet. They seem to think I'll be walking, back to my old self, in no time. I think they just don't want me to leave, that they enjoy my company. That's why they're keeping me here longer."

Chance leaned back. They were in the post hospital at Fort Davis. Chance's left arm was in a cast, his left hand bandaged. It itched like a son of a bitch. He couldn't imagine how uncomfortable Grace Profit was with casts on both ankles, and a bandage wrapped around her forehead. Both hands were wrapped in gauze, too.

"And Savage?"

Chance shrugged, and brushed the bandage on his cheek. It itched a mite, too. "We dragged the bodies out of the church. One of Lo Grande's men was still alive, so we tied him up, put a sock in the hole in his shoulder, and turned him over to the alcalde. The priest and alcalde fixed you up as best as they could, and procured a wagon for you. By then it was just about dawn, and Moses and I brought you back here." He coughed. "I think we'd worn out our welcome in Boquillas."

"I asked about Hec Savage."

"Well, the priest suggested I bring his body back to Texas. I said he wasn't fit to be buried in Texas. Then Moses Albavera told me —"

Albavera interrupted. "I said, 'That's just like you, a damned Texan. Savage isn't fit to be buried in your damned state, but he's good enough to be planted in Mexico in some town whose church he just blasted halfway to hell. You're as bad as Savage.' That's what I told him, ma'am."

Chance looked rather sheepish. "Moses was right. We buried the captain in the cemetery at Fort Leaton. The soldiers looking for the captain, thinking he had declared independence from Texas, were still surrounding the fort. They had a couple doctors with them. We rested there a day. Then rode up here."

Boots scraped across the plank floor, spurs jingled, and Chance rose off the cot. He stood beside the tall Moor as two officers, a man with a sheriff's badge, and a man in a plaid sack suit and bell crown hat stormed across the hospital floor. Weaving among the beds filled with sick soldiers — the post surgeon, a major named Hunter, said sick call had almost tripled since Grace Profit was admitted — they surrounded Grace, Albavera, and Chance.

The man in the sack suit whipped the hat off his head and pointed a finger at Chance. "Well?" he snapped. "We've been riding halfway across this godforsaken place looking for you and your captain, Sergeant."

"I turned in my report yesterday, Colonel Thomas. Sent it with Lieutenant Henshaw."

"Yes, you did, Sergeant. And I got it. I read it." He spit. "The same as I read that telegram that was sent from Sanderson. Am I supposed to believe that a stalwart Ranger with such a long history of bringing law and order like Hector Savage turned renegade? And took most of his command with him? Am I suppose to believe that you're the only honest Ranger there was in the entire E Company?"

"Not the only one." Chance felt his anger boiling. "There was Lieutenant Wickes . . . Rangers Smith, Magruder. And Babbitt and Turpen."

"Hec Savage served as a Ranger since the Rangers were organized. Before that he . . ." Thomas shook his head. "Two of his uncles were killed at the Alamo. I can't believe this."

The sheriff cleared his throat. "Well, Colonel, sir, there were witnesses in Murphyville. They saw Savage and some of his men taking that train. One man swore he saw Savage gun down the conductor in cold blood."

"I just don't believe it," Thomas said again.

"Believe it," Albavera said.

Thomas turned, and stared at the Ranger badge pinned on Albavera's vest. "Who the hell are you, mister?" he snapped. "The Rangers have never, ever, had a nig—"

"I'd watch it, Colonel," Grace Profit said.

Thomas turned, his face paling, shaking his head. He had started to sweat.

One of the officers, a white-haired lieutenant colonel with a well-groomed mustache, cleared his throat. "Well, there is one more thing. It's . . . well, sir" — his eyes turned hopeful — "the gold?"

Smiling, Chance turned to the empty cot he had been sitting on, unbuckled the strap securing Savage's leather bag, reached inside, and, grunting, pulled out the bar of bullion. The second officer, a captain with a pockmarked face, gasped as Chance placed the bar in his hands.

"There you go," Chance said.

Eyes locked on him.

"Where's the rest?" the white-haired officer asked.

Chance looked at him dumbly. He shot a worried glance at Albavera, who looked just as idiotic as Chance suddenly felt.

"Sir?" Chance asked weakly.

"That's one bar," the lieutenant colonel said.

The Ranger leader added, "Where are the other twenty-nine?"

"They'd be on the train," Chance guessed.

"The one you wrecked?" the Army captain asked.

"Well, yeah. The one Mickey rammed."

Silence.

Chance was also sweating. *Thinking. When we left . . . the posse from Marathon and Sanderson was there. Lo Grande's men were fleeing south. Savage had taken Grace, ridden south. He couldn't have carried more than one bar, could he? Certainly not thirty.*

He looked at Albavera.

Albavera stared at his boots.

"It had to be on that train," Chance said.

"It wasn't," the white-haired officer said. "All of those safes were empty."

Silence.

"Savage . . ." Chance shook his head. *Impossible.*

"The posse?" Albavera guessed. "Those men from Marathon, railroaders from Sanderson?"

Chance shook his head. "They didn't know what was on board. But maybe they could have figured it out. Maybe . . ."

Suddenly, Grace Profit started giggling.

"What, madam," Ranger Colonel Thomas roared, "do you find so amusing? By thunder, if you know where Captain Savage hid the rest of that bullion shipment, you had better tell me, and tell me now."

Grace wiped the tears from her face with her bandaged hands. "No, Colonel Thomas, Captain Savage took only one bar when he fled after the train wreck. I'll swear to that."

"Then," the sheriff asked mildly, "where's the rest of the gold?"

Grace began giggling again.

"I'll be a son of a bitch," Chance said, snapping his fingers. He looked at Albavera.

Both men said the name at the same time. "Don Melitón."

"What?" Colonel Thomas dropped his hat on the floor. "Don Melitón Benton?"

"That's absurd," the sheriff said.

Grace laughed so much she thought she might wet herself.

"He was shot in the chest," Chance said, looking at Albavera. "Said he was dying."

"*Said* he was dying," Albavera repeated.

"He was bleeding internally. He was spitting up blood."

"Likely he bit his tongue."

"He didn't look so good when we left him in Texas."

"He didn't look so bad when he and his men saved our bacon in Mexico."

The younger Army officer, still holding

the bullion bar, said, "I'm lost in this conversation."

Grace's giggles erupted into a roar of laughter that spread across the hospital. Soon all of the soldiers lying in their sickbeds were cackling, though none of them knew why.

"The don wanted to avenge his son's death," Chance said above the ruction.

"A quarter of a million dollars can buy a better son. Especially considering that the one I killed was a little creep," Albavera said.

"The man's richer than God already."

" 'Wise men ne'er sit and wail their loss, but cheerily seek how to redress their harms.' "

"Don't start sounding like that Shakespeare-quoting son of a bitch Lo Grande."

They headed out of the hospital.

"Sergeant Chance," Colonel Thomas wailed, "and you, the big nig— stop. Where in blazes are you going?"

"Meoqui," Chance called back.

"Mexico," Albavera added.

The door slammed behind them. Despite one arm in a cast, Chance easily swung into the saddle. "You're not coming with me," he told Albavera.

"The hell I'm not." Albavera mounted his horse.

Colonel Thomas barged out of the hospital, stopped on the porch, and pointed his finger, but couldn't find any words. He just stood there, trembling, silent.

Chance ripped off his Ranger badge. "This won't do us any good in Mexico." Looking at Albavera he said, "And it's none of your affair."

Albavera unpinned his own badge, and let it fall to the ground. "I'm coming with you, Sergeant Chance."

"Why?"

"Because" — Albavera grinned — "I care."

Chance let out an exasperated curse, swung his horse around, and kicked it into a trot. Albavera rode alongside him.

Inside the post hospital, Grace Profit kept laughing, and so did all the soldiers. The white-haired lieutenant colonel, the pock-marked captain, even the sheriff had joined in.

As they rode out of Fort Davis, Moses Albavera and Dave Chance had also started chuckling.

The employees of Thorndike Press hope you have enjoyed this Large Print book. All our Thorndike, Wheeler, and Kennebec Large Print titles are designed for easy reading, and all our books are made to last. Other Thorndike Press Large Print books are available at your library, through selected bookstores, or directly from us.

For information about titles, please call:
(800) 223-1244

or visit our Web site at:
http://gale.cengage.com/thorndike

To share your comments, please write:
Publisher
Thorndike Press
10 Water St., Suite 310
Waterville, ME 04901

1142